DASHING THROUGH THE SNOW

A Holiday Regency Duology

LAUREN SMITH

BEWITCHING THE EARL

CHAPTER 1

Strange, how one's future can hang upon a single moment. One can feel trapped, frozen, while the world spins wildly by. Daphne Westfall was caught in such a moment, unable to move forward now that her life had been turned upon its head. Ever since her father's death, she dwelt in a nightmare that had no visible end.

She shivered on the snowy sidewalk, hand extended toward passersby, praying someone would have mercy on her. They dodged her with lips curled in sneers of disgust. Another gust of wind blew in from the river and whipped her threadbare skirt about her legs. She stamped her feet and then pressed her legs tightly together, hoping to conserve warmth, but she still couldn't feel her toes. Her hands were dry and cracked, her once clean nails layered with the grime of the streets.

Tears stung her eyes. Just a few pennies before night-fall would keep her out of the White House Brothel in Soho. She bit her lip and mentally fled from that option. To go there would finally break her.

Her aching stomach rumbled. But she had to be pragmatic if she hoped to fill her aching stomach, warm her shivering body beside a fire and sleep in a warm bed.

Daphne resisted the urge to touch the secret pocket in her dress, where she'd hidden her mother's pearls. Another woman might have sold the pearls to eat, but Daphne couldn't bring herself to do it. The single, elegant strand was all she had left of her mother, the only thing the courts of England hadn't been able to pry from her fingertips as they carried her father to prison.

When her father had been convicted of counterfeiting, Sir Richard Westfall's estate had been seized by the Crown and his property sold to settle his debts to his victims. Daphne had been cast out into the cold with nothing but a single dress and her mother's pearls tucked away in a hidden pocket.

"Please—please, sir," she whispered to a passerby. "A few pennies..."

The man spat on her open, trembling palm. She shrank back with a wince and hastily wiped his spit off on her gown. More tears escaped as shame threatened to suffocate her.

Sell the pearls and you won't face this anymore... a dark voice whispered in her head. But she couldn't.

A man and a woman paused on the street a few feet away and stared. Hope surged. She knew that woman. Lady Esther Cornelius, a friend, once.

Esther stared hard at her, then whispered something to her companion who, although a good distance away, tossed a small pouch of coins. In the past, she would have hidden from a familiar face, ashamed to be seen in such a state, but right now all she could think about was her hunger. To her shame, she leapt at the pouch, landing hard in the icy puddle along the alley. She caught the pouch and clutched it to her chest. When she looked up, Lady Esther and her companion were walking away.

Daphne sniffed, her nose burning as she tried to keep her tears at bay. How she wished she could curse her father. He loved her, just as she loved him, yet he had destroyed her life, her future...everything.

She wasn't sure how long she sat there, shivering and clutching the small pouch to her chest, before she tucked it safely in her skirts and glanced about. Her attention caught on the figure of a tall, handsome man leaning against the wall of a shop across the street. His exquisite clothes and refined appearance marked him for a gentleman.

Fear crawled up her spine. Why would a gentleman be watching a beggar woman? Perhaps he was not as gentlemanly as he appeared. Would he steal the coins, take her mother's pearls? She wouldn't let him. She pushed to her feet and hurried down the street, fighting the urge to run.

She glanced over her shoulder. He followed on the opposite side of the street. She quickened pace. The man suddenly vanished from view as a crowd of people swept past him. She stopped beside a row of coaches parked along the street close by and scanned the crowd.

"Miss Westfall." She started to turn toward that voice when strong fingers seized her arm.

Her shoulder collided with a hard chest. She cried out. The door of the nearest coach opened and he pulled her inside. She clawed at the masculine arm that held her.

"Do not scream, Miss Westfall. You are in no danger."

Daphne twisted free of his hold and lunged for the door. He yanked her onto the seat opposite him.

"Miss Westfall, please. I am attempting to render aid."

She stilled at his urgency. He was the too-handsome man she had glimpsed across the street. How had he gotten behind her so quickly?

"Render aid?" she demanded, hating how frightened she sounded. "Kidnapping is not the kind of aid I require."

"That's fortunate, for it's not the aid I'm offering."

He released her arm and leaned back against the cushion. "My name is Sir Anthony Heathcoat. Some call me The Lord of Arrangements."

"The Lord of Arrangements?" She had never heard of him. "What does this have to do with me?"

He smiled gently. "Everything."

She studied him. His expression lacked pity or lust. Perhaps his aid was nothing more than letting her rest inside a warm coach, away from the icy winds.

"I know about your father," Anthony said.

Daphne tensed. He wasn't the first man to seek vengeance on her because of her father.

"Easy, lass," He lifted a hand. "I've no desire to harm you. Allow me to speak. Afterwards, if you don't wish for my help, I will allow you to return to your position on the street with an extra few pounds for your trouble."

Shame heated her face and she glanced away. Never in her life had she believed she would be sitting in a coach with a man discussing her life as a beggar.

She raised her chin and met his gaze. No threatening shadow darkened his eyes. "Very well. Speak your piece."

"I am aware of your father's crimes," he said. "Counterfeiting is a serious offense. He's lucky they didn't send him to the gallows."

Daphne tried to swallow the sudden lump in her throat.

"I also know that his conviction resulted in his property being used to repay his victims; at least, those who were members of the peerage."

Another painful gulp. She couldn't speak. That had been the worst indignity. Her father had betrayed friends in society, tainting them with his dishonor. She had not been allowed to hear the more gruesome details from her father's solicitor, but she had heard whispers that one man had shot himself after being associated with the scandal.

"I have never believed the sins of the father should pass to his children," he said. "It is unjust that you should suffer for his crimes. I wish to help you."

"How can you?" she asked, feeling strangely numb.

"Have you noticed how the *ton* always favors a good marriage? The right union can erase even the worst sins from public memory." He smiled. "Perhaps even for someone shadowed by scandal."

Shadowed by Scandal? The man had a way with words. But marriage? No sane man would marry her. Even the shabbiest modistes had refused to employ her as a simple seamstress because her family name was so blackened.

"But... I have no prospects, no connections. No gentleman would ever—"

Anthony's soft chuckle stunned her into silence. "No need to fret, Miss Westfall. I am quite convinced I can find half a dozen men who would consider it a privilege to take you as a wife. If you are agreeable, that is."

"Agreeable?" she repeated. Perhaps it was warmer in the coach then she'd realized, for her head began to swim.

"A marriage auction," he said. "Polite society doesn't discuss this form of...courtship, but the general arrangement is this: you meet the interested gentlemen, then they bid for your hand."

"Bid?" The word escaped in a frightened squeak.

Anthony nodded. "The money they bid will be placed in a secure trust for your use. Contracts are signed and a male trustee of your choosing is appointed to ensure your husband honors the terms. This provides you with money to live comfortably. Of course, one hopes, your new husband will offer you even more as his wife."

It sounded mad, but... Daphne bit her lip as she considered. An arranged marriage? Women of title and wealth were contracted in marriage to men who offered the best terms. But she wasn't a woman of wealth. And to be sold into marriage? She stared at the roof of the carriage. Put that way, it sounded little better than the White House Brothel. Still, allowing a stranger to bid on her? Marry her? Could she agree to something so wild?

"Would...would there be a way to ensure these candidates are not prone to hurting their wives? I could not marry someone who..." She trailed off. She'd learned men could be cruel and abusive if it suited their desires, and she had no wish to give away her relative safety in marriage to a man who would hurt her. She'd seen evidence of that enough when she'd witnessed a woman accosted the other night on the street and robbed of her coins. The man who'd stolen from her had beaten her severely and no one had stepped in to help her because she was a prostitute.

His expression sobered. "Of course. I will conduct a most detailed interview of the candidates, and you will have my word, only good men will bid upon you."

She slid her hand into her dress pocket and stroked the smooth pearls. "You really think men will bid upon a...woman shadowed by scandal?"

Anthony nodded. "The men will be aware of your situation, and I can assure that they will not judge you for it."

Anthony smiled and Daphne was startled at the kindness in his expression. "Not all men judge a woman for her father's crimes." A twinkle appeared in his eyes. "Especially when she is intelligent—and beautiful."

Heat crept up her cheeks. "When must I decide?" she asked.

"I can give you a week, but I would prefer that you weren't wandering the streets. You could catch your death. If you agreed now, I can have the auction proceed as early as tomorrow and provide you a warm bed for the night, along with hot food."

Her stomach cramped at the mere thought of food. She should fear this stranger's motives—she should decline and flee, but instinct--or intuition--urged her to trust this man. She pressed a hand to her stomach. Or maybe it was starvation that overrode common sense. "Please, consider accepting now," he said.

She studied his earnest face in the dim confines of the coach. "What do you gain by helping me?"

Anthony didn't reply immediately, but she noted a hint of melancholy that dimmed the earlier glint in his eyes. "I find that bringing people together, people who suit, gives me purpose. Too many people focus on money and power. I want to create a force for love." He grinned and suddenly looked years younger. "A tad romantic, I know, but I cannot help myself. I have a certain talent for bringing couples together, and often they end up in love matches."

Love... Daphne hadn't thought of love in so long, she questioned whether such an emotion still existed. Anthony might have a talent for making matches, but she would never be fortunate enough to find love. But a man who cared for her even a little—a man who wanted children... Oh my, she hadn't considered that possibility. Such a man would provide a life far beyond anything she'd dared hope. For the last several months, she'd felt frozen in a way that had nothing to do with wind and snow . . .unable to move, to change her fate in any way.

"I...I will do it," she said at last, her tone strong despite her racing heart.

"Wonderful! Do you have any possessions we need to fetch, or can we go straight to the house?"

"I have nothing save what I am wearing," she admitted, another blush of shame warming her face.

"Not to worry," Anthony said, but the sorrow in his eyes was almost too much to bear. She focused on the small window of the coach while he opened the door and gave the driver an address.

A marriage auction. But what choice had she? She pressed her hand against the pearls hidden in her dress and closed her eyes. The edges of her frozen world seemed to thaw just a bit, and her body warmed with the promise of safety and a chance to live again.

CHAPTER 2

Lachlan Grant strode into the card room of Berkley's club, scowling at any man who dared appear to think about getting in his way. The coach ride from Edinburgh had been long and tedious and he wasn't in the mood to deal with foppish Englishmen preening before one another. He didn't even wish to be out this evening, but remaining alone one moment longer in his brother's townhouse would have driven him insane.

No, no longer his brother's...

Like everything else in the months since his older brother's death, that residence still felt like William's. William's title, William's home, William's life. Lachlan had simply stepped into his boots to fill the void.

I never wanted to be the Earl of Huntley.

A bitter taste clung to his tongue and he scowled, his mood blackening further.

Now he was saddled with a bloody title and all the duties and responsibilities that came attached. He had gained a fortune he'd never wanted, and the price had been the brother he'd treasured most.

Lachlan scanned the tables, desperate to join any card game, even though his heart rebelled. He felt reckless, angry, and ready to do something utterly foolish--*anything* to ease the ache in his chest.

He was the last of the Grant family, for neither he nor William had married. It was one of the reasons they had been so close, only two years apart in age. William had turned thirty a mere six months before he'd passed, and Lachlan had just turned eight and twenty, far too young to lose his brother.

A burst of laughter from a nearby table drew his focus. A group of young bucks leaned around a Faro table, excited by their winnings. He started toward the table, but someone stepped into his path and he stumbled into the man.

"My apologies," he muttered.

The other man caught him by the shoulders and they both stood back. Lachlan blinked in surprise as he recognized that dark hair and angled chin. "Anthony?" The dark clouds gathering on his inner horizon lifted somewhat.

"My God, Lachlan!" Sir Anthony Heathcoat slapped him on the shoulder in greeting. "How long has it been?"

"At least four months," Lachlan chuckled.

His friend sighed but his eyes remained warm. "Four months? That long? You've been well, I trust?" This question came more carefully and Lachlan knew why. Anthony had been just as close to William as he was to Lachlan, but he'd been out of the country and had missed the funeral. William's unexpected death had left many of their friends still coping with his loss.

"I admit, I have been better." Lachlan scrubbed a hand along his jaw. "Never wanted to run Huntley Castle. Not that I have a choice now."

Anthony nodded, his eyes shadowed. "Come and have a drink. I want your opinion on something."

Lachlan followed Anthony. Encountering his old friend had softened his reckless mood. They entered a quiet reading room with a crackling fire and thick plush chairs. After settling, Anthony waved a boy over and ordered two glasses of brandy.

Lachlan rested his forearms on his knees and leaned close to Anthony. "What can you possibly need my advice on?"

Anthony met his gaze with a sudden hint of mischief. "I'm holding a marriage auction tomorrow evening. I was hoping you might join us and bid on the bride."

A bark of laughter escaped Lachlan, but he sobered

when his friend frowned. "What the devil is a marriage auction?"

His friend chuckled. "It's exactly as it sounds. I have a lovely young lady staying at my home and I'm inviting some marriage-minded men to meet her and speak with her for a few minutes. Then you bid upon her. The highest bidder takes her as a bride. The money he bids is placed in a special trust for the lady, to be handled by a third party, a man she trusts and chooses."

"The women involved are willing participants?"

Anthony drew back. "What do you take me for?"

"A far better man than I just implied. I apologize. So, tell me, what is this actually about?"

"It's about aiding ladies in distress, women who are desperate for a match. Most men agree to pay a small fortune to secure a bride."

"And you have men agreeing to purchase a bride?" Lachlan never thought to meet a man willing to give a fortune to a wife when the law allowed husbands to claim their wives' property. Lachlan wasn't one to marry for monetary gain, but he knew many men did.

"You'd be surprised. Not every man is as jaded as you about love, old friend. Some are quite happy to find a sweet young woman to marry so that they might make a good life together. Now..." Anthony paused as the boy returned with their brandy on a tray. Once he departed, Anthony said, "Now, would you consider coming and bidding on the woman?"

"Bid on a bride? You want me to *buy* a woman? God's teeth, Anthony, I have no wish to marry yet. Besides, I have no need to buy a wife, you know that." Mere weeks after William's death, women were seeking invitations to visit him in Scotland. Half of the English *ton* wanted to traipse across his threshold, invade his life and disturb his grief, all for the chance of leg-shackling the newest Earl of Huntley.

Anthony sipped his brandy, eyeing Lachlan thoughtfully. "I remember all too well your wilder days, but with William gone, a wife might ease some of your burden."

Lachlan frowned and swirled the contents of his glass.

His friend's eyes narrowed. "You know I didn't mean it that way."

They drank in silence for a moment before Anthony shrugged off the tension and smiled. "I thought you might be interested in knowing that the young lady is Daphne Westfall. She's very beautiful and quite sweet. I was hoping you would at least consider meeting her."

Westfall...

The name hit him like a blow to the gut...a name carved in blood upon his heart. On the study table near his brother's body had been a letter that explained the shame and responsibility William felt over his dealings with the notorious counterfeiter Sir Richard Westfall. The Huntley title and lands had survived the fallout from Westfall's forgeries, but William had never been one to withstand the loss of honor.

"Westfall?" Lachlan's mouth ran dry at the name. "She wouldn't happen to be Sir Richard's daughter, would she? The man convicted of counterfeiting bank notes?"

Anthony gave a slow nod. "Indeed, she is. Do you know her?"

Lachlan had never shared the contents of the letter with anyone, not even his mother.

"No, but I hear she is a nice lass, despite her father's crimes."

He'd heard no such thing. Hadn't even known the old bastard had a child. But the revenge he never thought he'd get for William might now wait within reach.

"So, you'll come? I promised Miss Westfall I would bring good, decent men to bid on her. She's fallen on hard times, and a good match would secure her future."

Lachlan composed his features into a polite show of interest. "Of course. I'd be happy to meet the lass and bid on her."

Heathcoat grinned. "Marriage will suit you well. I had a feeling it would take only a nudge."

With a grim smile, Lachlan agreed. Sir Richard was in prison for his crimes, and so would his daughter endure a prison of another sort.

She was going to marry him, and spend the rest of

her life paying for her father's crimes by forgoing the rich trappings that her father's forgeries had given her. She would learn to live with no frivolity, no joy, no love...nothing.

Just as he was condemned to live without his brother.

We can suffer together.

DAPHNE FELT LIKE AN IMPOSTER IN THE BLUE GOWN that Anthony had given her. He'd insisted she keep it, but she'd promised she would find a way to return it once she had new clothes of her own. Fear turned her mouth bitter as she tried not to think about her future after tonight, and she reached instinctively for the pearls in the pocket of her new gown.

As she entered the drawing room of Anthony Heathcoat's townhouse, she reminded herself that this was the safest option remaining. If she secured a husband tonight, she would avoid the brothel and not go hungry again.

A group of seven men stood by the fire, all talking quietly to one another. When she cleared her throat, they turned as one, each instantly assessing her. She folded her hands in front of her to control their shaking as she endured their speculative perusals.

She'd never thought much of how brood mares felt

when being sold at Tattersals, but now she felt quite sorry for the creatures.

"Gentlemen, may I present Miss Daphne Westfall?" Anthony approached, lifted one of her hands to his lips and kissed her gloved fingers. "Are you all right, my dear?" he whispered.

"Yes, I just feel a little..." Her trembling hand said what she could not. He gave it a gentle squeeze.

"They are good men and will treat you fairly."

"Thank you," she said. She meant it. Anthony had saved her from the streets and she would never be able to repay his kindness.

"Good. I will introduce you to each man. They will place their bids in their envelopes. The highest bidder will return and we will sign the contracts. This will secure your monetary assets."

Daphne's throat constricted. She still couldn't believe she was really doing this, meeting with men in hopes that they would want to marry her. How was this different from prostituting herself? At least, she shared her body with only one man, and she didn't live with the shame of a brothel address.

"Gentlemen, please form a line so I may make your introductions to Miss Westfall."

The men formed a queue, and one by one she was presented to each. They were all charming, friendly, and genuine. With each introduction, she grew more relieved. She had a minute or two to speak with them and found she liked each one. Anthony had kept his promise.

The last man who approached her was different. She had to tilt her head back to see his face. He was incredibly tall, with broad shoulders. She felt tiny in his presence. He was a little more muscular than the others and a bit intimidating. She almost retreated a step, if only to see his face better.

"Miss Westfall, this is Lachlan Grant, the Earl of Huntley."

"It is a pleasure," Lachlan's deep voice was heavy with a Scottish brogue.

"My Lord," she replied, staring into his dark blue eyes. They were a lovely deep sapphire, yet a strange gleam flashed in their depths and then vanished behind a polite smile. Had she merely imagined that? Perhaps so. She had heard more than once that Scotsmen tended to be brooding and intense, and it seemed Huntley was no different.

"You're from Scotland? Whereabouts, if I may ask?"

"The town of Huntley is a half day's ride north of Edinburgh." His eyes remained locked on her with an almost predatory gaze. She shivered, trying to think of how to continue their conversation and draw out more of his personality.

"I've never been north of Edinburgh. I imagine it must be lovely."

There it was, a momentary softening of his eyes and

mouth. "Aye, 'tis stunning, especially in the spring when the heather blooms."

"Would we live there most of the year, if your bid is successful?" It was something she asked of each gentleman. She needed a home, a place she could feel safe, a place to escape the judgment of the *ton* for her father's crimes.

"We would. I only visit London once or twice a year. Would that suit you?" he asked.

"Yes, whatever you do will be fine for me, I'm quite sure." A home in the Highlands...she loved the idea, but she wasn't sure she was ready to marry someone as serious and brooding as the man who stood before her.

"Now," Anthony smiled at the men. "Place your bids, and then please wait outside." Several of the men offered Daphne warm, hopeful smiles before writing down their bids and sealing their envelopes.

Daphne's gaze was drawn to Lachlan as he scratched his numbers on the bit of paper he held. His eyes met hers and a bolt of shock ran through her as if she were *owned* by him in that instant. The sensation frightened her and yet she couldn't look away from him even as he placed his envelope on Anthony's palm and strode from the room.

The final men handed their envelopes to Anthony before leaving the room. After the last man left, Anthony and his manservant, Finchley, opened the bids. Daphne watched them rearrange the pieces of paper in order as the higher bids moved to the top. Her heart pounded so hard against her ribs that she had trouble breathing. Which of the strangers was to be her husband?

"Ahh, here we are." Anthony glanced her way. "We have our winner. I shall thank the others and send them home." Anthony exited the room. The click of the door sounded far too loud in the awkward silence. Daphne clutched the edge of a chair for support, her nails digging into the floral pattern of the fabric as she struggled to calm herself.

The door opened and Daphne sucked in a breath. Sir Anthony entered, followed by the Earl of Huntley. Once again, she became the focus of that brooding gaze. Wasn't he pleased to have been the highest bidder? The tight purse of his lips suggested otherwise. A pit formed in her stomach and she struggled to breathe. She was to marry him...the man who spoke of Highland heather in the spring, but who looked like a wolf about to devour her. Which was his true nature? Perhaps he was a man torn between his duality of nature. Perhaps she might never know the real Lachlan Grant.

Anthony approached her while Huntley waited inside the door, hands folded behind his back like a military general.

Oh dear...

"Miss Westfall, Lord Huntley was by far the highest bidder at fifteen thousand pounds, which he has agreed to place into an account where the trustee of your choice will oversee the funds for you."

Daphne barely listened. Instead, she stared at Huntley and he at her. A slow smile curved his lips. It was not a cruel smile, no, but it warned her that she was pledging herself to a wolf. She was tempted to look away, to yield to that dominating stare, but she held her ground and lifted her chin.

Yet her instincts warned her to run far and fast from Lord Huntley.

"Sir... Anthony, may I have a minute to speak with you?" she asked, her voice wavering. Huntley shared a look with Anthony before he nodded and left the room.

Anthony approached, concern in his eyes. "You're trembling. Are you all right?"

"Lord Huntley, is he a good man? You promise that I'm safe with him?"

"I promise," Anthony vowed. "Huntley is a long-time friend. I would trust him with my life. He's rich and has excellent lands—"

"I don't care about that. I care about *him*. Is he the sort of man to care for his wife? Not...harm her?" She bravely forced the question out, even knowing it was not polite to speak of such matters.

"He's never harmed a woman. If he seems a bit cold, it's because his older brother, William, died only two months ago. He was close to William. His brother's death changed him, hardened him in some ways. But I promise you, he is a good man."

She saw only honesty in Anthony's eyes and she trusted that more than anything else. "Very well then, I agree to marry him."

"Good." Anthony then called for Huntley, who reentered the room. They assembled about the card table, where Finchley laid out several documents.

"Here's the trust agreement, Huntley. I filled out the forms with the amount you bid. All you need do is sign, as will Miss Westfall. Finchley and I will witness the contracts to assure they are binding."

Daphne watched Huntley bend over the table and scrawl his name before he straightened and held the quill out to her. She accepted it, her gloved fingers brushing his. A spark of heat flared between them, and just as quickly vanished. Huntley's eyes darted away as he stepped back. She leaned over the table and penned her own name.

"Excellent. Huntley, you can collect Miss Westfall tomorrow after you have procured a special license."

"Actually, I would like to marry in Scotland, unless the lady objects." Huntley looked to Daphne.

"Marry in Scotland?" Daphne had to force strength into her voice. She hadn't expected to leave so soon.

There's nothing to tie you here, not anymore.

"Aye, there's a little church not far from Huntley

Castle. It's tradition for the men of the Grant family to marry there."

"Oh... I suppose that would be all right." She had no friends left in London, none that would be seen with her. She had no real reason to stay here. In fact, it was quite possible that if word got out about her wedding, the victims of her father would come to the church and make trouble on her wedding day.

"We are agreed then?" Huntley asked. His blue eyes seemed to swallow her whole.

"Yes." With that single word, she felt she sealed a bargain with the devil. A most handsome, intimidating devil...

"The paperwork is all in order," Anthony said. "Anyone care for a glass of sherry to celebrate?"

Huntley shook his head. "Not tonight, old friend. I have a wedding to prepare for."

Anthony turned to Daphne. "What about you? Sherry, my dear?"

"Yes, please," she whispered. She needed a drink.

Huntley approached, grasped her hand and raised it to his lips. Their eyes met and held once again.

"Tomorrow," he promised softly.

"Tomorrow," she echoed. Then with a kiss to her knuckles that left her body burning with a strange sensation, he left the room.

Daphne watched him go, wondering if what she had agreed to would save her or damn her.

<h1 style="text-align:center">CHAPTER 3</h1>

Lachlan climbed out of his coach the following morning, stretched his legs, and climbed the steps of Anthony's townhouse. He paused at the door, holding his breath for a moment. The moment he went inside, his life would change forever. He knew that he could turn and run from this, change his mind about his plans, yet he didn't. Every emotion that had raged the night before was now locked away in a dark corner of his mind. Instead of focusing on his brother's death and the man responsible, he focused instead on the woman, Daphne, the bastard's daughter.

When he stood there in the drawing room the night before, as nervous as the other men, he had hated himself for showing such weakness. And then she had entered, a tiny creature with soft curves, dark hair and warm brown eyes. She had been as timid as a dormouse, her eyes as round as saucers as she'd gone through the introductions. Missing was the spoiled hellion he had expected from a man like Sir Richard Westfall.

He *wanted* to despise her on sight and rally his vengeance, but it hadn't been easy to hate her. He had managed it, but only just.

Lachlan growled in frustration as he rapped the knocker of the door. A moment later, a butler answered.

"I'm here for Miss Westfall," he announced. The butler nodded and opened the door wider, allowing him to step into the vestibule.

"Ahh. There you are, Huntley!" Anthony descended the stairs, Miss Westfall at his side. She wore a soft green carriage gown with a blue satin sash around her waist. The colors emphasized her dark hair and alabaster skin. Lachlan clenched his teeth as his body responded to her subtle beauty. He did not want to desire this woman, but perhaps he could allow himself that one weakness. She would be his wife, after all, and he did plan to beget heirs upon her. It was his duty now, and hers as his wife.

"Anthony," Lachlan greeted his friend with more warmth than he felt for Miss Westfall.

Her eyes were downcast, her lips parted, and for a brief instant he caught a glimpse of a woman beaten down, her spirit already broken. That was what he had wished for, wasn't it? A broken woman? Yet he'd wanted to break her himself, not collect the pieces with pity.

"Are you ready to leave?" he asked her. "I suppose you have quite a few clothes and other possessions to take with you."

At this, she raised her eyes and he saw sorrow in their honey brown depths.

"I have none. Even this gown is borrowed." She plucked at the skirts, revealing two dainty black boots.

"Borrowed?" he echoed with shock. How was it she had no clothes, no possessions? Surely that damned criminal of a father had left her plenty to live on.

"Yes. I... I thought you understood the circumstances I was in, my lord. I would not have agreed to the auction otherwise."

Lachlan was left speechless, until his friend gave a short cough.

"Er... Huntley, might I have a word with you?" Anthony jerked his head toward the door and released Miss Westfall's arm so he and Lachlan could talk in private.

"What is the meaning of this? Where are her clothes?" Lachlan growled. He had no desire to buy anything for the woman. His entire plan of revenge called for doing the exact opposite, allowing her barely enough to survive.

"Huntley, I didn't want to mention this, since it seems to be a delicate matter, but the reason I held the auction was to get the poor woman off the streets."

"The streets?" Miss Westfall had been selling her

body to survive? "You promised me a bride, not a trollop."

Anthony's eyes flashed dangerously. "She isn't one. She was, I suspect, considering the possibility when I came across her. She was standing in an alley, scrambling for coins tossed her way. Do you have any idea what she must have gone through? A gentle born lady left begging for scraps?"

The pain in Anthony's eyes was genuine, and Lachlan wondered how bad off Miss Westfall really was. He glanced over his shoulder at his future bride, who stood at the foot of the stairs, eyes once more downcast, one hand tucked in the pocket of her gown.

"You must take care of her. I know that William's death has been hard on you, but perhaps this marriage will heal you--heal you both."

Heal him? Nothing could mend the bleeding bits of his tattered heart. William's loss had left a gaping hole inside him, and nothing and no one could ever fill that.

Lachlan turned and walked past Miss Westfall toward the door. "We should be going. We have a long journey ahead of us."

She looked up at his approach, and for a second he saw hope in her eyes, calling to him, but he smashed down the urge to respond in kind.

"Ready?" he asked coldly.

She nodded and looked at his arm expectantly. He did not offer it.

Anthony called to him as they stepped outside, "Huntley, I meant what I said."

Lachlan did not reply as he opened the coach door for his acquisition. She climbed inside and he followed, settling back on the seat opposite her.

The coach rattled into motion and for a long while Lachlan wouldn't look at her. He kept picturing her in a tattered gown, ankle-deep in icy water as carriages and people passed, no one looking her way, no one caring about her. He mentally gave himself a shake.

I will not pity her, I will not let this creature crawl beneath my skin.

She was the daughter of a man who had destroyed many lives, a man in prison for crimes that had led William to take his own life.

Lachlan felt her gaze on him and, at last, looked her way.

"What?" he demanded in irritation.

"Why did you do it?" she asked, her head tilting as if in puzzlement.

He crossed his arms over his chest. "Do what?"

"Bid on me. It's abundantly clear that you do not like me. Why did you attend the auction? Have you had second thoughts? You had plenty of time after seeing me to walk away. You did not have to write anything down on that paper. I would've been happy to go with any of the other gentlemen."

The thought of her going home with another man, of having his vengeance denied, filled him with quiet rage.

"I wanted you. That's why I placed my bid." His growling response would have made any sensible woman know that the discussion was over. But not Daphne. The timidity he'd seen in her the previous night wasn't there anymore.

"You certainly aren't acting like a man who wants me." She seemed to regret what she said. "I don't mean—"

"Oh, I *want* you, lass. I have no doubt that I'll enjoy bedding you." He managed a sardonic smile that caused her to lean away from him. He chuckled darkly at her reaction.

"Don't be afraid. I won't touch you until we are properly wed, and only when I'm certain you want me too."

Her face flushed red and she sucked in a breath. "You mustn't talk so openly of—"

"Of bedding? Lass, you'd best get used to it. We Scots aren't so squeamish as you English."

"I really must insist you do not do that with me."

"Do what?" he challenged with a wicked grin. The more he teased her, the more that other version of himself seemed to return, the rogue who would take her in his arms and kiss her senseless right here in this coach.

"Please don't tease me about..."

"Sex? Miss Westfall, I'm a man with appetites, and I

plan to teach you to have your own as well." He couldn't help it. He moved to the seat beside her and reached up to cup her face. She tensed and tried to withdraw. He may have planned for misery in her married life, but he wasn't as cold hearted as to make her unhappy in his bed. Even he had limits.

"Stop resisting, lass," he said, and he loved the way her eyes flashed in open defiance.

"I'm not resisting, nor am I willing." She growled softly, the sound reminiscent of an angry cat he'd once startled in a barn as a boy. He'd learned then that cats had dangerous claws.

"I said I wouldna do anything to you and I meant it. But damned if you don't need a kiss to cool that temper of yours."

She arched a brow and knocked his hand away from her face. Then she moved to the other side of the coach, scowling at him. "I would not have a temper if you would behave like a proper gentleman."

He let her go, keeping to the promise that he wouldn't touch her until she was willing. He was a bastard for marrying her for revenge, but he was not a devil and would never force a woman to do anything she didn't wish to when it came to sex. Still, he saw the flush of color in her cheeks and the way her breath had quickened. She'd been aroused, even if she was angry at him for teasing her. Now he was looking forward to what it would be like to give her pleasure. His body was already humming with the prospect.

I could teach her to want me when I so choose, and leave her without my touch when it suits me.

He would derive some satisfaction knowing he could leave her aching for him whenever he wanted to. She blushed again and glanced out the coach window, clearly determined to avoid him and the subject of sex. There was a fair amount of amusement to provoking her humility and embarrassment and he would take his humor when he could.

She continued to ignore him and he let her. She would panic when she realized that they would not be sleeping in separate rooms tonight. The little chit would squirm because she hadn't yet realized that she had no maid and he would have to be the one to undress her.

Time passed as the coach continued north. Daphne fidgeted in her seat and tried to sleep against the side of the coach. He had left his more comfortable conveyance back at Huntley Castle. Not that he should be concerned with her comfort, that wasn't part of his revenge.

She finally settled with a soft sigh, her eyes closing. At first, he'd wanted to crow in triumph, but the expression on her face gave him pause. Her full lips tilted down in an open frown and a little wrinkle of worry creased her sleeping brow. A ripple of guilt disturbed him enough that he continued to stare at her for some time.

When he was convinced she was fast asleep, he reached over and lifted her onto his lap. She tensed. For an instant, he feared he'd woken her, but then she relaxed and burrowed deeper into his arms. His body was taut with arousal, but he suppressed his baser urges and instead focused on her weight and warmth in his arms. She was the daughter of the man who had driven William to suicide, yet here she was, lying in his arms, trusting him not to hurt her, trusting that he would be a good husband.

Will I?

The question had an easy answer.

I would've been...before.

But losing William had broken him and his mother. Their original family of four was now two, and here he was bringing home the child of the man who had brought death to their home. He'd kept the truth of William's involvement in Westfall's counterfeiting a secret. As far as his mother knew, William had killed himself but left no reason as to why. Lachlan didn't want his mother filled with the same vengeance that burned inside of him. If his mother ever discovered Daphne's true identity, she would cast her out. Therefore, Lachlan could not tell her who Daphne was. The burden of losing a child in such a way was torture enough, and he did not want to add to that misery.

Plagued by worries, he leaned his head back and tried to sleep, still cradling Daphne in his arms. When sleep came, dreams consumed him, dreams that made his heart bleed and his throat hoarse with silent screams. Yet buried beneath the nightmares of losing his brother lay a warm softness against him that brought comfort.

"SLEEP IN THE STABLES?" DAPHNE WHISPERED TO Lachlan, facing away from the frowning innkeeper. They were a day's ride from Scotland, and there wasn't another inn for miles. They couldn't press on because of the storm that had blown in and still raged.

"'Tis the only space left," the innkeeper insisted. "The rain, you see. Everyone stopped here. The roads are bad for miles around."

Lachlan glanced away and she swallowed hard.

"Can you tolerate some hay, lass?" he asked, his tone cool.

She nodded stiffly. They'd woken up in each other's arms only half an hour before, in a strange and wonderful sort of intimacy that had shocked her. His hold had been protective and gentle, his eyes soft and inviting. Yet here he was, treating her coldly again. What was she supposed to do?

Lachlan slapped down several fat coins on the counter "Then we'll take the loft, but I'm not paying full price." The innkeeper collected them and slipped them into his apron pocket.

He led them to a muddy courtyard, where icy rain pelted their skin before they reached the protection of the stables. Over a dozen horses were tucked away in stalls. The warm scents of hay and grain were oddly comforting to Daphne as she kept pace with Lachlan.

"Use this ladder," the innkeeper said, "and be careful not to roll off the ledge in the night." The innkeeper retrieved several thick woolen blankets and offered them to Lachlan, who took them under one arm.

Lachlan turned to Daphne. "You go first. I'll be here to catch you if you slip." He gave her a gentle nudge. She approached the wooden ladder, a tad apprehensive. Heights were not something she enjoyed.

"Go on, lass," Lachlan growled and gave her bottom a gentle swat.

"How dare you!" She was torn between mortification and anger, both emotions almost choking her. The innkeeper laughed at her sputter of outrage.

"Climb, or I'll do it again," Lachlan warned with a twinkle in his eyes that she didn't like. The swat hadn't hurt, of course, not with the layers she wore, but to strike a lady in such an intimate place, especially when they weren't alone...

Daphne clenched her teeth, used one hand to lift her skirts and the other to climb. She had to go slow. When she reached the top, she toppled over into a mountain of fresh hay. There was space for both her and Lachlan to sleep, but not much more than that. She stilled as she realized that she and Lachlan would be sleeping mere inches apart.

Nerves stormed the inside of her belly and she fought off a little shiver. *We're not married yet.*

Lachlan emerged over the edge of the loft and tossed the blankets to her. She caught them and waited until he knelt beside her amid the mountains of hay.

"Make yourself a nest and get some rest. I'll find some dinner." He tucked the blankets more fully into her lap before he shifted back toward the loft's edge. She set the bedding aside and stepped toward him.

"Lachlan—"

He paused, already halfway off the ledge. "Aye?"

Suddenly tongue-tied, Daphne blushed. She wasn't sure what she'd meant to say, only that she'd wanted to say something.

"Be careful not to fall."

He answered her warning with an inscrutable expression before dropping from view.

Once he left, she arranged the hay to lay more evenly, then spread one blanket as a bottom sheet and the second as a cover. It would have to do.

She almost laughed. Of course, it would do. It would do very well. This bed was a far better accommodation than she'd had these last two months. There was nothing so dreadful as curling up in the nook of a doorway or huddling beneath bushes in Hyde Park. Those were the places she'd grown accustomed to sleeping. Here she had a roof over her head and warm blankets. By comparison, it would be easy to endure, even if they went hungry tonight. Given the crowds due to the storm, it was possible the inn might run out of food, as well.

She settled back in the hay, curled into a ball and closed her eyes. She listened to the pattering rain on the stable roof and the rustle and occasion snort of the horses below. There was a gentle cadence to it all that exuded a sense of peace. Since her father's incarceration, she'd carried the weight of his sins squarely upon her shoulders. Yet now, at this moment, that burden was lessened. Daphne inhaled slowly and let her thoughts turn to the future, to Lachlan.

He was a Scottish earl, with a vast estate in Scotland, yet he'd agreed to marry an English woman who Sir Heathcoat had made clear was in need of financial support. What sort of man agreed to that? Was he desperate for a wife?

The ladder to the loft creaked and Daphne squeaked in surprise, clutching the blanket to her chest, even though she remained fully dressed.

"I dinnae mean to scare you," Lachlan chuckled as he appeared at the loft edge. He reached up and set down a tray containing covered dishes.

She stared at the fully laden tray in awe. "How did you carry that?"

"It wasn't hard, a wee bit of balance was all." He joined her in the makeshift bed and they shared the food in a quaint silence. Lachlan was clearly not a talkative man, which Daphne did regret. She had loved to talk to her father and her friends...before everything had gone wrong.

"Have more travelers arrived?" she asked.

"Aye. There will be no beds, and likely the stables will fill up, as well. We'll have to stay in the loft unless that distresses your delicate feminine sensibilities." The sudden coldness in his tone surprised her.

"Oh, no, here's quite fine," she rushed to assure him. Perhaps his pride had been pricked by having to sleep above animals in a stable.

"I know you are used to finer things, but let me warn you, sweet bride," his tone was still cold and she shivered. "There will be no fine clothes or expensive things in Huntley. It is not my way and it won't be yours."

Daphne didn't miss the way he said this. Each word seemed to have a dreadful importance to it, but she couldn't see why. She was not foolish enough to ask for an explanation.

"I'm quite accustomed to going without," she murmured.

"Having to borrow a dress or two isn't going without." His tone was now angry and a fierce scowl crossed his face. It might have made her flinch, but she was safe and warm and fed for the first time in days, aside from her night spent in Anthony's home. She wasn't going to let Lachlan bully her, even with words.

"I have gone without," she said, her tone as hard as steel. "Did your friend not tell you? He found me begging in the streets, my only gown ripped, my belly empty, and my limbs frozen."

She paused. Her body practically shook with fury. How dare he assume she was some spoiled child who'd never faced hardship? "For the last two months, I would've given *anything* to have a roof and a dry place to lay my head. I was on the verge of..." She choked on the words, but his silent stare dared her to continue. "I was going that very night to a brothel, my last hope for food and a warm bed." She drank the last of her wine in a long gulp and stared at him hard. "But Anthony found me. He rescued me before I made that mistake. Do not *ever* lecture me on going without, Lord Huntley. I have been ripped from my home. My life was destroyed because my father was careless and cavalier when it came to the law. I am paying for his sins. I only hope you, my future husband, will not judge me for them."

She kept her composure as she turned her back and lay down on the bed she'd made. That tiny distance was the only barrier she could make between them and she hoped he would respect it.

Only then did the tears she'd held back begin to flow. She heard him mutter something that sounded like a curse before he lay down beside her and curled one arm around her waist. He pulled her back a few inches to nestle her into the curve of his body. Of course, he wouldn't leave her alone. Even now, after all she had said, he wanted to remind her that he owned her. That she was bought and paid for. She tensed and tried to pull away from him, but she was tired and cold.

"I'm sorry, lass."

The words surprised her, but only half as much as the kiss he placed upon her cheek. The tenderness of it startled her enough that she shifted onto her back to stare at him.

"Why must you be so cruel, Lord Huntley?"

His blue eyes filled with shadows. "I... I am angry. Very angry at someone and it keeps my temper short." His cryptic response was apologetic, but it was clear he would speak no more on the matter.

"You shouldn't hold on to anger, my lord. It doesn't help." She too had held onto anger for a long time. Anger at her father. But all too soon she realized anger didn't provide shelter, get her friends back, and didn't fill her belly.

"When a man's heart is broken, sometimes anger is all he has left." Lachlan's words were hoarse with emotion. Was he speaking of the brother he'd lost? Or was there more? Had he loved a woman and lost her?

"Go to sleep." His tone was even now. "We've a long journey ahead of us."

Daphne was certain there was no way she could sleep, not with the frantic pulse of her thoughts, but somewhere close to dawn, sleep did claim her.

NOTHING WAS GOING ACCORDING TO PLAN.

Lachlan scowled in the darkness of the loft as he held Daphne close for warmth. They had no proper room to share and neither of them had been able to bathe or change into nightclothes. They slept with animals. He'd wanted to be in control of her misery, to exact revenge on his terms, but the opportunities failed to appear.

Of course, after what she'd just told him, he couldn't shake the guilt of wanting his revenge. The need to avenge William was as strong as ever, but now there was a compulsion to protect Daphne, to care for her, which warred with his need for vengeance.

How can I protect her from me? He should send her back to London and let Anthony find one of those other love-struck lads who bid on her and give her to one of them. But the thought of giving her away now? He couldn't. She would be *his* wife.

The anger which had been a part of him since William's death usually burned like wildfire, snapping and snarling as it devoured his soul in its greedy flames. But at this moment, that rage had become a single candle flame.

He nuzzled the nape of Daphne's neck, inhaling her sweet scent and feeling the silken tresses of her hair slide against his cheek. She let out a soft sigh and scooted back against him. One of her hands touched his where he'd wrapped it around her waist, and she laced her fingers through his. She wasn't awake, or she would not have done that, yet he almost smiled at the thought that she trusted him, at least in sleep.

"Have I made a mistake, lass?" he whispered, knowing she wouldn't hear. "Because I want to keep you?" He wanted to keep her, yes, but for the wrong reasons.

Daphne slowly turned, still asleep, and wrapped herself around him, her face pressed to his chest, her leg slipping between his as she clung to him. A sharp pain burst close to his heart as he held her. How could he hurt this woman? She was not the spoiled brat he had hoped to torture by denying her material possessions. No, Daphne was a fighter, a survivor, like him.

Had she been anyone else's daughter, he would have fallen in love with her then and there, but he couldn't. She was the reminder of everything he'd lost. It would be an insult to William's memory if Lachlan abandoned his revenge and fell in love with Westfall's daughter.

So, I am damned either way...

CHAPTER 4

The following day, Daphne held her breath as she stepped out of the coach and faced Huntley Castle. It was a beautiful medieval grey stone house abutted by extensive gardens on either side. Much of what might have been old-fashioned in architectural style to some seemed classic to her, and not run down.

She wasn't sure what she'd believed his home would look like. A dank, dreary place, perhaps? This home was certainly not any of those things. Rather, despite the winter, it appeared to be bustling with life and color. Candles were lit in windows and servants moved about the grounds tending the gardens, preparing them for the spring, still many months away.

"Not what you expected?" Lachlan asked.

She ducked her head, but couldn't control her blush.

"I'm not quite sure what I was expecting, but it is lovely." She admired the towers and the stained-glass windows along one wing. Statues lined the gravel pathway up to the front entryway. Rosebushes, now dormant in the winter, would be stunning come spring.

Lachlan instructed their driver to attend to his luggage. She had none.

"This way." He didn't offer his arm, but stayed close as they walked up to the house. The door opened and a fleet of servants came out to greet them. The faces Daphne glimpsed were cheerful and curious, despite the black bands of morning on the arms of their uniforms. Their positive response to her gave Daphne a flutter of hope.

They might like me as their new mistress. I might be happy here, after all.

"Ahh, here we are," Lachlan greeted the servants warmly before he turned to her. "This is Mrs. Stewart, the housekeeper." He nodded to a matronly woman and then to a man in a black suit. "And Mr. Frampton is the butler. This is Miss Daphne Westfall," he informed the staff. "We are to be married as soon as possible."

"Married?" An older woman emerged through the doorway, her face mired with confusion. "You only left for London five days ago!"

Daphne had a moment to study the woman at the top of the steps. Her dark blue dress was adorned with a white apron of fine lace, which signified she was a woman of high social standing. Daphne's heart jumped into her throat as she recognized Lachlan's features in this woman's face.

"Daphne, this is my mother, Moira, the Dowager Countess of Huntley. Mother, this is Daphne Westfall." Lachlan finally offered Daphne his arm as he escorted her up to meet his mother. Lachlan's mother speared her son with a penetrating gaze, not hostile, but certainly unamused. Daphne might have laughed as she realized his mother was the one he'd inherited that intense stare from, but, at the moment, she was struggling to remember to breathe. Daphne resisted the urge to cling to Lachlan like a frightened child. It wasn't that she was afraid, but the shame of who she was and her family situation made her shift restlessly.

"Lachlan, you went to London to attend to business. You made no mention of an intent to find a bride." Lachlan's mother turned toward Daphne and suddenly smiled with genuine warmth. "It's wonderful to meet you, Daphne. I'm sorry we weren't ready to greet you, my dear. My son, as usual, forgot his manners and didn't send us any advanced notice."

"Oh please, don't be upset with him. We left London quickly and there wasn't time to write. It's nice to meet you." She dipped into a curtsey.

"Ach, an English lass," Moira chuckled and gave her son a rueful smile. "I suppose you never will do things as expected. Well, come inside, Miss Westfall. I'm sure you're tired after the long journey."

"Indeed, we are."

Lachlan and Daphne followed Moira into the house, which was even more beautiful than the outside. Cherry-wood banisters with delicately carved spindles led to the upstairs corridors. High windows allowed sunlight to illuminate the portraits hanging on green satin walls. There was an unexpected brightness to the castle that surprised Daphne. With Lachlan's anger and grim moods, she'd expected to arrive at a dark estate sinking into the moors, not this place of sunlight and fresh air. It was clear that the house matched Moira rather than her son. She was a warm, smiling woman who had laugh lines around her eyes and mouth.

"Where shall we put Miss Westfall?" Mr. Frampton inquired of Lachlan.

"The blue room in the east wing," Moira said before her son could speak. Daphne didn't miss Lachlan's sudden frown. Was the blue room a good room or a bad one?

"If you follow me, miss," Mrs. Stewart said to Daphne, "I'll show you to your room."

"Rest and have a bath, Miss Westfall," Moira said. "We shall dine in an hour, if that suits you."

"Yes, that would be fine, thank you." Daphne peeked at Lachlan, but he was already striding away. The sight of his retreating form sent a flutter of panic through her.

He was the only person in this castle she knew and he was already abandoning her.

"Don't fret, my dear," Moira gave her shoulder a motherly squeeze. "He'll be back soon enough. He never likes to let the dust of travel linger and is likely going to have a bath himself." Moira was still smiling but there was a hint of concern that transformed the laugh lines around her eyes into something akin to sorrow. Daphne knew why. She, too, sensed something wrong, but couldn't put her finger on what it was.

She trailed after the housekeeper, who led her up a grand staircase and down a corridor. They passed through a drawing room with oak paneled walls and eighteenth- century furniture. The delicate chairs with gilded arms and embroidered upholstery were exquisite. The desk, which sat at the far end of the room, was covered with books, many open, their pages reflecting the early evening sunlight. Daphne could only imagine how beautiful this room would be with the fireplace and chandelier lit.

The room was far more beautiful than her father's townhouse, and yet she remembered her father's pride in their little house in Mayfair. She could still see his face as they entered the white painted entryway for the first time. She'd just turned fourteen and the thrill of living among titled peers and wealthy aristocrats had been exciting. It had been her father's dream for years to live in that part of London.

"She's beautiful, eh? We shall certainly fit in here, won't we?"
Her father's brown eyes had twinkled merrily.

If only she had known how desperate he would become, trying to maintain that way of life, that he would destroy them both.

Daphne paused behind Mrs. Stewart as the housekeeper unlocked the bedroom door and smiled at her.

"In here, miss. This is the blue room."

Daphne entered and glanced around. The bedroom had robin's egg blue walls and a bright walnut, four poster bed. Framed watercolor sketches of Highland wildflowers hung on every wall. The warmth of the room was both feminine and welcoming.

"Once you and his lordship are wed, we shall move you to the chambers for the Countess of Huntley in the opposite wing. I'll have the footmen fill your bath. Do you have luggage?" Mrs. Stewart was now surveying her closely, and Daphne had to swallow the sudden lump in her throat.

"She doesn't have any clothes, Mrs. Stewart," Lachlan said from behind her, making both ladies jump. "Mrs. Stewart, tomorrow, be so kind as to fetch the modiste from the village. I wish to have Miss Westfall fit for clothes. You might as well make inquiries about finding her a lady's maid, as well, unless one of the upstairs maids will do?"

"We do have Mary. We can spare her if you wish to elevate her to a lady's maid," Mrs. Stewart said.

"That will be acceptable," Lachlan replied, then glanced at Daphne. "Mrs. Stewart, you may return to your duties. I should like a moment alone with Miss Westfall."

Daphne wrung her hands as the housekeeper left. Lachlan closed the bedroom door. They were alone in a bedroom, which shouldn't have worried her. They were engaged, after all, and she had slept with him in a hay loft, yet this felt more...scandalous.

"We have to have a story," he said quietly.

She tried not to appear restless under his intense stare. "A story?" she echoed.

"Aye. How we met. I meant to discuss this with you in private before we arrived, but I've been distracted these last two days. My mother will not approve if she thinks we met at an auction."

"Oh...yes. I understand." Daphne relaxed a little. "Perhaps we ought to stick to the truth as close as we can? You met me through Anthony, a mutual friend. You heard I fell on troubled times, you thought marriage might be beneficial to us both."

Lachlan placed his hands on his hips as his gaze roamed the lovely room, looking anywhere but at her.

"Aye, that might work, but my mother will be surprised I did not marry for love."

At this Daphne had nothing to say. She too had wanted to marry for love, yet here they were, no love between them.

"Then tell her the truth, that you rescued me from the streets. I can bear the shame of my situation, if it eases your mind."

He spun to face her. "Why must you always do that?"

"Do what?"

"Accept the shame of your condition? You never fight, lass, you simply..." He made a frustrated noise and raked a hand through his hair.

"Never fight?" she whispered. Her body vibrated with anger. "I have fought, Lord Huntley. I fought every day to keep myself clothed and to find a dry place to sleep. I begged every friend for work, I tried to find any employment I could, but..." Her voice trailed off.

"But what?"

"But my father committed a terrible crime, and was punished for it. The reach of his ruination went deep. Not even the street sweepers would take me on."

A pause filled the air between them, and when Daphne spoke next, it was with a heavy air that almost dragged her to the floor. "I am *tired,* Lord Huntley. I am tired of fighting. When you rescued me, I thought...I thought perhaps I might have a moment of happiness, that I might have a home. And if not that, then perhaps a little peace. If I have caused you trouble, if I am not the woman you imagined I would be, then why not send me away?"

Daphne began to tug at the gown she wore, desperate to be free of it and everything else that did not belong to her. She'd made a grave mistake in agreeing to marry a stranger. She wasn't going to stand here and take any more of his judgment when he didn't know what it was like to starve and beg.

Just then, his hands clasped her face and tilted her head back. She had only a glimpse of the emotions that warred upon his face before he lowered his head and kissed her.

Lachlan's mouth moved over hers, bruising her with his intensity, yet she welcomed the passion. The blaze of heat that flowed between them left her dizzy and she curled her arms around his neck. She'd never been kissed before, but it felt wonderful, terrifying in a way, but absolutely *wonderful*. One of his hands fisted in her hair at the nape of her neck and the other gripped her hip possessively as he pulled her closer.

"God, you taste sweet," he murmured between kisses. Daphne threaded her fingers through his hair, tugging on the strands as her body pulsed with a sudden awareness of Lachlan's strength. He was so much taller. His strong arms could so easily harm her, but they held her gently, firmly, and he kissed her until she felt faint. It made her think of the first time she drank a glass of sherry—the delightful buzz, the warm tingling that flowed through her body, but there was something else, a sharp pain deep in her womb.

She rocked her hips, needing to be closer. "Lachlan, I feel..."

"I know, lass." He lowered his lips to her neck and nipped her shoulder, which sent fiery tingles down her spine. His fingers played with the buttons of her gown and she couldn't help but giggle. It was the first time in so long that she'd laughed.

The sound broke through whatever wildness seemed to hold him and his hands dropped from her body. He stepped back and the distance between them became a chasm.

"Apologies. That was presumptuous of me. Dinner is in one hour." His tone was polite but distant.

She nodded, her heart now aching from his sudden coldness.

"Very good. I'll fetch you then. I'll have a maid find you something to wear this evening. The modiste will come tomorrow to fit you for some proper clothes." He didn't meet her eyes as he spoke, and his hands were curled into fists at his sides.

Was he angry? Why? What could she have done to upset him? Daphne bit her lip as she watched him leave. She'd never met a man so determined to walk away from her.

She collapsed onto the bed and stroked the blue satin coverlet as she tried not to cry.

He isn't worth your tears, the voice inside her insisted, but it didn't prevent the prick of those treacherous tears. She reached into the pocket of her gown and felt for the pearls, relieved as the silken beads slid between her fingers.

For a long moment, she didn't move as she studied the beautiful blue room and the single tapestry hanging behind the headboard of the bed. A unicorn was encased in a circular fence with maidens dancing around it. The scene of the ladies in the forest with the unicorn teased her imagination and her longing. Her mother had loved to tell her stories about maidens fair and unicorns as pure white as snow. The ache in her heart grew deeper, pulsing like an old wound struck anew.

I don't deserve to be here, not after what father did.

The thought filled her with a sinking uncertainty. Could she handle being the Countess of Huntley? Could she handle living with Lachlan? What had she agreed to by coming here and marrying him? Lachlan's behavior baffled her. One minute he was furious, the next he was cold, and the next he was kissing her until she grew dizzy and breathless.

Could she really marry a man whose moods changed so unexpectedly? Then again, what choice did she have? If she broke the contract, she would be sent back to London. The contracted money wouldn't last forever. Perhaps Lachlan's mercurial moods would settle once they married.

She could only hope that would be the case.

A knock came at the door and she glanced up, expecting to see Lachlan, hoping for a chance to speak to him and try to fix whatever had gone wrong at the end of their kiss. Her heart sank as a young maid of perhaps sixteen or seventeen entered the room. Her arms were full of clothes, which she set on the bed.

"Afternoon miss, my name is Mary. I'm to help you while you are here. I've been properly trained as a lady's maid." The girl was bright-eyed and quick to smile, but blushed when she did so.

"Thank you, Mary." Daphne returned the girl's smile.

Mary began setting brushes and hair pins out on the vanity table. It reminded her of home. She missed Eugenia, her maid. When her father had been convicted, she had been evicted from the townhouse, she had urged the few remaining loyal servants to seek new employers for she could no longer pay them. Eugenia had pleaded to stay with her, but Daphne couldn't hurt one of her few remaining friends by dragging her down too. If Eugenia had stayed with her, they both would have ended up on the streets without work. It was better for Eugenia to find a new lady to serve.

"I brought fresh clothes for you." Mary walked over to the bed and held up a simple, dark blue walking dress and the necessary undergarments. "I know they aren't much, but we are similar in size and they will do until the modiste arrives. Mrs. Marchby usually has quite a few gowns ready-made that she can adjust to fit most ladies who need something quickly. Should I call for a hot bath?"

"Yes, please." Daphne was looking forward to soaking in a tub. She'd only had the chance to bathe once at Anthony's, and she was desperate to do so again.

Mary pulled the bell cord by the bed, then set about retrieving fresh bed linens from the dressers.

"Mary, could you tell me more about the house and the servants? I should like to know as much as possible about my new home."

"Of course, miss." Mary's delighted smile and happy tales about life on the estate eased Daphne's weary heart. Huntley Castle sounded like a wonderful place to live. She only hoped Lachlan would not regret bringing her here.

Daphne and the maid spoke in whispers as footmen carried in buckets of hot water and filled the copper tub in the dressing room. The young men glanced their way, trying to hide their smiles.

Mary finally intervened. "Off with you now! She's got plenty of water." One of the young men dared to steal a kiss from Mary when he thought Daphne wasn't watching. But she saw the tender scene reflected in the mirror and smiled. Maybe someday she and Lachlan would be that spontaneous, feel that sort of love, and steal kisses when they thought no one was watching. If the kiss they'd shared a short while ago had been a bonfire, his kisses would warm her through the coldest winters, burning through the dark and healing her heart.

"Ready, miss?" Mary returned and helped her out of her clothes.

When Daphne was undressed, she stood naked in the dressing room, clutching the pearls to her chest. Where could she put them and feel confident that they would not be lost? Mary didn't miss her possessive hold over the necklace.

"Shall I find a small box to store those in for you, my lady?"

The word *no* was on the tip of her tongue, but this was her new home and she had to make herself comfortable here. Being able to leave her mother's pearls somewhere safe during the day would be necessary.

"That would be nice. Thank you."

"Of course." The maid smiled and carefully collected the pearls from Daphne's hands, then left her alone to bathe.

Daphne sank into the large copper tub, allowing the hot water to slip over her skin, its warmth sinking deep into her tired muscles. The hot water reminded her of being wrapped in Lachlan's arms, how he'd held her close in the hay, his body heat warming her. A tremor shook her and the spot between her thighs pulsed with a sharp ache. His lips had pressed into her hair...hair that now hung damp against her neck. Daphne reached up and touched the locks, feeling once again his lips so close to her neck, wishing she could feel more of his delicious, forbidden heat.

Last night in the stables, she had felt warm and safe. But then, any place was preferable to London's icy alleys. She had woken once during the night to find Lachlan curled against her, his lips buried in her hair, his hands both possessive and tender as he held her. Whatever plagued him during the day seemed to vanish at night. His worry-creased brows had softened and for a moment she had a chance to admire his masculine beauty. His full lips, lips she now knew to be soft and hot, had looked so inviting. His proud aristocratic features seemed to be chiseled out of marble.

If only I could understand him and his changing moods.

His older brother's death had to play some part in it. She understood that kind of heartbreak. Losing her mother to a weak heart, her father to prison, and her security to the courts, she'd had her heart broken over and over again. Lachlan had clearly been close to his brother and losing him...that could break even the strongest man. It was understandable for him to be rough and unfeeling when he was protecting his heart, but Daphne wished he knew he didn't have to guard against her. They could band together in their grief and become stronger for their union. She just had to make him see that.

After she finished her bath, Mary helped her dress. Luckily, the maid was right, they were close in size, and the plain white stockings and sensible, dark blue gown fit well enough. Mary handed her a lovely red and green tartan shawl.

"'Tis the family colors, my lady. I thought his lordship would like to see you wearing it tonight at dinner." Then Mary held up a rosewood box. "I've put your pearls inside, and if you leave the box on your vanity table it will be untouched." The maid set the box in Daphne's hands and Daphne couldn't resist peeking in to see that her mother's necklace lay safety inside the black velvet interior of the box.

Her throat tightened. "Thank you, Mary. I'm sorry I acted so silly, but they were my mother's and I would..." She swallowed past the lump in her throat. "They are all I have left of her."

"I understand, miss," the maid assured her before heading to the dressing room.

Daphne turned away to hide her embarrassment and to set the box on the dark brown vanity table beside the bay window. For a moment. she gazed at the box, remembering how her mother used to twine the pearls around her fingers as she dressed for dinner. Daphne's father would then enter the room and smile.

"How's my two beautiful girls?" he'd ask and then he would take the pearls and fasten them around Daphne's mother's neck and kiss her cheek, making her blush. It had been a romantic sight that Daphne, as a little girl, had safely locked away in her heart. Papa as he had been

before they lost her mother and before he ruined her life.

"Are you ready for dinner?" Lachlan's voice came from the doorway. She jumped yet again. That man had the worst habit of sneaking up on her. She hadn't even heard the door open.

"I'm as ready as I'll ever be." She tried to smile at him as his cool gaze swept over her.

"You look acceptable." He crooked his arm and she slid her hand through his arm, relief fluttering through her. Was he finally playing the part of a gentleman now that they were in his home?

"Thank you," she replied a little stiffly.

She accompanied him down the corridor until they reached the grand staircase. As they descended, she brushed her fingertips over the polished banister. Huntley Castle was lovely, but would it ever feel like home? Daphne vowed at that moment she would do everything in her power to make this place somewhere she could belong. And, if she was lucky, win Lachlan's heart, as well.

CHAPTER 5

Lachlan couldn't get the memory of that kiss out of his head. Daphne had tasted as sweet as strawberries, her soft lips utterly tempting, and her curves made for his hands. It was a miracle he managed to stop. If he hadn't heard her giggle, he might not have been able to. He would have laid her flat on the bed, her skirts tossed up over her waist and buried himself within her. He'd wanted her to clutch at his shoulders and writhe in ecstasy. The old Lachlan would have reveled in such reactions. Knowing a man could give pleasure to a woman so fully that she lost her control and sense of self had been one of his joys in life.

But that laugh of delight had been a douse of cold water. It shocked him from his haze of lust and, for that, he was grateful. Marrying her wasn't supposed to be about making her happy or giving her pleasure. It was about justice. It was about revenge. It was about *William*. He could not dishonor his brother's memory by becoming distracted by her. Oh, he would bed the pretty lass and likely enjoy it, but he was not going to allow her to have a happy life here. Her marriage would be penance for William's death.

"You're scowling again," Daphne whispered as they entered the large dining room.

Lachlan tried to ignore how delectable she looked, even in a simple servant's day gown and a tartan shawl wrapped around her shoulders. Freshly bathed, her hair smelling sweet and her skin glowing, she looked too innocent, too good to be Richard Westfall's daughter. If only she wasn't... If only.

"I'm not scowling," he muttered.

"You are..." she said in that sweet voice. He was tempted to smile, but his mother waited for them, drawing his attention to other matters. They must have looked like a happily affianced couple, their bodies close as he escorted Daphne to her chair.

"There you are, Lachlan. I wondered if you two had become distracted."

He forced a smile for her, even though it felt like a grimace.

"Come and sit by me, Miss Westfall." The Dowager Countess patted the seat beside her.

"Thank you." Daphne tried to pull free of his arm, but Lachlan escorted her all the way over to his mother and pulled back the chair for her. It gave him another chance to touch her, to brush his fingertips over her shoulders when he pushed her chair closer to the table after she was seated.

"Please, call me Daphne, my Lady."

"Then you must call me Moira." His mother beamed at Daphne. She smiled back, and for a moment Lachlan couldn't remember why he'd brought Daphne here. All thoughts of anger and vengeance were obliterated like shadows beneath a noonday sun. The open joy in her voice as she spoke to his mother was entrancing.

I shouldn't be captivated, not by her. Anyone but her... The guilt of his brother's loss prickled like an incurable itch, just out of reach.

"Lachlan, dear, when is the wedding to be?" Moira asked when he sat down across from them.

"The day after tomorrow," he replied.

His mother's brow knit with confusion. "So soon? That's hardly sufficient time to prepare."

"I need only to meet with the vicar at the Kirk of Huntley and schedule a quick service."

His mother was openly frowning now. "But your bride needs a proper trousseau."

"She doesn't require such fine things." He smiled at his mother, his tone teasing, yet as he turned to Daphne, he added a bite to his gaze. "Do you?" A spark of fire blazed in her eyes, and her lips parted in protest before she composed herself.

"Quite right. In fact, I insisted that we not make a fuss. It seems so unkind to focus on a wedding whilst the family is still in mourning for William. A quiet, simple wedding is proper."

"Really Lachlan, you must be willing to spend a little on your bride. This doesn't happen every day. I know society dictates we stop living while we mourn, but I, for one, think it is wrong. Weddings should be a happy affair and we should act accordingly. We are quite comfortable and can afford to buy her a trousseau."

He didn't miss the way Daphne shifted in her chair at the mention of money.

"If you don't wish for a trousseau for her, fine," his mother continued. "But we must still invite a few friends to the wedding."

Lachlan did not want anyone to be there, but a few witnesses would be required.

"What about Cameron McLeod and Eliza?" Moira asked. When Daphne showed open confusion, Moira patted her arm and added. "Cameron and Lachlan have been friends since they were wee bairns. They live only a short distance away. Cameron recently married. Eliza is a sweet lass."

"Oh, that would be lovely." Daphne's shoulders sagged in relief and Lachlan now frowned. He didn't want his close friends to see him marry the daughter of the man who had driven William to his death. Not that anyone except him would ever know the truth, but his victory was grim and he didn't wish to celebrate it.

"Please, Lachlan." Daphne breathing his first name drew him from the thoughts that shadowed his heart.

Candlelight illuminated her features, showing her full and beseeching eyes. That soft part of his heart he thought he'd buried with William resurrected itself.

"I should like very much to meet your friends." Her smile was tentative and shy.

He tried to cling to the edges of his anger and bitterness. *Tell her no, just say no.* But the refusal never made it past his lips.

"Er... I suppose I could invite them. We will need witnesses, after all."

"Wonderful!" Moira exclaimed. "We will make a party of it. I know we must still mourn, but I could do with a bit of laughter in this house. I believe it's what William would have wanted."

Both women turned to him, hope shining in their eyes. Lachlan knew he would never win an argument if both his mother and bride aligned. He stared down at the food as dinner was brought in, but did not think he could eat. Conversation moved around him and he felt much like a large stone cast in a stream. The rivers of words flowed around him, unstoppable, soothing. He hated how easily his mother and his fiancée got along. He threw in a word or two when questions were sent his way, but the ladies seemed content to talk on without him.

He had made the foolish assumption that by bringing Daphne here, he could control her happiness and keep her defeated and miserable. But he hadn't planned that his mother would take to Daphne so quickly. Since William's death, she'd been quiet, her heart wounded by her grief. Now he saw the glint of joy in her eyes and he welcomed the return of her smile. If he ruined Daphne's happiness, it would make his mother retreat into her pain all over again and he could not do that to her.

I should never have agreed to meet Daphne. Damn Anthony and his foolish ideas.

He could still break the contract and send Daphne back to Anthony. But Lachlan couldn't stomach the thought of another man claiming her.

He listened to his mother and Daphne talk, but the longer he watched them, the more his stomach turned to knots. He shoved his chair back and stood. Moira and Daphne turned to him, eyes wide in surprise.

"Excuse me. I'm afraid I don't feel well." He offered no other explanation, but simply left the dining room.

The corridor outside was dark, with evening shadows playing tricks upon his eyes. He paused at the base of the grand stairs to face the portrait of his older brother. William stood proud in his kilt and black coat. His face held an eerie, life-like quality. The artist had captured the hint of sorrow in his eyes and the worry lines around his mouth. William had always been one to fret over even the smallest of details.

Brother, why did you do it?

He closed his eyes. The memories were there, swirling just beneath the surface like the waters of a deep loch. He couldn't block out the past; it came rushing up to meet him, drowning him.

The late fall at Huntley Castle was always exquisite. The gardens were just beginning to lose their summer blossoms and the walkways were littered with colored petals. The trees were turning a brilliant array of reds and golds, which set the sky on fire when the sun began to set behind the edge of the castle.

Lachlan soaked in the beautiful view as he rode up to the front steps. As he dismounted, he felt that the world held out every answer, every dream to him. He smiled as he dropped the reins into the hands of the waiting groom and took a step toward the door. Out of the corner of his eye, he saw William at the window of his study, watching him. Lachlan waved, eager to see his brother. He'd only just returned from a month in London.

But William hadn't waved back. He hadn't seen Lachlan, at all. His gaze had been distant, seeing things beyond the window's view. Then he noticed the pistol in William's hand.

Why—

Lachlan rushed into the house, but he only made it a few feet before the shot rang out.

"William!" Lachlan plunged into his brother's study, skid-

ding to a halt inside. He saw William's leg stretched out from behind his elegant desk.

"Will—" the name choked him. William didn't move.

Lachlan stumbled forward, his legs leaden and his hand shaking as he approached the desk and leaned over to stare down at the pistol laying close to William's right hand. And when he turned his gaze away, he saw the crimson splatter staining the wall.

The contents of Lachlan stomach threatened to rise. He covered his lips with the back of his hand, a strangled sound escaping his lips.

"Oh God...Oh God..."

The rustle of people in the doorway shocked Lachlan back to life. He felt as though he'd been split down the middle, like a lightning strike hitting an old oak tree. Part of him, the carefree part, was gone. What remained was a shell. That part of him took charge, sending a footman for the doctor, even though William was clearly gone. He ordered his mother to be kept away. She couldn't be allowed to see her son like this.

How long he stood there as the world passed around and by him, he wasn't sure. The body was covered and taken away, blood wiped from the walls. Only the dark, almost black, stain on the carpet remained.

Lachlan's knees shook as he collapsed into William's desk chair. His eyes burned as he fought to breathe past the agony that ripped through him like a storm upon the coast. He struggled to suck in a painful breath as he stared at his brother's desk.

That was when he'd seen the letter. Neatly written in

William's hand, the quill placed at the bottom of the page. The remaining ink had dripped down to form a tiny black pool beneath his signature.

MOTHER,

I am sorry for all the pain my passing will cause you and Lachlan. I cannot bear the shame I have brought upon myself. In the coming days, you will learn of my involvement with a man named Richard Westfall. He was an investor I foolishly trusted with some measure of our family fortune. I assure you that we have not lost enough to ruin us, but Richard has been arrested for crimes of counterfeiting banknotes. He was using his notes to payout returns to his investors. I have accepted and used these funds and I encouraged many men I trusted to invest with him, who lost everything because of me. The guilt and shame of my involvement is too much to bear. I was never the man to run Huntley. That burden now falls to Lachlan. No doubt he will prove to be a better son than I ever was. Please pray for my damned soul. I hope I shall someday have the peace that I was deprived of in life.

Yours always,

William

LACHLAN TOOK THE LETTER AND LOCKED IT IN THE DESK

drawer. His mother could never be allowed to read it, yet he could not bring himself to burn the letter. Their mother would be devastated to learn the depths of William's struggle to find peace within himself.

Moira would blame herself for failing to see William's despair and not intervening to save him. If he could make one good come from this nightmare, he would spare their mother that particular agony.

Lachlan pulled himself out of the past, his heart heavy and his soul empty. He stared again into the layers of oil that formed his brother's face and saw the hollow, haunted look that had rarely left his brother's face while he lived.

You left us, Will, and you made me step into your life, a life I didn't want. I cannot forgive you for this.

Lachlan closed his eyes and drew in a shaky breath, then made for the library at the far end of the house. The servants kept a fully stocked liquor cabinet in the room, and tonight he had every desire to drink himself into oblivion.

I want to forget you, Will. Forget you, forget Daphne and her warm brown eyes and petal soft lips. I want to drown it all away.

He knew the relief from his pain would be temporary, but he would do anything right now for a few blessed hours of numbness.

CHAPTER 6

"Tell me, my dear, how did you meet Lachlan?" Moira asked after Lachlan abruptly left dinner.

Daphne struggled to compose herself lest she betray the truth of her circumstances.

"At a private dinner party hosted by Sir Anthony Heathcoat. He was very sweet to invite me. I only knew him a little." Daphne did her best to stick to the broad elements of the truth.

"And you love my son?" The hope in Moira's eyes made Daphne's heart stutter. She wanted to love Lachlan, but the man was making that more than difficult.

She swallowed hard. "I want to love him, yet I must admit, we are both still strangers in many ways."

Moira rested one elbow on the table, her dessert plate abandoned. "You still wish to marry him then?"

Using her fork, Daphne carefully played with a bit of bread pudding on her plate as she considered how best to answer. Finally, she looked directly into Moira's eyes. "Your son rescued me when I needed a friend the most. Our desire to marry was a natural course of action that stemmed from that, and I wish to be worthy of him as a wife and a friend." Daphne meant every word. He had saved her from life in a brothel. The least she could do was make their marriage a good one, and perhaps banish whatever demons seemed to haunt Lachlan.

"Lachlan never ceases to surprise me." Moira gave a soft laugh, rich with amusement. "He was the more stubborn of my boys. The lover, the fighter, the one who broke the rules more often than not. I always believed he would wait forever before marrying." A flash of melancholy crossed her face before she offered Daphne a wry smile. "I assumed William would marry first. He was always so conscious of his duty to the estate."

"What was his brother like? Lachlan hasn't spoken of him." Daphne tried to still her racing heart, but she wanted to know more about Lachlan's family.

Moira appeared surprised. "William? He hasn't told you?"

Daphne shook her head.

Moira's pale blue eyes filled with tears and sorrow tempered her smile.

"William was my firstborn. You never forget your first bairn. I thought my body would break apart when he came into this world. He was such a quiet, wee lad. He was smart and kind, but there was a sadness to him as well. Do you know what I mean?"

Daphne's throat tightened. "Yes, I do." She'd had a friend once, a lovely girl from a good family, but no matter how warm the sunshine or how lovely the day, the girl was always...perhaps sad was the wrong word. Maybe, unaffected by the world, for good or ill.

"And Lachlan? What was he like as a boy?"

"Lachlan was my little warrior, fit for the clans of old. There were always biscuits to steal, trees to climb. He was fearless. But I grow concerned that something changed with William's passing." Moira blushed. "I cannot explain it, but the light in his eyes seems dimmer." She reached out and touched Daphne's cheek in a motherly caress. "Except now, for just a moment, when he watched you laugh, I saw a glint of the old spirit in his eyes. Mayhaps this marriage will be a good thing for you both."

Daphne's heart raced at the thought of her laugher having that effect on Lachlan. For two months she had felt so helpless, so useless, but now she had a chance to help someone.

"I know he doesn't seem to care about your trousseau, but I was thinking you might fit into my wedding gown. It's a bit old in style, but I believe I was about your size when I wore it. We can have the modiste make the necessary alterations, of course."

Her heart swelled and she had to resist the urge to hug Lachlan's mother. "Thank you, I would be honored."

"I think, my dear, it is time I retire for the evening. I'm not so young as I once was." She smiled again. "You know the way back to your room?"

"Yes, I'll be fine."

She and Moira rose from the table and parted ways. For a long moment, Daphne stood in the dim corridor, thinking of Lachlan and his brother. When she began walking again, she sought out the main stairs, but paused at the sight of a portrait she'd missed earlier that day. The morning sunlight had favored the stairs, leaving the walls in shadow and she hadn't looked closely. Yet now, moonlight basked the portraits on the wall with a milky light. The face staring back at her was unmistakable.

It had to be William. The clothing was modern, and his features were so much like Lachlan's. Yet she saw an eternal melancholy in his eyes, just as Moira had described.

"He was a good man, my brother." Lachlan's slightly slurred voice came from the shadows by the entryway straight ahead of her. Daphne bit her lip to keep from gasping and her stomach churned with a deep uneasiness. Lachlan had an obvious talent for sneaking up on her when she least expected him.

"Your mother told me a little about him," Daphne admitted.

Lachlan emerged from the shadows, his tall body

imposing in the darkness. She had the sudden image of him overpowering her, catching hold of her body and kissing her, uncaring of whether she wished him to or not. His waistcoat was gone and he held a bottle of Scotch in one hand. His cravat was missing and his hair was tousled, as though he had run his hand through it repeatedly.

"And did she tell you how he died?" His voice was soft, but Daphne sensed danger in the question. He turned away from her and she thought for a moment he'd forgotten her, lost in memories.

"Er...no, she didn't."

He spun to face her and stepped closer, the contents of his bottle swishing in the silence of the house.

"He took his own life." Lachlan stood only a few feet away now. She inhaled the heavy perfume of Scotch as it rolled off him. He'd been drinking too much. She shouldn't stay alone with him, not when he was in such a condition.

"My lord, perhaps I should fetch someone to—"

He caught her arm, firmly but gently, and kept her close to him, caged by his body.

"No need to get anyone. I've been deeper in my cups than this." He chuckled. "Do I frighten you?"

She gazed into his eyes, searching for any aggression or brutality. She saw only sorrow and curiosity.

"Frighten me? No," she finally replied.

"Good." He set the bottle down on the foot of the

stairs and placed one hand on the banister, trapping her against it. She leaned back, the wood railing pressing into her spine until she could not retreat any farther. He reached for her hip, his fingers curling into the loose fabric of her gown, as he secured a firm hold.

"And now?"

Daphne's blood pounded in her head and she felt suddenly dizzy. "Only a little."

She raised her chin as he tilted his head slightly. His lips, so often curved in a frown, twitched as though tempted to smile.

"I'd never hurt you, lass." He lowered his head, giving her plenty of time to resist, to push him away, but she didn't want to. Their mouths met in a slow kiss that burned like a warm fire. She tasted the Scotch on his lips and was lost in the headiness it created within her. She had forgotten what it felt like to be warm, to feel a fire obliterate the cold inside of her.

She curled her arms around his neck, pulling him closer, needing more of his touch, and his heat. When he kissed her, she felt like she was falling, breathless and free, into a world where the past no longer mattered. Only this moment existed, the brush of soft lips and sweet sighs...

"What are you doing to me?" he demanded in a panting whisper between kisses.

I'm loving you. The thought rose unbidden to answer him and it startled her. She barely knew Lachlan, but it was true, she *wanted* to love him, was even at this moment falling in love with him.

He reached up and cupped her face, their eyes meeting briefly before he deepened the kiss once more, and plundered her mouth in the most sinful way. Daphne moaned as ripples of fire stirred throughout her body. She couldn't resist threading her fingers through his dark hair, tugging on the silken strands. He growled against her lips and used one hand to drag her skirts up to her waist.

He gripped the back of her left thigh and lifted her leg up to crawl around his hip. Daphne didn't fully understand what he wanted her to do, but her primal instincts took over and she rocked against him. To her delight, she found the hard press of his muscled thigh against the apex of hers, intense and overpowering. Sensations shot through her from the simple but intense friction. Lachlan leaned against the banister, his thigh rubbing harder against her sensitive mound through the thin layers of her underclothes.

"Ride me," he murmured, showing her the natural rhythm of their bodies moving together.

Once she matched it, it was too much to bear. His tongue played with hers and her breasts ached against her stays as he assaulted her every sense. His taste, the hint of Scotch, the smell of leather and man mixed with his rough caress and the sting of his hand fisting in her hair as he began to kiss her ruthlessly. He was conquering her with every weapon at his disposal and she was more than ready to surrender. If he had wanted to take her there on the stairs, she would have let him.

The building pressure and the dark need for some kind of release became unbearable. She whimpered as he rubbed his thigh over and over against her mound. Then he suddenly changed direction, rolling his hips in a slightly different direction, and the explosive release of a frightening pleasure was unbearable. Daphne cried out against his lips and he pulled away from her with a curse. The abrupt separation made her stumble on the steps. She barely caught herself against the banister before she fell.

Without a word, much less an explanation, Lachlan started up the stairs, leaving her alone, legs shaking and body aching with a loss she didn't understand. How could he have touched her so intimately, so... She blinked back tears. He'd roused deep feelings within her, not simply passion, and then he'd left her alone, cold and confused. The evening sunset had faded an hour ago, leaving soft purple beams of moonlight painting the walls with a melancholy splash of color.

Daphne stared up at the portrait of Lachlan's brother and shivered. His pained eyes seem to gaze right through her.

"What am I supposed to do?" she asked him in a barely audible whisper.

The handsome, tragic man in the portrait offered no

reply, leaving Daphne feeling more alone than she'd ever felt before.

"YOU'RE GETTING MARRIED?" CAMERON MCLEOD burst out laughing.

"It's not amusing," Lachlan barked. He glared at his best friend. Cameron couldn't seem to stop grinning and was barely restraining himself. Laughs still escaped as snorts and hisses, which made him sound one gasp away from giggling like a girl.

"For heaven's sake," Lachlan punched his shoulder in only a partially playful manner, but Cameron's good-natured grin didn't fade. His eyes were alight with mischief.

"Well, don't go silent on me, Lachlan. Describe this paragon of a girl who has captured your heart."

"She hasn't," he replied. She'd captured his interest, his arousal, but not his heart.

At this, Cameron sobered immediately. "You...you don't love this lass you're planning to marry? But you always swore you wouldn't marry, not unless you fell madly in love."

Cameron frowned as he and Lachlan strode toward the small stone church. The Kirk of Huntley was a quaint Gothic structure that had been around for hundreds of years and would likely be there long after he was dust. He paused as he reached a heavy oak door and grasped the handle, unable to look his friend in the eye.

"That was before I became an earl. I have a duty to marry and provide for an heir." The words tasted like poison. Marrying out of duty was bad enough, but marrying for revenge was worse, yet here he was intending to do just that.

Cameron placed his hand on the church door, preventing Lachlan from opening it. "Do you even *like* your future bride?"

"I like her well enough. She's fetching and sweet."

Cameron rolled his eyes, but his gaze was serious when he finally lifted his hand from the door.

"'Marrying for anything other than love is damned foolish.' Those are your words, Lachlan."

Lachlan exhaled slowly, closing his eyes for a brief moment. "Losing William has made me stop thinking like a foolish and unrealistic child. It's time I settled down with one woman and made the best of it. If you do not approve, you don't have to witness tomorrow's wedding."

"Not come? I wouldn't miss it. I only want you happy." Cameron followed him into the church, their voices lowered out of respect as they walked down the aisle. The echo of their boots on the stone floor summoned the vicar, John McKenzie. Lachlan greeted the middle-aged vicar and shook his hand.

"My lord, what service can I do for you?" The vicar's

bright blue eyes appeared amplified behind the spectacles perched on his nose.

"A wedding. I need a wedding tomorrow."

"Oh? And who's the lucky man?" John glanced at Cameron and chuckled. "I seem to recall marrying you only last month."

Cameron laughed and pointed a thumb in Lachlan's direction. "It's him, if you can believe it."

McKenzie blinked in surprise. "You, my Lord?"

"Why is everyone so shocked that I am to be married?"

John smiled. "Hardly a year ago, you said you would never marry, not unless someone made you." The humor faded from his eyes. "There isn't a...reason that a ceremony is required in such short time, is there? You know how I—"

"No," Lachlan couldn't keep the sarcasm out of his voice. "The lass still clings to her precious maidenhead. I simply want the wedding to be done quickly." Lachlan didn't care for their assumptions, and had grown tired of everyone questioning his motives. That the truth was far worse, didn't help matters.

The minister pursed his lips and, after exchanging a glance with Cameron, shrugged.

"And what's the lucky lass's name? Is she from this area?"

"No. She's English."

Both Cameron and McKenzie stared at him.

"You're bringing a Sassenach to live here? With you?" Cameron started laughing again.

"There's a bit of a problem with her residency," McKenzie replied more seriously, "and the banns…"

"Aye, I figured as much." Lachlan glanced around the church, noting some of the wooden rafters were a bit fractured. "And what of your church? Perhaps a bit of timber could find its way here?"

McKenzie glanced up at the same rotted timbers. "I suppose the banns can be read today three times and… well, we could have the church ready for a ceremony tomorrow at nine in the morning. Does that suit you, my lord?"

"Aye, that does." Lachlan glanced once more at the stained-glass windows and the kaleidoscope of pale colors cast over the wooden pews.

"And this is to be a private affair?" John asked.

Lachlan finally faced the minister again, expecting more questions. "Yes. Cameron and Eliza will witness."

"Very well. Is that all you need, my lord?"

"Yes, that is all." He and Cameron bid the minister farewell and then they exited the church.

"Cameron, why don't you bring Eliza up to Huntley Castle for a few days? Mother thinks it would cheer Daphne." He wasn't too keen on doing anything that would cheer his future wife, but it would cheer him, which was something he desperately needed. The anger he'd clung to for so long was waning and he was filled with an empty loneliness that he couldn't seem to escape. Having Cameron around for a few days would remind him of the happy man he'd once been, before Willian's death. He wanted Daphne to see him as he used to be, the man who might have fallen in love with her under different circumstances.

"I'm sure Eliza would be thrilled, and it will give me a chance to meet this woman and see if I can figure out why she has you twisted up in knots."

"I'm not twisted up in knots."

"So you say. But never in my life have I seen you so boorish. Growling like a wounded bear one minute and snapping your jaws like a wolf the next."

"McLeod..." he warned, and inwardly cursed at how the name escaped his lips in a clear growl.

"Ack, now I've done it. You're calling me McLeod." Cameron feigned distress as they reached their mounts, tied up outside the church yard.

"Be there tonight for dinner," Lachlan said as he and Cameron climbed into their saddles. His horse shifted and snorted. With a light smack on the gelding's neck, Lachlan gripped his reins and readied to leave.

"Tonight, it is." Cameron nodded to him and rode off, his home being only a few miles away.

Lachlan began the quick journey back home, wishing the distance was greater. He wasn't yet ready to face Daphne. Not after last night. He had groped her like a randy lad and she had purred like a cat in response, something he hadn't expected. The startled look of pleasure in her eyes told him she had never climaxed before. She wasn't simply a virgin, she was completely uneducated in the ways of pleasure. He tried to bury the heavy guilt he felt, knowing he would enjoy giving those lessons.

I shouldn't enjoy her, not anything about her, yet I do. It felt like a betrayal of William's memory.

For the next half hour, he was lost in thoughts of Daphne as he rode home.

As he approached the castle's entrance, he spotted a feminine figure kneeling among the rose bushes. There were no buds to admire, though, only frost on the remaining greenery. Intrigued, he rode closer, wondering if one of the maids was out...but then he recognized Daphne.

He took a moment to admire her. She worked a small pair of clippers in her gloved hands to cut a bit of a rosebush, then lifted the stem close to examine it.

"What are you doing?"

"My lord!" She gasped in shock and leapt to her feet before she spun around, her cheeks flushing. "I was retrieving a stem of this rose. I thought I might grow it inside the hothouse I discovered behind the castle."

"The hothouse? That place hasn't been tended to in years." He slid off his horse and patted its flank as he waited for Daphne to join him. She wasn't wearing a cloak, only a thin shawl, yet she seemed unbothered by the chill.

"Where's your cloak?" he asked sharply.

Daphne's face was still red. "I don't have one."

"But the modiste came today to bring you clothes." He had seen to that personally before he'd ridden off to seek out Cameron.

"She gave me plenty of ready-made dresses and other necessary things, but she did not have a completed cloak."

"Oh…" He felt like a horse's arse for snapping at her. Lachlan stripped off his great cloak and hung it over her shoulders, noting that it pooled on the ground like a black train. He wanted her unhappy. He didn't want her catching cold and becoming ill.

"Really, my lord…"

"Lachlan. Please call me Lachlan. As your future husband, I must see to your care. That includes giving you a cloak when you are cold." He took his time, making sure it fastened securely beneath her chin. She trembled at his touch and clutched the frozen branch to her chest like a talisman.

"I thought you said you did not fear me," he whispered, stepping forward until their bodies pressed. He couldn't resist her, not when he thought of last night—the way she felt so perfect in his arms, and the way she reacted to him. The tension between them built as she raised her eyes to his.

"I don't fear *you*..." Her admission only deepened the blush staining her cheeks.

He brushed his gloved hands down the pale column of her throat. "Then what do you fear?"

"I fear how you make me feel." Her brown eyes, the color of a doe's and just as frightened, glanced away from him.

"You should never be afraid of passion. Sometimes, when all else has been stripped away, it's the only thing you have left in life," he murmured, and the truth of the words hit him deep. Passion was all he had left. Love and trust, faith, hope...all of these had perished when William died.

"You have more than that, I've seen it in your eyes. Passion is a spark, and a spark dies quickly unless it has fuel to sustain it." Daphne's eyes softened and her lips curved in a smile so full of hope that it made his heart bleed for the past.

She reached with her free hand and stroked his cheek, then cupped his face and stood up on tiptoes. She pressed her mouth to his in a way that sent his senses spinning like no chaste kiss should. He took in the fall of her thick dark lashes before he closed his eyes and returned her kiss. He realized with a stunned sense of clarity that this moment was not about passion. It was about *them*, together, their souls reaching out to one another.

He should've stopped it, but he couldn't. Kissing Daphne was like breathing. He couldn't do without her.

Lachlan tried not to think about the danger he was putting himself in by caring for the woman he planned to marry out of spite. When she finally broke away from him, she raised a hand to her mouth, touching her slightly swollen lips, which had become a lovely shade of dark pink.

"Lass..." Lachlan choked on the words he didn't want to say. "We do not have to go through with this."

She blinked, her gaze still hazy with desire. "What?"

"You don't have to marry me. I have been thinking about this and it's not fair for you to marry a stranger. I'll waive any rights to the money I set up in your trust, if that's what you're worried about."

She swallowed and spoke quietly but firmly, "I swear I didn't agree because of the money." She blushed and looked at the ground for a second. "I did need security, but after I met you and we arrived here, well, I want *this*... I want to be a part of your life. Do you wish to cry off? Is it because of something I've done?"

He placed his hands on her shoulders. "What? No!"

"Then why?"

"I'm not a good man, Daphne. I'm broken." The honesty shocked him.

"Everyone has something a little broken inside them. Perhaps our pieces fit. Don't you think we should at least try?" She bit her lip. The hard set of her face told him she wanted to marry him. The poor fool.

I tried to do the right thing. I tried.

"Perhaps we should," he agreed, fighting the temptation to kiss her again. "Let me escort you back to the house." He held out his arm and after a moment's hesitation, she slipped her arm in his. They walked side by side to the house, her with her rose branch, him leading his horse. He was struck by the strange domestic contentment of her companionship without a word needed between them.

"I met with the vicar today," he said at last.

"Oh?"

"It seems the church was in need of a bit of repair. I offered to donate timber to the parish, and Mr. McKenzie is overlooking the residency issue since you're not a resident of the Parish. He shall call out the banns three times today to satisfy the legal requirements, and then we can marry tomorrow."

"Are you sure that will be legally binding?"

"Yes. Sometimes Scottish law can be looser than English law, but do not worry, you will be the Countess of Huntley."

"I don't care about that. Titles never really mattered to me." She was smiling a little as they walked.

He shot her a sideways glance of disbelief. "Titles don't matter?"

"Not to me. My mother was the daughter of a duke,

but she married down for love. I think I'm more like her than my father, at times. I care little about the *ton* and it's love of rank. It always seemed a silly thing to me."

"Oh?" He stiffened at the mention of the man who had unknowingly brought them together.

"Yes. I love my father, but he was focused on advancing our position in society. I believe he felt he had to earn his place to make up for my mother marrying down, but he became addicted to his social climb. It was very lonely growing up with him after my mother died."

Her quiet words cut through the anger that usually filled him when that man was mentioned. But to hear about him through her eyes, the rage vanished. She, too, had lost someone she'd loved.

"How old were you when she passed?"

"I was eleven. She was fine one minute and the next, she had a bad headache. She went to sleep after tea and never woke up. It was her heart that failed, according to the doctor." She looked down at her feet. "I cried for weeks. I still miss her."

Lachlan pulled her close as he pictured her waiting for her mother to wake up, and how frightened and grief stricken she must have been when she didn't.

"I..." She hesitated as they reached the steps. She tucked her rose branch under one arm then lifted something from the pocket of her gown and held it out. When she uncurled her fingers, he saw a string of pearls coiled on her palm.

"These were my mother's. It's all I could save when the Court took my house to pay the victims of my father's crimes." Her voice wavered on the last word, but when she raised her head to look at him, fierce pride gleamed in her eyes.

"You don't wear them?" he asked, surprised at her humility.

"No. They're too precious for that. I couldn't even part with them for food and water when..." She couldn't finish her sentence.

"When you were living on the streets?" There was a time he would have taken a dark pleasure at the idea of her on the streets, cold, hungry, alone and endangered. But now the thought filled him with a hard rage, almost as suffocating as the hatred he bore for her father.

"Wear them tomorrow for the wedding," he ordered. "I want to see them on you."

"But—" she started to protest, but he placed a finger to her lips.

"*Please.* I insist. For your mother's sake. No doubt she would have wanted you to wear them."

"They won't look fetching with my plain white gown."

Regret prickled his insides, because he'd insisted that he didn't want her to have a fancy wedding trousseau.

"We could have the modiste return..."

"No," she replied. "You wanted simple, and simple I shall be." She tucked the pearls back into her gown pocket. She let go of his arm as he met a groom at the steps of the house. She did not wait for him, nor did she look his way as she entered the house alone, her head held high.

If he ever doubted she was the granddaughter of a Duke, that moment alone would've proven him wrong. And damned if the picture didn't make him smile.

CHAPTER 7

Daphne trembled as she gazed at herself in the full-length mirror. Her new maid had helped her dress in her lovely but simple purple evening gown. Would it be good enough to please Lachlan? He'd claimed he didn't want a fancily dressed wife, but that didn't stop her from wanting to look pleasing. His friend Cameron McLeod and his new wife Eliza had arrived for dinner and Daphne couldn't shake the feeling that they would be studying her closely, measuring her to see if she made a suitable match for their friend.

"You look lovely, my lady. Truly." Mary sighed dreamily. "Purple complements your fair skin."

Daphne pressed a hand to her cheek, trying to see the beauty Mary spoke of. She had to admit, she did look...*better*. Two months of scraps had left her gaunt and feeling worn in ways she hadn't been prepared for. Having a warm bed and regular meals had been more than a relief, it had been restorative.

I am finally safe, I finally have a home.

Her eyes suddenly burned and she closed them, fighting her emotions.

Mary touched her shoulder, giving her a gentle squeeze. "My lady? Are you all right?"

She cleared her throat. "Yes. I am. 'Tis nerves, is all. I'm anxious about meeting Mr. McLeod and his wife."

Mary grinned. "There's no need to be nervous. Mr. McLeod is a perfect gentleman, especially toward the ladies. I suspect his Lordship will be the one in trouble."

"Oh?" Daphne reached for the white elbow-length gloves that had been laid out across the bed's coverlet.

"Yes, Mr. McLeod—Cameron, that is--loves to tease his Lordship. Ever since they were lads, or so I've heard. Mr. McLeod will no doubt tease him about you, as well." Mary put the brushes and extra pins into the drawers of the vanity table.

"What could he tease Lord Huntley about in regards to me?" Daphne asked.

The maid shrugged, reluctant to speak.

"Please, tell me."

Mary glanced around, as if afraid someone would hear, then said in a low voice, "It's quite well known that his Lordship has certain beliefs on marriage," she began. "He'd always proclaimed he would marry only for love.

Now that he's marrying you... well, Mr. McLeod will be sure to prod him about his reasons."

"Oh dear," Daphne sighed, and a headache began to form behind her eyes.

Lachlan didn't love her and would likely be upset if his friend teased him about it.

"I wouldn't worry about it, my lady," Mary replied with a little giggle before a distant gong sounded somewhere. "Ach, dinner's ready."

Lachlan had a gong? That was unexpected. Only the finest houses boasted such a thing. Not that Huntley Castle wasn't fine, but despite the exquisite furnishings, the estate had a rustic feel to it that made her forget she was in one of the finer houses in Scotland.

Daphne left Mary to tidy up the bedchamber. Lachlan waited for her at the bottom of the stairs, one arm resting on the newel post. The sight brought back wild, forbidden memories of last night's kiss. A kiss that had led to one of the most exquisite pleasures in her life. Her face heated and she tried to focus on anything but Lachlan and the memory of his thigh rubbing against her in that unexpected way.

"Dinner and new acquaintances," she repeated over and over until her nerves replaced the flush of arousal. She bit her lip as she reached Lachlan. He smiled, and for the first time it was warm and genuine. He held out his arm to her and she accepted his escort.

"Don't let Cameron fool you," Lachlan said as they neared the dining room. "He's quite a trickster."

"And Eliza?"

"By far, she is Cameron's better half. You will take to her, lass, do not fret."

She held her breath as they entered the dining room. Candelabras had been lit, lending a seductive glow to the long, polished dining table and the gray walls around them, which bore stately portraits of Lachlan's ancestors.

Moira stood waiting for them at the far end of the table, beaming. Firelight from the white marble hearth illuminated a couple close to Moira. The man, Cameron McLeod, was almost as tall as Lachlan, with blond hair. They dressed in similar style, but where Daphne felt they stood apart most was in their expressions. Already, she could see the trickster she had been warned about in his face. Lachlan, on the other hand, had a certain wildness about him, something that seemed untamable, and she longed to let go and be wild with him.

The woman at Cameron's side, Eliza, was a pretty woman with reddish-brown hair. She wore a fashionable gown but, like Daphne's, it was simple in cut. That came as something of a relief. The gowns from the modiste were quite good, but she feared they would not appear worthy of a countess. Of course, she was content to wear simple clothes, but at the same time, didn't want to make a poor impression and embarrass Lachlan.

"Ahh, Lachlan, you finally prove the mystery woman exists!" Cameron laughed heartily. It was an open, kind laugh, and despite the mischief that lurked there, Daphne knew she would like and trust Cameron.

Eliza poked her husband in the ribs with an elbow. "Oh, hush." She beamed at Daphne, approached, and grasped Daphne's hands.

"So lovely to meet you," Eliza said. "I'm Eliza McLeod, and this is my very silly husband, Cameron."

"It is so nice to meet you as well." Daphne couldn't stop smiling as she looked at the couple. She chanced a glance at Lachlan. He seemed more relaxed than he had ever been since they'd met.

"You look well." Moira gave Daphne a motherly hug that threatened to return burning tears to her eyes. She was suddenly ridiculously happy. She was making new friends, ones who probably didn't know about her father or her shame. She was being treated like a daughter, a fiancée and a friend.

"Shall we begin?" Lachlan asked.

Eliza and Daphne took adjacent seats at the table. Lachlan moved to its head while Cameron and Moira sat opposite Daphne and Eliza. As the courses flowed in and out of the room, Cameron regaled the diners with tales of his and Lachlan's childhood.

"...And there was the time we snuck into the bakery in the village, you remember that?" Cameron asked between sips of wine.

"I do. I also recall forbidding you from sharing that particular story," Lachlan said, his tone teasing. He leaned back in his chair, smiling. Daphne was fascinated by this change in him. *He seems so at home, so alive and warm around Cameron.* The ghosts of the past seemed, for now, to have been banished by their guests.

I wish I could always see him like this, smiling and happy.

Eliza snickered. "Go on, tell us what happened, Cameron."

Cameron toyed with his fork, grinning devilishly. "Well... Lachlan climbed into the back window of the bakery and started stuffing cherry tarts into his trouser pockets. But he forgot about the fat green toad we'd recently captured at the loch." He paused to let Lachlan shake his head with a rueful smile.

Daphne couldn't resist asking, "And?"

"The old baker came storming into the storeroom and saw Lachlan standing there, pockets full of tarts and me halfway out the window. He grabbed us both by our necks and gave us a good shake. Then he demanded we empty our pockets. Lachlan reaches down, pulls one out and slaps it into the man's hand. There, covered in red cherry sauce, is that toad, bug eyes wide and its throat pulsing as it croaked. The baker yelped and tossed the toad in the air. It landed on the bakery racks by the bread. Lachlan and I dove out the window and took off running before he recovered."

"I still hear that old man's bellows in my nightmares," Lachlan laughed. "If he'd ever caught us..."

"Neither of us would've been able to sit down for a month, that much is certain," Cameron finished. "So, you see, my dear Miss Westfall, you are marrying a veritable outlaw. I hope you're prepared."

Daphne beamed at Lachlan. "Have no fear, Mr. McLeod, I shall keep the cherry tarts safely under lock and key.

"Nonsense. You need only keep plenty about for me to eat." Lachlan's casual tease felt so natural, so wonderfully sweet. It was the way she'd dreamed a husband would be with his wife. She longed for a man who would be sweet and amusing and intimate with her in all the aspects of his life. And right now, she felt that she and Lachlan had that chance.

Perhaps I might find a way to banish the ghosts in his heart the way Cameron does.

Lachlan grinned boyishly. "Enough about us, Cameron. I wish to hear Eliza play. It's been some time since anyone has used the music room."

"Eliza?" Cameron looked to his wife and she blushed and nodded.

Moira clapped her hands and stood. "Let's be off. I, too, long for some music." She joined Daphne and Eliza. "Do you play, Daphne?"

"Me? Oh... No, but I sing a little," she admitted.

"That's a good thing, for I do not," Eliza mused.

The music room was just off the dining hall. A thick, lushly carved harp sat in one corner and a pianoforte held a prominent place with several chairs facing it. A servant had thought to light a fire in the room and the candles on the two tables by the chairs were lit. Eliza seated herself at the piano, facing the small crowd over the gleaming wood of the instrument. Daphne joined her, but remained standing. A treacherous flutter of nerves made her place a hand to her stomach. Lachlan was watching her keenly, the intensity of his focus making her inwardly flounder.

"Do you know the song, *Drown it in the Bowl?*"

"Why, yes I do," Daphne said. It was a very unusual song, not one she would expect to sing in parlors, but she was happy she knew it well enough to sing while Eliza played.

"Ready?" Eliza asked.

"Yes." Daphne's voice wavered, but she cleared her throat as she listened to the notes of the piano, then closed her eyes and began to sing.

"The glossy sparkle on the board,
The wine is ruby bright,
The reign of pleasure is restor'd,
Of ease and fond delight.
The day is gone, the night's our own,
Then let us feast the soul,

If any care or pain remain,
Why drown it in the bowl."

Daphne opened her eyes and saw the open admiration of Cameron and Moira. It buoyed her spirits and she sang louder. As her gaze met Lachlan's, a shock ran through her, sizzling along her skin as she continued,

"This world they say's a world of woe,
That I do deny;
Can sorrow from the goblet flow?
Or pain from beauty's eye?
The wise are fools, with all their rules,
When they would joys control:
If life's a pain, I say again?
Let's drown it in the bowl."

She pictured the moment the officers of the law came to her house and dragged her father away; the spectators in the street who watched her eviction mere weeks after her father's sentence was announced. The cold, frightening agony and loneliness of the streets, the smooth comfort of the pearls against her fingertips, kept like a talisman against the ill will around her.

Her voice carried stronger now and she saw not only the past but a future, one she hoped to share with Lachlan. Sunny days on heather-filled meadows and nights in bed, his kisses setting fire between them.

"That time flies fast the poet sing;
Then surely it is wise,

In rosy wine to dip his wings,
And seize him as he flies.
This night is ours; then strewn with flowers
The moments as they roll:
If any pain or care remain,
Why drown it in the bowl."

Eliza played the refrain once more, then lifted her hands off the keys and laid them in her lap. Her eyes met with Daphne's and she was surprised to see the woman's eyes aglitter with tears.

"You sing beautifully," she said at last.

Daphne's throat constricted, and she looked at the small audience before her. Cameron was wide-eyed in admiration and perhaps a bit of shock, while Moira had a bittersweet smile upon her face. But Lachlan... His face was a storm of emotions.

Then, without a word, he stood and strode from the room, slamming the door behind him. Cameron exhaled a low, painful sigh before he rose and joined Daphne and Eliza.

"Eliza, why did you pick that song?" He brushed the back of his fingers over his wife's cheek. "You know it was his favorite."

"Whose favorite?" Daphne asked. "Lachlan's?"

Cameron's face turned to hers. His usual gaiety had vanished, replaced by deep grief.

"William. It was William's favorite."

"I'm sorry." Eliza stood, crossed to Moira, and

hugging her. The older woman wiped away stray tears. "I had forgotten. Please, forgive me."

"No, it was beautiful. Thank you," said Moira, then looked at the shut door. "But I fear the moment has affected poor Lachlan differently."

"I'll go talk to him," Cameron said, but Daphne caught his arm.

"Let me. I want to."

Cameron studied her. "Perhaps it would be best."

Daphne rushed from the music room and caught sight of Lachlan farther down the corridor. She followed him and realized he was headed toward the terrace. The back door to the hothouse was located near the terrace.

Lachlan entered the hothouse. Daphne slipped in behind him. The interior of the glass structure was warm, its windows fogged with moisture. A few abandoned yet blooming plants interspersed those that had withered and now stretched helplessly over dusty pot edges, their decaying vegetation filling the air with a bittersweet scent of death. Empty watering cans littered the floor, and wind whistled eerily along the windows while pale moonlight illuminated the house in creamy patches of light and shadow. She had settled her bit of rose bush here earlier in the day, having filled its pot with fresh soil.

Lachlan stood in the back of the room with one hand braced against the glass, his head bowed like a dark lord over a magical garden that slowly died around him.

"Lachlan," Daphne whispered. Her slipper trod on a dead leaf. The sharp crackle caused her to flinch. He did not move or speak.

She came up behind him, curled her arms around his waist and rested her cheek against his back. He tensed but did not pull away.

"Tell me about him."

After a long moment, he relaxed. The sigh that escaped him held a century of pain. "My brother was a good man," Lachlan said, "but plagued with sorrow. All of his life, a shadow hung inside him. No matter how bright the day or how pretty the girl smiling at him, he never..." The words roughened in his voice and she held him tighter. "He never saw the good. You understand?"

"I do." She rubbed his stomach with one hand. He reached up to take her hand and held it for a long moment. The simple connection seemed to root her, giving her hope that she could grow here beside him, two well-tended plants, twining their hearts together as plants would their roots.

"I never knew what to say to banish those clouds. I loved him fiercely, but my love was not enough."

He thought his love wasn't enough to save his brother? No wonder Lachlan and his mother suffered such pain. An accident was unexpected, but suicide... There was a helplessness to people who lost loved ones this way.

"What happened to him was not your fault," she

said. "Your love was enough, but sometimes sadness is too much to bear, and it comes from deep wells that are of no one's making. It doesn't mean they do not love, do not care." She remembered all too clearly the young woman whose family had cared about her, but she too had taken her life by plunging into the Thames one night and perished. "Focus on his *life*, not his death. Times when he knew and felt your love for him. Those are the memories you must burn into your heart. Only light can banish shadows."

Only love can banish sorrow... Daphne held him, willing Lachlan to feel her heart speaking to his, to feel her love. *I want to love you. Let me. Let me help you heal.*

He turned to face her, but she didn't let go. When he looked into her eyes, she saw a glimmer on his cheeks where tears had run down his face.

"You're not at all what I expected. Not what I wanted," he murmured as he cradled her face in his hands.

"Not what you wanted?" The words hurt, but he suddenly smiled, though it was tinged with melancholy.

"No, you're far *better*. I don't believe I will ever deserve to have you as my wife."

She relaxed and smiled back. "Lucky for you, I'm bought and paid for. I'm all yours."

His hoarse chuckle tickled her ears as he leaned down and placed a soft, lingering kiss upon her lips. With that kiss, she was pulled deeper into him, this beautiful wild Scotsman with his broken heart that called to her own. He kissed her slowly, wrapping her in his strength and warmth until every worry and every fear she had faded away. There was only this moment.

Tomorrow, this wonderful man will be my husband. Tomorrow...

CHAPTER 8

Lachlan stood at the entrance to the church, his black breeches and black waistcoat accented with gold embroidery. A red and green tartan sash was pinned at his chest with his father's brooch, which bore the Huntley seal. Beside him, Cameron stood unusually silent. A faint breeze rustled the dead leaves that were covered in frost, making the leaves look like shards of ice dancing between the tombstones when morning light illuminated them.

The castle's coach arrived and stopped at the end of the cobblestone path that led to him and the church behind him. He held his breath as the coach door opened. Eliza and his mother emerged, both smiling broadly before they stepped aside.

From the darkness of the coach, a slender hand

appeared on the frame of the door. Then a dainty foot in an elegant white shoe took its first step outside. His breath caught and his chest tightened. Daphne exited the coach, the fullness of her gown now filling the doorway. He swallowed hard as she stepped to the ground. The pale crème lace netting over the white skirts was old-fashioned, but the silver threading in the shape of swans on her pale blue bodice was exquisite.

His mother caught his eye and smiled again. He recognized the gown as his mother's wedding dress.

Daphne looked like a fairy queen. Her dark hair, bronzed by the light, flashed with hints of auburn and gold. How had he not noticed that her hair was more than simply dark? Daphne lifted her head and their gazes locked. She reached up, her fingertips touching the pearls around her neck. Emotion flooded him, blinding him with an intense inner light and heat that stole his breath and stopped his heart.

The vulnerability in her gaze was overshadowed by a trust so deep he knew he could never hurt this woman, *never* betray her. Whatever his reasons for bidding on her that night at the marriage auction no longer mattered. She was to be his wife, his partner in life. He would seek her counsel, seek her love and support. It was what he always longed for, even as a foolish young lad. Love had always been his dream.

Now I have it, at a terrible cost. Indeed, had he not lost his brother, had he not been driven by vengeance, he never would have met her—and she, in turn, never would have saved him. *I have been rewarded with a priceless prize.*

Daphne lifted her skirt and started down the gravel path. The sun lit glints of silver on her gown so she glowed and sparkled like a gemstone. He'd never been one for angels and God, at least, in the literal sense, but in that moment, as he watched her approach, he *believed* in something better, something wondrous and endless. It made him feel small, yet connected to everything around him—the wind in the trees, the stones collecting moss by the road, even the chatter of the larks in the heather. For two long months, he'd barely lived, his grief so strong, it threatened to drown him. But seeing Daphne coming toward him, hope shining her eyes, he breathed again for the first time in ages. His gratitude, his affection for her, was over-powering.

When his bride reached him, he raised her hand to his lips and knelt on the ground on one knee, then bowed his head, sending a silent prayer to the heavens that he would never lose her, his precious pearl. All his anger, all his sorrow had been banished by her light.

"Lachlan, what are you doing?" Daphne asked in a confused whisper. He pressed her hand to his cheek before he finally let go and stood.

"I..." He had no words, no way to tell her what lay in his heart at this moment.

"Forgive him, Miss Westfall," Cameron chuckled. "He seems to have swallowed his tongue."

"Aye, I have," he agreed with a smile and held out his arm to her. They entered the church together, the stained glass lighting up the pews with brilliant splashes of color.

The vicar, Mr. McKenzie, waited for them at the altar. Eliza and Cameron flanked them as the priest began his speech. Lachlan spoke his vows and stared at Daphne, smiling as they swore to love, honor and cherish each other until the day death parted them. The priest then pressed her right wrist against Lachlan's, and wound a plain white cloth around their hands. It was an old handfasting custom. Lachlan saw Daphne's puzzlement and fought off a chuckle. Then the priest spoke in Gaelic, and, in quiet whispers, Lachlan translated for her, "Two souls made one, two hearts made one. Let none tear asunder what the heavens have brought together."

Daphne's eyes widened as she looked up at him, but he saw only excitement with a hint of nervousness within her eyes, no fear.

"All right, lass?" he asked.

"Yes." As she spoke, a loose curl from her coiffure brushed her collarbone. He was arrested by the contrast of that lock against her pale skin, and the gleaming pearls that hung around her neck like frozen dewdrops along a delicate spider's web.

My lady in pearls.

"You may kiss your bride," Mr. McKenzie announced.

Lachlan leaned down, his free hand still curled in hers, their other hands bound fast, and kissed her. Tonight, he would see her in his bed, wearing nothing but those pearls, and he would make her smile, make her laugh, make her as happy as she was making him in that moment. When their lips broke apart, he heard her breathless sigh and reached up to brush her chin with his fingertips.

"You finally belong to me."

She caught his wrist and stroked his skin beneath the cuff of his shirtsleeve. "And you to me."

"Indeed." *I will not let the past destroy us.* The pain of William's death was finally muted, like a painting left in a sunny room, the colors bleached white, leaving barely a hint of what had once been so vivid. Daphne would paint new memories for him, ones of joy, not sorrow.

His throat tightened as the priest removed the hand bindings.

"I present Lord and Lady Huntley."

Cameron clapped loudly along with Eliza and Moira, who both wiped their eyes. For some glorious, ridiculous reason, Lachlan laughed, unable to contain the joy in his heart.

"I suppose you have a feast ready at home, Mother?"

Moira smiled despite her tears. "Of course. It's not every day my wee bairn takes a wife."

"Wee bairn?" Cameron laughed harder than Lachlan. "He's not been wee in over twenty years!"

"Mother, you mustn't embarrass me in front of my wife," he teased. "No man wishes to be thought of as wee on his wedding day."

Cameron laughed. "Indeed! Or Daphne will worry what else is wee on you tonight when you—*Oomph*!" Cameron doubled over as Eliza elbowed him hard in the chest.

Daphne giggled and Lachlan curled an arm around her waist.

"I promise, lass, there's nothing wee about me." He laughed again as she blushed scarlet.

The small wedding party exited the church and for the first time in two months, Lachlan embraced the warmth of the sun on his face. Daphne was his wife and tonight he would show her a world of pleasure. Perhaps Anthony had been right after all.

She will heal me. She's already begun to.

MARRIED. I AM MARRIED.

Daphne couldn't stop smiling as she waited in Lachlan's bed chambers. It was close to midnight, but she wasn't tired. They'd spent the remainder of the day feasting and playing games in the drawing room with Cameron and Eliza. It had been the most fun she'd had in such a long time.

She plucked nervously now at the nightgown she'd changed into. The only thing she wore aside from it was her mother's pearls. Lachlan had stopped her in the corridor just before she'd left to change for bed. He caught her by the waist and leaned close to whisper, "Wear the pearls, and nothing else."

She couldn't very well wait in his chambers completely naked, but she assumed he would insist upon her removing her nightgown once he arrived.

The sound of footfalls outside the door made her tense. She curled her fingers into the fabric of her nightgown.

Lachlan entered. He carried a delicate decanter of wine and a pair of glasses. He froze when he saw her standing there by his bed, barefoot, her hair unbound, wearing nothing but her nightclothes. He blinked and then gave his head a little shake.

"I thought you might wish for a drink." He gave the decanter a slight whirl and she nodded. A drink would help calm her nerves.

"Yes, that would be nice." She fidgeted for a moment before sitting down in the chair next to his desk. He poured two glasses and, after slipping one glass into her hand, drank his in two long gulps. He refilled his glass and brought it to his lips.

"Lachlan..." she began, noticing his hands shaking a little. Was he nervous? The thought was laughable. The worldly Scotsman, nervous on his wedding night?

"I..." He chuckled and set his glass down. "I am a wee bit..." He didn't finish, but his cheeks darkened to a ruddy shade beneath the candlelight.

"You're not the virgin, I am," she blurted out, and then covered her mouth with her hand, stifling a nervous laugh. Lachlan approached and played with the strands of her hair with his fingers, making her shiver with a secret thrill.

"I've not been with a lass that I cared about the way I do you." He brushed her long dark hair away from her neck. She reached up and touched the pearls at the same moment he did. Heat flared between them when their hands met.

"You care about me?" the words that escaped her were barely above a whisper.

His short nod was followed with a smile so faint she almost wondered if she'd imagined it.

Daphne held her breath a long moment before she replied, "I feel the same about you."

His look of boyish wonder as he cupped her face and gazed into her eyes melted away every concern she'd had about marrying him.

"I doona deserve you, lass. But I swear on my bones that I will strive every day, with every breath, to care for you and make you happy." There was an almost violent flash of pain in his eyes. She threw her arms around his neck, clinging to him. She slipped off the chair and they tumbled onto the floor, Lachlan holding her in his lap as he leaned against the bed's frame.

Daphne breathed in his comforting, enticing masculine scent and pressed her lips to his neck. His hands tightened around her waist as he held her very still. She examined his face, the hard jaw with a hint of stubble, his blue eyes now as dark and endless as the surface of a lake.

She trailed her fingertips down his nose to his lips, memorizing every curve, every faint line, even the barest hint of freckles on the bridge of his nose, which she hadn't noticed before. He was beautiful physically, but there was something else, a nobility in his face that seem to come from within. It had nothing to do with bloodlines or titles, but a nobility of the soul. She realized she trusted him more than she had ever trusted anyone except her mother. Her father's crimes had cost her much, including her trust in others, but now, for the first time, she felt like she could trust another person. She could trust in Lachlan.

I want to give him everything, all that I am.

"Are you ready to go to bed?" she asked, stroking his lips. He moved one hand up and down her back, the way a man would calm an untamed horse.

"Aye. Are you?" he asked. Worry marred his face until she nodded.

She slid off his lap and they stood, smiling hesitantly, both embarrassed.

"Why don't I take off my shirt?" He stepped back and reached over his head to pull off the white garment. Once exposed to view, his bare chest made her mouth run dry. He tossed the shirt away and lifted one of her hands to his chest, placing her palm over his heart.

"I am yours, lass, look your fill. *Touch.*" He stroked the back of her hand. "As you will."

Daphne explored him, marveling at the muscled plains of his abdomen and the corded steel of his arms, awed that something so beautiful could be hers. Then he unfastened his trousers and removed his shoes. She stepped back with wide eyes when she saw his fully bared body. He was unashamed and waved her closer with a coaxing hand. He stepped back and leaned on the edge of the bed, inviting her near.

"I doona bite," he chuckled when she drew close enough. She placed one hand on the top of his hard thigh, a secret delight surging through her when his muscles leapt beneath her fingers.

"Now for you." He reached for the front of her nightgown, unfastened the buttons at her breasts and then lifted the gown over her head.

When she stood naked before him, she stiffened, her nipples pebbling in the cool air. He parted his knees and gently pulled her to stand between his thighs so he could touch her. He cupped one breast, and his rough, calloused palms sent delightful tingles through her. She clenched her thighs as wetness grew between them.

Lachlan plucked one nipple, the gentle tug making her hiss out a soft moan. She arched her back, clutching his shoulders as she offered him her other breast. He bent his head and fastened his mouth to it, kissing, sucking, nibbling until she couldn't stop from trembling. Everything he did was thrilling, even frightening, but exquisitely wonderful. She reached for his erect shaft, needing to touch him as intimately as he was touching her, but he caught her wrist.

"There will be plenty of time for that, lass, but not yet. A man needs to pleasure his woman thoroughly before he sees to himself." He slid his hands down to her bottom and lifted her onto his lap. His shaft slid between her wet folds and she whimpered as a hard edge of need rolled through her. She needed him to do something to her, to ease the hunger she barely understood.

"Lachlan, please, I want you to—"

"Shhh..." He kissed her hungrily, their lips melding as he clenched her buttocks and rocked her against him in his lap. She arched, her knees sliding on the bedding on either side of his slender hips. Daphne was desperate to feel him inside her, even though she was afraid he wouldn't fit, that he was far too big, but her hunger was stronger than her concerns. They broke the kiss and she implored him with begging eyes to give her what she needed, what they both did.

"Aye. You'll be the death of me, wife." He fell back on the bed with her before he rolled them over so that she lay beneath him. Her knees gripped his hips, trying to close even though his body lay between them. Blood surged from her fingertips to her toes.

He lowered his mouth to hers, and his kiss burned like morning light through the darkness of her weary soul and she surrendered everything to him. The unexpected pinch she felt as he slid inside her faded beneath the fire of his kiss. He spoke to her between kisses as he withdrew and thrust back inside her. She recognized the words, the Gaelic from the wedding ceremony.

"Two souls made one, two hearts made one. Let none tear asunder what the heavens have brought together." She closed her eyes as the tension building inside her broke in a sudden crest. The pleasure was as pure as it was explosive. Daphne gasped in sweet agony. She clung to him, her inner walls fluttering around him and she pressed frantic kisses along his cheek, lips and chin as he thrust twice more and collapsed on top of her, his weight heavy but welcome.

Lachlan kissed the shell of her ear, smiling as he lifted his head to gaze down at her. A deep peace settled inside her, as if she stood in a meadow at dawn, with the birds beginning to chatter softly, sunlight beginning to bathe the ground, and a breeze rustling the grass.

There was something about a *beginning*. It seemed to fill one's soul with hope, with *love*. What she and

Lachlan had shared this night was a new dawn, a beginning all their own.

Lachlan brushed stray wisps of hair back from her face and swallowed hard. "How do you feel?" he asked.

Daphne smiled, feeling like her whole body could float away. "As though you gave me wings to fly."

With a chuckle and a glint of mischief in his eyes, he nuzzled her cheek. "I've not even showed you the best parts."

"Oh?" She couldn't possibly imagine that what they had just done could get any better.

"Aye, there's a few hours yet before we should sleep. And I know just how we can pass the time." He kissed her, and she was swept away by his embrace, his touch and his passion. Lachlan had given her the one thing she longed for above all else. Happiness. She would cling to it as long as she could.

CHAPTER 9

"You're in love with her."

Lachlan tensed. He and Cameron leaned against the short wall of the terrace. Before them, in the field between the gardens, Daphne and Eliza played with a sheepdog that belonged to one of the tenant farmers who had come to speak with Lachlan's groundskeeper.

"No, I like her. She's a bonnie lass and—"

"You can lie to yourself, old friend, but never to me." Cameron's teasing tone softened, "I know you've convinced yourself you don't deserve love, not after losing William, but you're wrong. You deserve her. You deserve joy in your life. It's what he would have wanted for you."

Cameron touched Lachlan's shoulder. The truth of his friend's words seemed to reverberate through his body with the sound and clarity of the bells hanging in the tower of the Kirk of Huntley.

He *loved* Daphne.

He should've known the first time he spoke with her that she would leave a burning imprint upon his heart and soul. Lachlan was finally seeing things clearly. It mattered that her father had driven William to his death, but she was not her father. His sins were not hers, and would never be hers. She was a victim, just like William, yet she hadn't surrendered, hadn't given up, even when she had reached the end of her rope. She'd agreed to marry a stranger, and done her best to fit in here. She had even fallen in love with him. Even now, without knowing it, she had changed him, dragged him kicking and screaming from the hollow hole in his heart and forced him back into the light of the living, How could he not love her?

Daphne tossed a red ball and the sheepdog scampered across the lawn, stumbling to a stop as he nearly tripped over his prey, then clutched it in his mouth and returned it to her. He shook his black and white coat and pawed the ground before dropping the ball, his tail wagging so hard that his whole body shook. Even at this distance, Lachlan could see the joy on Daphne's face.

"There it is again," Cameron said. "That love-struck look you made fun of me for when I first told you I planned to marry Eliza."

Lachlan couldn't resist a smile. "I suppose I am owed this teasing, aren't I?"

"Indeed, you are, and more." Cameron chuckled. "I think it's time Eliza and I went home. You need a proper honeymoon with your bride, and should not spend it entertaining guests."

Lachlan grinned. "As much as I like you, I would prefer to return her to bed and not leave for days except to eat."

Cameron slapped Lachlan's shoulder. "Let me collect my wife. We should arrive home in time for dinner."

Lachlan shook hands once more with his friend. As he watched Cameron walk away, he realized he'd neglected their friendship for too long. William's death had robbed him of so much: his joy, his friends. Marrying Daphne was already bringing his life back into focus. He wouldn't let the things that truly mattered escape him again.

Lachlan remained on the terrace, watching Daphne chase the dog, who now barked excitedly and dodged her in a game as old as time. The heartache in his chest was nearly gone, something he never thought possible.

"My lord?"

Lachlan turned away from the terrace. His groundskeeper stood there before him, hat in hand.

"Yes?"

"The farmers said the black fallow deer herds are in

need of thinning. I thought we might give them permission to go shooting on our lands, if you approve."

"Of course. You'll see to it they get the meat they need?"

His groundskeeper nodded, then laughed. Lachlan followed his gaze back to the field. Daphne held the dog's front paws, making him stand on hind legs. The furry beast was licking her face enthusiastically.

"Oh, I'll see to it. You got a bonnie bride to tend to quickly, or else you might be replaced in her affections." The groundskeeper chuckled as he walked away.

Lachlan leaned against the stone terrace railing and watched his bride. Her hair blew loose in the breeze, her face flushed. She waved at him and he waved back, a boyish giddiness growing inside him. After so much darkness, so much pain, he had a moment of pure contentment.

Daphne left the dog and walked up to the steps.

"It's a wonderful day. Come and walk with me." She held out her hand.

He descended the stairs and took it, loving how their fingers intertwined, and headed toward the gardens. Once there, he tugged her against his body, delighting in her gasp and sigh as he covered her mouth with his. Daphne gave freely of herself and he whispered soft words of encouragement against her skin when she clung to him. The velvet warmth of her kisses cocooned him inside a private heaven that he never wished to leave.

He wasn't sure how much time passed before they broke apart. That single kiss had seemed endless. He never knew that simply kissing a woman could fill him with such pleasure.

Lachlan grasped her hands and grinned. "Let's go inside and continue this."

She giggled. "That sounds like a wonderful idea."

As they walked back to the house, Lachlan had to stop himself from whistling. In the distance, he heard the crack of gunfire.

"What's that?" Daphne asked, looking over the fields beyond the castle.

"The farmers are hunting deer. The herds need thinning. I have quite a few on Huntley lands, and I let the tenants hunt during the winter to keep the poor beasts from starving. The extra meat will be a welcome for the tenant farmers come wintertime."

"Can I meet the tenants?" she asked. "I would like to know as much as possible about your life here."

"*Our* life," he corrected.

"Our life," she echoed with a blush.

"I can take you to meet them tomorrow." Lachlan paused as he reached the door and stole one more kiss before he gestured for her to precede him.

"Lachlan?" His mother's voice stopped him in his tracks.

Moira stood in the hallway, her face pale. She clutched a piece of paper. She stood only a few feet from his study, or rather, William's study. Moira's eyes darted to Daphne, a mixture of horror and pain so stark it made him suck in a breath.

She knew.

"Moira, are you all right?" Daphne let go of Lachlan's arm and started toward her. Moira retreated a step as though Daphne would attack her.

"I need to speak with you, *alone*." Moira told him, refusing to look at Daphne.

"Lachlan, should I...?" Daphne began.

"Go upstairs to my chambers and wait from me." He moved toward his wife.

"But—"

"Go." He pushed her gently toward the stairs.

Once he was sure Daphne had reached the upper floor, he escorted his mother into William's study and closed the door.

"You *hid* this from me." His mother shoved the paper at his chest and he caught the slightly crumpled letter. "I found it locked in his desk drawer. You *knew*, didn't you? William never locked those drawers, but *you* did." Moira's eyes were rimmed with red as she looked at him, then she collapsed into a chair in front of William's desk, her head bowed.

"I couldn't let you know the truth." He set the letter down on the escritoire, his throat suddenly tight. Why hadn't he burned the letter? He should have, but he'd foolishly been unable to let go of it. They were William's last words and he couldn't let go.

His mother lifted her head. "He said he was involved in something with Sir Richard Westfall. That's Daphne's father, isn't it?" It was less a question than an accusation.

"Yes." He wanted to lie to her, but he couldn't.

"You knew before you married her, didn't you?" Moira sniffed. Tears trickled down her cheeks. His mother's agony cut through him hard enough that he could feel his heart bleeding.

"Aye. I knew."

"But ...how could you? The daughter of the man who-- Why? Did you think to find some justice in it or did you have other designs for her? What were you thinking?" her words crumbled into a breathless inhalation as she fought off a sob.

"I married her to hurt her, to hurt *him*. I didn't love her, mother. It was a marriage arranged from spite and vengeance. I wanted to make her miserable. It was my only way to hurt him, through her." A great weariness settled on him.

"What?" Moira's voice cracked. "You brought her here for that? Lachlan, I want her gone, I can't have her here, not when..." she choked on a sob and wiped her eyes. "She's a sweet girl and she doesn't deserve to suffer your vengeance. She's not her father, can't you see? Living with a man who despises her isn't fair to her, not when she's innocent of her father's crimes. You must send her back to London. Annul the marriage."

"It's too late for that," he whispered.

His mother stared at him, horror filling her face. "Then you must live apart."

Lachlan was silent for a long moment. "No. I can't send her away. Because... I love her. I love her *wildly*, Mother. I don't care about her father, not anymore. I want to look forward, not dwell in the past. She's the only thing that matters to me now. William would not have wanted me to forsake my love if he knew how happy I could be."

Moira rose from the chair, her blue eyes dull and her lips trembling.

"You should have told me." For a long moment they stared at each other, a chasm growing between them, one that he feared he could not repair. Then she turned her back on him and left.

For a long while he didn't move. He stood behind William's desk, thinking back to the day he'd ridden up to the house and saw his brother in the window, heard the shot that rang out across the grounds, and the awful silence that followed. His heart had frozen in that instant as he had tried to reach his brother. Too late. Always, too late.

"I'm sorry, brother," he whispered to the silent room. He could almost feel William there, as though he paused on the other side of an invisible veil. The hairs on the back of his neck rose and he closed his eyes, speaking again. "I *love* her. I can't cling to both love and hate. She fills my heart, so there's no room left for anger and pain and hatred."

He thought for a brief moment that a hand touched his shoulder. An infinitesimal pressure, one of reassurance and comfort. He reached up and placed his hand where he felt the slight weight.

"There is nothing to forgive," the words came in William's voice.

His mother would need time to heal, to understand. Right now, he needed to speak to Daphne. She deserved to know the truth. But first he had to prove his love for her. Only then could he confess the truth behind his original intentions in marrying her.

As he exited the study, he heard something roll along the wooden floor. He glanced down and saw two dozen white beads that had scattered when his foot brushed them. He knelt and picked one up. They were pearls. Not his mother's, because she hadn't worn any.

With a gasp, he frantically tried to retrieve the pearls, clutching them in his palm. Blood roared in his ears as he reached into the nooks and crannies of the hall, desperate to reclaim every precious orb. But Daphne had gone upstairs, so how...?

"May I help you, my lord?" The young maid, Mary, knelt beside him, cupping her hands to receive what he'd collected so far.

"Take these and put them somewhere safe. We must find every one," he said. His voice began to fill with panic, trying not to think about the implications of this moment.

The maid tucked the pearls into her apron pocket. "My lord, the countess is gone."

His stomach grew heavy as his fear began to materialize, but still he refused to believe it. "Gone?"

"She was crying, and I feared you didn't know. She called for a coach and left."

There was no more denial left in him. Daphne must have listened at the door. He stared at the floor where the pearls had fallen. She always touched them when she was anxious. She must have ripped them from her neck before she fled, when she heard the awful truth behind their marriage.

"How long ago did she leave?"

"Half an hour?" Mary guessed.

"What? Why did no one summon me?" He stumbled to his feet.

The maid stepped back but was brave enough to answer, "She was most upset when you were in the study and begged the staff who saw her not to say a word. But when I saw you come out, I knew someone had to tell you." Her gaze shot to the open door behind him and he understood. No one bothered him when he was inside his study. They believed he went in there to seek peace, to feel close to William, and it was true.

"I'll take care of the pearls, my lord," Mary promised, one hand touching the pocket of her apron.

"Thank you." Lachlan sprinted down the corridor and called for the nearest footman to have a horse saddled. He donned a coat and gloves as he rushed down the steps to the drive. He studied the road leading away from Huntley Castle but saw no sign of the coach carrying Daphne away from him.

Lachlan nodded at the groom who brought him his fastest gelding and mounted. He prayed he would not be too late to reach the other half of his heart before it, too, was lost forever.

CHAPTER 10

Daphne could barely breathe.

She lay curled up in the coach, a fisted hand pressed against her mouth to mute the sound of her sobs. Why had she gone back downstairs? She had hoped to render aid to Moira in some way, who had clearly been distressed, but then the words she'd overheard had stopped her cold and eventually broken her soul.

Until that moment, she'd survived everything. Her father's scandal, the loss of her former life, her home and friends, but none of it hurt quite like losing her heart. Everything had been a lie. Every kiss, every look, every vow to love and cherish each other. All she'd had to hear was that her marriage to him was a lie and she'd fled the house.

I was nothing more than a part of Lachlan's vengeance.

She reached for her neck. The skin was bare, yet it stung where she'd grabbed her mother's pearls and ripped them off in panic as her world fell apart.

She'd had recurring dreams of drowning in her youth, of being pulled down into an endless darkness, her mouth and lungs filling with water. Lachlan's words were worse than those nightmares. They weren't just pulling her down, they were burying her so far below the surface that she would never survive.

"It was a marriage of spite and revenge."

Tears leaked from her eyes as she recalled the heat of his kiss, the whispered words of affection in her ear, and their bodies pressed close.

All lies. He had treated her well. So, when had he planned to spring his trap? She didn't want to stay and find out what his form of revenge would be.

She tried to breathe again, but air got trapped between her mouth and her lungs, unable to flow. The coach rocked suddenly and a voice outside shouted, "Halt!"

Lachlan's commanding tone was all too clear. It jolted Daphne's heart back into rhythm. The carriage bumped to a sudden stop.

"My lord?" the driver called out.

Daphne heard steps on the left side of the coach. She jerked open the door on the right and tumbled into the road. They had reached the forest a mile from the castle. Her attention swept the tall, dark woods, the thick trunks and the cover of the head pine trees. There was nowhere to run, but she couldn't stay here.

"Daphne?" Lachlan's voice sounded hoarse and panicked.

She wiped tears from her face and ran past the horses and the stunned coach driver. She heard a curse and the rush of boots on the dirt road behind her. A hand caught her arm, dragging her to a halt. The pull sent her spinning back around to face him. He caught her in his arms and for an awful instant her body wanted to surrender, to burrow into him and believe the lies he'd told her, if only for a little while. She regained control and shoved at his chest.

"Let go of me, you monster!"

"Daphne, please listen," Lachlan begged, holding her tight despite her struggles.

She kicked his shin. He cursed, bent to grasp his leg and let go. Stunned by her sudden freedom, she didn't immediately turn to leave. What would be the point? She could not outrun him.

Lachlan straightened, letting go of his shin as he panted and stared at her. "Please, let me explain."

"Why should I?" The words cut her, but she kept her head high. Her father may have committed terrible crimes, but she was also the granddaughter of a duke and a lady in her own right. What pride she had left wouldn't allow her to be pathetic, not even when her heart was bleeding.

"I know what you heard." Lachlan's face reddened. "My motives the night we met were inexcusable. Monstrous, yes. My heart was blackened with grief and you came into my life offering what I thought I needed." He swallowed hard, then his words dropped to a whisper as he gazed at her like a drowning man would stare at a rope tossed to him from shore. "And I was right. You *were* what I needed... I just didn't know the reasons why."

Daphne wasn't sure she understood what he was saying.

"I didn't need revenge. I needed...*love*." The last word was spoken so softly she thought perhaps she might have dreamt it. He reached for her and she didn't draw away, even though she knew she should. With gentle fingers, he brushed away the tears on her cheeks.

"You don't love me," she said, her voice hitching. "You don't intend to hurt people you love."

The smile he gave was bittersweet. "I agree. But every time I tried to hurt you, to revenge William's death, I stopped. I couldn't go through with it. Did you not hear what I told my mother?"

"That you married me out of spite and vengeance? What happens when you are in one of your black moods? When you miss William and all you see in my eyes is the daughter of the man responsible? Will you still love me then?"

"You are not your father. I see that now." He raked a

hand through his hair. "You didn't hear the rest. You didn't hear me say that I love you. I love you madly. I love you with a wildness that frightens me."

He took a step closer to her, his blue eyes stark with desperation. She didn't step away, but her heart raced. She had to master her reactions as he held out a hand to her. Loneliness and confusion battled with hope and longing until the crescendo of emotions became too overwhelming to be kept inside. She sniffed as her nose and eyes began to burn.

"Will you say something, lass? Anything?" he begged.

"How do I know you mean what you say? Any of it?"

Lachlan looked away, then locked eyes with her again. His throat worked as he tugged at his cravat. "I don't know a way to prove it to you. I'm a man full of stubborn, foolish pride, but..." He took her hand and knelt down on one knee. The memory of the last time he'd done this came flooding back. The tears which followed burned her cheeks, but she didn't move to wipe them away, or dare to breathe.

He paused, his blue eyes misty. "I found your pearls. They'd spilled across the floor and I picked them up, every single one and..." He shook his head, as though unsure of what to say, then, "I was never supposed to be an earl. That was William. But he's gone, and I am here, making a bloody mess of everything I hold dear. I under-stand why the pearls are so important to you. You, you are *my* string of pearls, Daphne. The thing I reach for when I'm full of joy or when I'm frightened of the world around me. You are the most precious thing to me. You are my hope."

He stroked his thumbs over her cheeks, his gaze impossibly soft. "In my eyes, you are the most exquisite gift a man could be given. I'm afraid to let you go, to have you scatter and vanish like a broken strand of pearls." He bowed his head. "But if you must leave, I love you too much to force you to stay." Lachlan drew in a deep breath, pressing her hand to his cheek.

"You'd really let me go?" she asked.

"Yes, but you'd take my heart with you, lass." He choked on the last few words. And, in that moment, she saw him in a way she hadn't before. She saw Lachlan's heart beneath the tall muscled form that remained on bended knee before her. His heart was in his eyes and the pain of his past, so vividly exposed, that she hurt with him. There was no menace, no anger or hatred there, only love and the fear of losing it. But it all brought one question to mind, one she still didn't know the answer to.

"*Why* do you love me?"

He answered without hesitation, "Because of who you are. Not as the daughter of a wretched man, but as a woman who cares about strangers and fights for her life and refuses to surrender to fate. A woman who smiles and dances and finds joy even after enduring so much sorrow. You love with all your heart and make me want to be the best version of myself. I can't breathe when I think of you hurting, lass. You've become a part of me, and I hope that there's a little bit of me inside you too. I cannot imagine my life without you." He pressed his lips to her hand. "I made a vow in the church to you. Two souls made one, two hearts made one. The heavens brought us together and only you can break us apart."

Daphne stared down at him, too afraid to hope that all he said was true.

"Lachlan, even if I believe you, it won't erase the fact that my father caused your brother's death. Your mother will never forgive me."

He was on his feet, tugging her into his arms, embracing her so tight that she had to shove at him to get room to breathe.

"All that matters, is that you are my wife, my love. What your father did was a true dishonor, but William was his own man. He took his own life by his own choice. I didn't want to face that truth, but I have to. Tragedy brought you to me, but I promise to let only hope bind us from now on."

She pressed her cheek to his chest, her heart still heavy with concern. "What about Moira?"

"She likes you. She wanted you gone to protect you from me and my thirst for vengeance. But my only plan is to love you. Madly, wildly, deeply." He leaned back so he could cup her face.

"Lachlan," she breathed, trembling, wanting to believe him, to trust him.

He brushed a thumb over her lips so intently that he seemed to be imprinting their shape upon his memory. "Aye?"

"You cannot lie to me, ever again. I need...I *deserve* a husband who loves me enough to give me honesty. If you won't be that man, then I have to leave." She was amazed at the strength in her voice. She meant every word. She would protect herself no matter the consequences.

Lachlan nodded. "Aye, you're right. And you have my word. I am your man, lass. Always." The word was breathed so softy it sounded like a prayer.

By the forest's edge, a deer wandered out and watched their reunion with mild interest.

"Then take me home." Home to Huntley. Home with him.

Please let him be a man of his word. Please let him love me.

Lachlan laughed with such joy and relief that he swung her around in the air before he set her back down.

"Ach, lass," he murmured, kissing her. "You'll be the death of me if I lose you."

"Then don't lose me." She bit her lip but finally smiled after a moment. She was so afraid to hope they could be happy—

Crack!

The report of a rifle exploded around them and the

deer bolted across the road. Lachlan grunted and stumbled, still holding her in his arms, but she saw pain streak across his features before he dropped his arms and crumpled to the ground.

Blood suddenly covered her face and his.

"Lachlan!" She screamed, falling to her knees by his side.

"My lord!" The driver leapt from the coach and dashed over to Lachlan.

"He's bleeding!" Daphne touched Lachlan's head. Blood poured from a deep cut along one of his temples.

"He's been shot."

"What?" Daphne frantically ripped at the hem of her dress, freeing a bit of fabric. She pressed it to the wound, staunching it. Terror pounded inside her.

Shot. Blood. Death. The three words cut through her over and over as she pressed the cloth tight to Lachlan's head.

"Seamus! You shot his lordship!" Both the driver and Daphne looked in the direction of sounds coming from the nearby underbrush. An old man and a young boy emerged from the foliage. The young boy carried a rifle. The old man shook the young boy by the shoulders and tore the rifle from his hands.

Seamus's face turned ashen as he stared at Daphne and the coach driver clutching Lachlan's body, blood coating their hands and the road.

"I dinnae mean to!" The lad's bottom lip quivered.

"Help me get him into the coach," she told the driver. She turned to the farmer and boy. "Do you have horses?"

"Aye."

"Fetch the nearest doctor. Send him to the castle."

The old man struck the boy's backside. "You heard her ladyship!"

Seamus sprinted back into the underbrush. The farmer helped Daphne and the driver lift Lachlan into the coach. The farmer stayed inside with Daphne, who kept the blood-soaked bit of cloth pressed tight to Lachlan's temple.

The ride back to the castle seemed to last forever. Daphne panted softly as she focused on Lachlan. His eyes opened halfway, as if he were dreaming and not losing a perilous amount of blood.

"My pearl," Lachlan said drowsily and raised one hand to brush her cheek.

She clasped his hand in hers. "I'm here." His eyes closed but his breathing remained steady. When they reached Huntley Castle, Daphne ordered the farmer and driver to carry Lachlan to the drawing room.

Moira rushed down the steps. "Lachlan!"

"He was grazed by a bullet." Daphne caught Moira's arm. "Have the footmen bring hot water and fresh towels."

Moira whirled and rushed into the house, calling for footmen. Daphne led the driver and the farmer into the drawing room, where they placed him on a chaise lounge.

She continued to keep the cloth firmly pressed to his wound the entire time.

"What else can I do, my lady?" the farmer asked.

"Watch for the doctor."

She wiped the blood on the side of Lachlan's head, wincing.

"What happened?" Moira's voice broke as she rushed into the room, two footmen following, their arms full of supplies.

"Hold this." She took Moira's hand and pressed it against the cloth to keep pressure on Lachlan's wound. Then she stood and took one of the cloths from a footman. She offered him a whisper of thanks before she dipped the cloth in the bowl of hot water. She returned to Lachlan and pressed a new, clean cloth to his temple.

"Daphne, what happened?" Moira demanded again.

"One of the tenant farmer's children was hunting and the bullet grazed Lachlan's head. If it's only a surface wound, he will be all right. Head wounds bleed more than others."

Moira's eyes were pinned to her son's pale face. "How do you know?"

"My father had friends who served in the military and shared rather vivid memories from the wars. One of them mentioned that a head wound such as this bled a lot, but wasn't fatal as long as the injured person was seen by a physician right away.

There was a commotion outside the drawing room and the boy from the forest appeared. Behind him came a gentleman in a black waistcoat and trousers. He carried a black medicine bag as he rushed to Lachlan's side.

Moira and Daphne gave the doctor space to examine Lachlan's head wound. Moira slipped a hand in hers and they clung to each other, holding their breaths while the doctor tended to Lachlan. He spent several minutes closing the wound with stiches and then cleansed it. When he finished, he faced them with a relieved smile.

"His Lordship should be fine. He'll need his bandages changed daily until the wound fully heals. No riding, bending over, or anything else that requires physical exertion until the stiches have been removed."

Daphne glanced at Moira and then she turned back to the doctor. "I believe we can manage that."

"What can we do for him now?"

"For now, you must let him rest. I will leave you some further instructions before I go."

"Thank you." Moira wiped away a tear before she shooed the footmen away.

"I'll be back with some hot tea," Moira said before she, too, slipped out of the room.

After Daphne thanked the doctor and saw him out, she returned to Lachlan's side and set a chair next to the chaise, thankful she could just sit beside him. She curled her fingers around his hand. He had protected her when she was desperate for help. Now she would protect him.

A few minutes later, Moira returned with tea and poured them both a cup.

"Is he doing better?" she asked.

Daphne had been paying close attention to Lachlan's breathing. It had deepened rather than become shallow. That was a good sign.

"Yes. I think so."

Moira swallowed hard and looked at Daphne. "I pray you are right. I cannot lose him, not like I did William."

Daphne placed a hand over Moira's wrist, squeezing it gently. "You won't lose him."

"You are so sure... How?"

Daphne smiled sadly. "Because Lachlan is a fighter. He won't let go of life, not without a struggle. It's one of the reasons I love him."

"You love him?" Moira's eyes softened with sorrow. "But you must know why he brought you here."

"I overheard you talking in the study. It's why I left. What I didn't hear was that his feelings had changed."

"He said he loved you. I know my son. He spoke the truth when he said he loved you. I didn't want to believe, but it was in his eyes, in his voice." Moira stroked Lachlan's cheek and he groaned.

"If he can love you, then I believe I can too," Moira said. "I already was fond of you, my dear. I couldn't have chosen a better woman for him. Fortunately, I didn't need to."

Daphne's throat constricted as she focused on Lachlan, afraid she might burst into tears if she looked at Moira right now. It was all she ever wanted, to be accepted and loved.

I'm so afraid it won't last, that this dream will prove false.

CHAPTER 11

Lachlan woke, his mouth dry and his head throbbing. A soft weight rested on his ribs. He moved and felt a feminine body slumped over his chest. He blinked, clearing his vision, and saw Daphne sitting beside him on a chair in the drawing room.

What had happened?

The last thing he remembered was standing on the side of the road, holding her in his arms, after she agreed to return home. He reached for his temple and touched bandages. The drawing room door opened a crack and his mother peered inside. She looked between him and Daphne.

He carefully slipped off of the chaise, then eased Daphne back in her chair. He touched his head again gingerly, fighting off a wave of dizziness.

"You need to stay down," his mother admonished, trying to force him back to the chaise.

"I will, in a moment. I wish to speak with you outside first." He pointed to the hall. They both exited the room and he leaned against the corridor wall to preserve his strength while his head pounded.

"Lachlan, you scared me." His mother embraced him with a gentle, careful hug, reminding him of when he was a wee lad and he'd come to her afraid of shadows. She'd held him just like this and whispered the words only mothers knew that could put a child's fears to rest.

"I'm all right, Mother." He kissed her forehead and then gently lifted her arms away so she would step back. He needed to see her face and he couldn't do that while she hugged him.

"I was so afraid," Moira's voice trembled. "I couldn't lose you too."

"You didn't. I'm right here." He looked back through the doorway, where he could still see Daphne's blood covered, sleeping form.

"She's a sweet, brave lass and I want her to stay," Moira said. "She loves you, despite the terrible reason you brought her here."

"I love her more than I ever thought I could love a woman. I thought, at first, fate was being cruel by letting me fall in love with the daughter of the man who drove William to his death, but she's suffered too. Greatly. And when I'm with her, my heart doesn't feel so broken."

Moira hugged him again. "Maybe we can finally heal."

"Aye."

"My lord?"

Lachlan turned. Mary stood behind them. She held a small rosewood box on her palm. "I collected each pearl. What should I do with them?"

Lachlan glanced at his mother. "I have an idea. Assuming you don't mind, Mother." He winked when she raised her brows.

"What are you up to, Lachlan?" she asked.

"Something wonderful."

A WEEK LATER, DAPHNE SAT CURLED IN A LIBRARY chair, reading by the fire. Beside her, in his own chair, Lachlan pretended to read. His head wound was nearly healed after she'd spent every day looking after him. This was the first day in which he'd insisted she take a few hours to do something she enjoyed and not fuss over him. When she'd suggested reading in the library, he'd agreed. Yet from the moment they'd sat down with their books, his focus remained on her. Every so often, she looked up and he hastily returned his attention to his book.

"You're watching me," she said. "Why?"

He smiled, set his book aside, and waved her over.

She put her own book down, crawled onto his lap, and wrapped her arms around his neck.

"I've been waiting for the right time to give you this." He reached into his trouser pocket and pulled out a small, velvet pouch. He offered it on his palm. She took it, loosened the drawstrings, opened the velvet. She paused and looked at Lachlan in puzzlement before she tilted the bag upside down. Pearls tumbled into her hand. This necklace held two strands of pearls.

"My pearls... But... they can't be. Mother's necklace had only a single strand of pearls."

"The others are a gift from my mother. She would have given them to you at some point."

"But, I cannot take hers, not when..."

"Hush, lass. She wanted you to have them. To let you know that you're as dear to her as you are to me."

Daphne peered closely at the double-strand necklace, her lips trembling.

She pressed the back of her fingers against her mouth. "I thought I'd lost them forever when I left that day. I'd thought I'd lost you too," she admitted.

"I'm not that easy to be rid of, you know." His tone was teasing and mischief lit his eyes.

"I know. You almost died and..." she choked, the terror of that day still fresh in her mind. She could have lost him forever.

"But I didn't, now dry those eyes. I don't ever want

to see you crying on my account." He wiped at a tear that trailed down her face.

She sniffled and raised the necklace to her cheek, brushing the smooth round orbs against her skin before she kissed them.

A piece of her past had been restored through Lachlan's thoughtfulness. Her heart had shattered violently from Lachlan's betrayal and she'd run fast and far from the dream world Lachlan had let her glimpse. When she'd broken the strand and the pearls had scattered across the floor, she hadn't stopped to retrieve them. She'd tried hard to forget the pearls over the last few days, not knowing what had happened when they'd fallen. They'd represented the life she'd had before her mother died, and she'd had to face the truth. That part of her life was over, had been over for years. She was living her new life, with man she loved with all of her heart. Yet he'd given her back this last bit of her mother and Moira had given her a set of pearls too. The unity of those two strands together was beautiful not because the pearls were lovely but because of what they represented. Time was healing old wounds. Willian's death and her father's imprisonment were the past. She and Lachlan were the future.

Lachlan took the pearls from her and fastened the clasp around her neck. Their gentle weight against her collarbones was comforting.

"I love you lass, never doubt it." Lachlan's winter-blue eyes held no frost, only the heat of a winter fire.

She brushed her fingers through his hair, careful not to touch his barely healed wound. "I love you too."

"Prove it," he said.

She brushed her nose against his. "You're quite commanding, aren't you?"

"Only when I expect to be kissed." He wrapped his arms around her waist and she laughed, but her heart was so full that she could scarcely breathe. She very slowly leaned her head into his, biting her lip as she paused an inch from his mouth.

"Do you know what I keep thinking about?" she asked.

"What?" His eyes fixed on her mouth.

"About our wedding, and the moment we entered the church together."

Lachlan's eyes met hers and held. "That is a day I will never forget. I could breathe again when I took you in my arms and pledged myself to you. You gave me my life back." He brushed a finger over the pearls. "My lady in pearls."

"You did the same for me." She closed the last inch between them. Their lips met and time froze, like an errant beam of sunlight that strikes a chandelier's crystal and fractures into a rainbow that illuminates the world around it.

We are two broken hearts made whole, two lost souls made one.

SEDUCING AN HEIRESS ON A TRAIN

CHAPTER 1

ondon, December 1888

The ticking clock in the corner of the waiting area counted down the seconds toward Oliver Conway's doom. Each second sounded like a hammer fall in the interminable silence. He clenched his worn black gloves in one hand and held his hat in the other as he waited to be summoned. Finally, the door to the bank president's office opened, and a portly man with kind eyes glanced down the hall to find him.

"Lord Conway, I will see you now."

Oliver swallowed and stood, then straightened his shoulders and entered the office of Mr. Kelly, president of Drummonds Bank.

"Please, sit, Lord Conway." Mr. Kelly waved at the pair of leather chairs facing the desk.

Oliver sat, his hands trembling a little. At the grown age of one and thirty he had few reasons to be afraid, but today this man held the fate of Oliver's family's future in his hands.

Mr. Kelly removed a pair of spectacles from his coat pocket and nestled them on the bridge of his nose. He pulled a stack of papers toward him. "I've reviewed all of the accounts this morning, my lord, and I'm afraid the loans your father extended two years ago are past due. I received the payments you've been sending, but it barely covers the interest currently owed."

Oliver's heart sank, and a bitter taste filled his mouth. "And the stock he purchased? We authorized the bank with permission to sell. What amount did it bring in?"

Mr. Kelly sighed, and his gray eyes, still showing that damnable sincerity and kindness, only increased Oliver's fears.

"The stock was worthless after the businesses your father invested in went bankrupt. I was able to recuperate a small amount, but it covered only the interest owed for the next month's payment."

Panic spread through Oliver. He had been fighting for over a year to save his family and his home from ruin after his father's death, and now all he had was his name and the title of Viscount Conway, which at the moment was a burden almost beyond what he could bear.

"Mr. Kelly, is there no way...?"

The banker removed his spectacles and set them on the desk. He leaned forward, his voice lowering.

"I have so few options, Oliver. Your father was a dear friend and..." Mr. Kelly paused, collecting himself. "But my hands are tied by bank regulations and investor expectations."

"So that's it, then? Astley Court, all of the tenancy properties and everything we own..."

"Will be property of Drummonds in thirty days," Mr. Kelly finished. "You've done a commendable job, but the debts were simply too great. The only way to..." Mr. Kelly stopped and shook his head.

"What?" Oliver pressed. "What were you about to say? I will do anything."

"The only option I see as a way out of this mess is to, shall we say...marry advantageously?"

Oliver didn't quite comprehend the banker's words because they were so unexpected. "Pardon?"

"An heiress, dear boy," Mr. Kelly said, forgetting their difference in social standing for a moment, not that Oliver cared.

"An heiress," he muttered, finding the implication distasteful.

"Yes. Find a pretty young lady with a fortune to her name and secure her hand in less than thirty days, and you will have access to money. I could get around some of the resistance here if you returned before the middle of January with a rich bride upon your arm."

Oliver stared down at his worn-out gloves and top hat, which rested in his lap. So it had come to this. Sell himself to the highest-bidding lady in London and find himself saddled with a wife, one he might not like, let alone love—all to save his home and family.

"Do it for Astley Court. Do it for your mother."

The thought of his mother, his younger brother Everett, and his sister Zadie all depending on him. It was all it took to make him decide.

"Thirty days," Oliver said, as if sealing the pact.

Still feeling like a man doomed and facing the gallows, Oliver thanked Mr. Kelly and shook his hand before he exited the office. He pulled on his gloves and cursed as he found yet another small hole in the leather. He had spent the last year putting every bit of coin he had toward the business debts his father's investments had accrued. The cost of his efforts, aside from his pride, had been clothing three years too old, and showing every day of it.

His mother and sister had suffered more, being forced to wear gowns well out of fashion. He and Everett were able to get by on what they owned since men's fashions changed far less and more slowly than the fashions of ladies. Zadie had held her head high, even when other girls had mocked her during her debut this season when she'd worn an outmoded gown.

His family had also reduced the staff at their country

estate by half and had sold their large townhouse in London six months ago. Now they only rented rooms when in town for the season. Oliver didn't want to think about what cuts they would have to make if he wasn't able to save Astley Court. A man without land and without a fortune... He shuddered, but resolved himself to the idea of learning a trade. He was not opposed to it, but the social circles his family ran in would surely find it distasteful, which meant he put Everett's and Zadie's futures at risk.

But if he could find an heiress...

No. He *would* find an heiress. He would do his duty, in whatever form that required.

As he left Drummonds and stepped out into the streets, someone called his name.

"Conway!"

He spun to find a man striding toward him, waving his arm. The tall, dark-haired fellow had the same green eyes as him.

"Cousin!" He laughed as he shook Devon St. Laurent's hand. Devon was second in line to become the Duke of Essex. Oliver's great-grandfather, Godric St. Laurent, and his wife Emily had had four children, and Devon's grandfather, second eldest of the brood, was the current duke.

"Care for a drink? I was heading to Berkley's."

"I would love to, but I surrendered my membership three months ago." It was one of the many frivolous luxuries both he and Everett had removed to slim down their family's expenses.

"What? Why?"

Oliver sighed. "It is a long story." His shoulders ached now. He had been waiting to see Mr. Kelly for over an hour, and he had been strung tighter than an archer's bow the entire time.

Devon smiled and clapped a hand on Oliver's shoulder. "Come on, we'll drink at a pub nearby, and you can tell me this long story."

Half an hour later, the two of them were two pints into a nice afternoon.

"All right, Oliver, tell me what's the matter." Devon's expression was back to that of concern. And like they had been as boys, Oliver found his trust in his cousin well placed as he shared his family's dire financial straits.

"Lord, Oliver, that's dreadful. Why don't you speak to my grandfather? I'm sure he wouldn't mind helping you out. You know how he loves Astley Court."

"I know," Oliver admitted. His great-uncle, the Duke of Essex, was a loving man, openhearted and kind, but even he did not possess the funds to help the Conways out of their massive debt.

"Why not?" Devon pressed. He rolled his half-empty pint glass between his hands.

"It wouldn't be enough. The amount we need to pay... It would put Essex House at risk. I cannot ask that."

Devon's eyes darkened. "It's truly that bad?"

"It is," Oliver replied numbly. He glanced around the pub, noting the men who sought to escape the winter chill. Most were laughing and talking, all in seemingly good spirits. It only served to deepen his melancholy.

"I feel I've failed," Oliver whispered.

"You haven't." Devon leaned forward and set his glass down on the table. "Debts happen, businesses fail. Your father made these choices, and they seemed good and sound at the time. It isn't your fault they failed. The world changed, and we're all still trying to catch up with it."

Oliver drained the rest of his pint, letting the stout ale go to his head. His stomach was empty, and his head ached from the lack of food. He had done his best not to eat at too many restaurants while he was in London. The expense was one more thing he couldn't afford.

"The banker said I need to find an heiress. Can you believe that? It was his *professional* advice."

"An heiress?" Delight suddenly burst on Devon's face as he grinned. "That may be something I could help you with."

"Oh?"

"You remember Adelaide Berwick?"

"The Earl of Berwick's daughter?" He nodded. He had spent much of his youth around the girl. She chattered endlessly and could be quite mean-spirited sometimes.

"She still wants you, Oliver. I know you didn't offer

for her when she came out last year, but she is still hoping you'll change your mind. Her father has settled a hefty sum on her as a dowry and a large sum to be given as an inheritance if he approves of the match. Old Berwick always liked you."

The Earl of Berwick was a good fellow, but his wife and his only daughter could both be unbearable. Still, Oliver considered it.

"Adelaide is a bit...much, don't you think?" he asked his cousin.

Devon shrugged. "Yes, I suppose she is. But she's as rich as Croesus, and that's what you need, isn't it?" His cousin chuckled. "Besides, if she truly drove you mad, you could always live apart in separate homes. That seems to be quite acceptable these days with those who marry out of necessity."

"I suppose you're right. I could stomach it. For Astley Court."

"There you are then. Cheer up. You're coming to Lady Poole's ball tonight, aren't you? Adelaide will be there. Propose to her, and I'll go with you to procure a special license. You'll be married by Christmas."

"Married to Adelaide Berwick by Christmas..." Oliver shook his head, trying not to laugh at the maddening twist his life had taken.

"Married, at least," Devon replied. "That ought to be some consolation."

They finished their drinks, and Devon paid the

barman. They then donned their gloves and hats before embracing the chill outside.

"Shall I see you tonight?"

"You shall." Oliver shook Devon's hand and parted ways with his cousin. He walked to the hotel his family were renting rooms at while they were in town. The Grosvenor Hotel on Buckingham Palace Road was an impressive structure modeled in the Baroque interpretation of French Renaissance architectural style. His father had been a good friend of the hotel's current owner, and whenever they stayed in town, they were able to rent a room far cheaper than most guests, for which Oliver was extremely grateful. It didn't hurt that having a titled lord staying there caused a flurry of interest from other guests, which the owner thought was good for business.

As Oliver entered its opulent entryway, his eyes rolled over the fluted twisting columns and the way the light from the chandeliers turned the white marble a soft gold. Bright-red roses filled half a dozen large crystal vases, and a group of young ladies in colorful gowns were gossiping as they donned their velvet manteaux, likely for an evening out at the opera or perhaps a ball. More than one lady in the group caught Oliver's eye, offering him a blushing smile before they dissolved into giggles with their friends as he passed.

In another life, Oliver would've enjoyed the attention. He was no fool. He had his mother's fair looks as well as his father's, and more than one young lady had thrown herself at him over the years. He had thoroughly enjoyed seducing a few, though never too far, just enough to please his ego and give the lady a breathtaking memory.

But he was older now, and there was a part of him that did long to settle down. He wanted what his mother and father had, a marriage based on love and respect.

But I won't have that with Adelaide. She will own me, and she'll never let me forget it.

He climbed the stairs to the third floor and then headed down the hall to the suite of rooms he'd rented. As he opened the door, he saw his mother and sister in the sitting room, talking excitedly about tonight.

"Oh, Oliver!" his mother exclaimed in joy as she saw him. She rose and came over to embrace him. "How was Mr. Kelly? Did he give us a very long extension?"

Oliver's gut knotted as he carefully planned his response. He saw his little sister, Zadie, who was only eighteen, watching him with anxious eyes.

She knows. She's always been able to read me like an open book.

"Mother, perhaps you should sit down."

His mother, still lovely even at fifty-two, now became concerned. "Oliver... What's the matter? What did Mr. Kelly say?"

Zadie gently ushered their mother into a chair, and

then she stood behind it, as strong as a soldier in Her Majesty's army.

"Where is Everett?" he asked.

"Here." His brother stepped out of the nearest bedroom. Everett could be Oliver's twin, though he was three years younger. He'd removed his coat and was waiting for Oliver to speak. They all were.

"Mr. Kelly could not grant us an extension. The entire amount of the debt has been called in, and we are destitute. We have thirty days to set our affairs in order and arrange for the sale of Astley Court and all of its sub properties, as well as the furnishings in the house."

That bitter taste had returned, and it broke his heart to see his mother wipe the tears in her eyes. No matter what Devon had said, he knew he had failed his family.

"I haven't given up," Oliver told them. "I have one last chance. Mr. Kelly suggested it, and I shall endeavor to do my best."

"What is it?" his mother asked. Even though her husband had passed more than a year ago, she, like Her Majesty, still mourned her husband and had not shed her widow's weeds. Her black silk gown whispered against the carpets as she stood and faced him with a strength that made him proud.

"If I can marry an heiress before the middle of next January, we'll be able to save the house, tenancies...all of it."

"An heiress? Oh, Oliver, no." His mother shook her

head. "I'll not have you become some dreadful fortune hunter."

"I won't be, Mother. I already know the woman I'm choosing, and she won't require any hunting." He tried to smile, but he knew the expression failed to reach his eyes. "You could even say that she's been hunting me."

"Who would be...?" Zadie asked, and then her eyes widened with horror. "Oh no, Oliver, not her. *Anyone* but her."

"Zadie." He held up a hand, trying to reassure her. "She's not that terrible."

"Not that terrible? She covered my hair in tar when I was twelve, Oliver. Mother had to cut it all off. I looked like a boy for almost a year!"

"Bloody hell," Everett said, then whistled. "I forgot Adelaide did that."

"She was just a girl then," Oliver said.

Everett shook his head in disgust. "Choose anyone but that one. There must be other heiresses."

"Everett, heiresses do not grow on trees," their mother said coldly. "If Oliver believes Adelaide is our only choice, then we must bear it." When Everett made a gagging noise, she added, "Or *you* could marry her." At which point, Everett turned as white as alabaster.

Zadie sank into the chair their mother had now vacated, while Everett shot Oliver a sympathetic look as their mother took his hands in hers and gave a gentle squeeze.

"You truly want this?" Margaret asked him.

Oliver squeezed her hands back. "Mother, it's not what I want, but it is what must be done. I won't lose our home, and I won't put Zadie's and Everett's futures at risk. They need a stable life and a reputation unsullied by destitution if they are to make decent matches."

For a long moment, no one said anything. Then his mother cupped his cheek and tried to smile. "You are a wonderful son to make such a sacrifice. I would give anything to keep you from doing this."

"I know, Mother." He closed his eyes, drew a deep breath, and tried to summon a smile. "Now, we have Lady Poole's ball tonight, and I for one would like to enjoy myself this evening before I propose."

He would not let himself think about what his future might be. Certainly not tonight with his last night of freedom before he shackled himself to an unwanted heiress.

CHAPTER 2

Rayne Egerton tried to quell the rise of nerves that fluttered in her belly as her father helped her down from their coach. Her father, Douglas Egerton, beamed at her with pride. She tried to smile back.

"Breathe, my dear. You'll do just fine. None of these ladies are any more special than you."

Rayne wished her father's words could comfort her, but the truth was, she felt out of place in England. They had only just arrived from a steamer ship out of New York, and London was proving to be more intimidating than New York had ever been. As much as she liked the country, the people seemed far less welcoming than she'd hoped. Even Americans with all their money weren't always welcome...or perhaps it was because of it?

"It's my first English ball, Father. What if I don't

know the right dances or say the wrong thing to one of the peers? The titles still confuse me." She had spent the last month reading a copy of *Debrett's Peerage* as she tried to understand the complicated system. Rayne still felt completely uncomfortable with all of the modes of address. At home, a woman was either a *Miss* or a *Mrs.*, and a man was simply a *Mr.* There were no earls, dukes, viscount, barons, or knights. Here it was all *Lord this* or *Right Honorable that*. And trying to keep their order of importance straight... It was all too much.

A footman at the door ushered them into Lady Poole's extravagant home. Great chandeliers lit the entry hall as she and her father joined the other newly arrived guests. She removed her ivory-colored silk-and-velvet dolman, something that resembled a half-coat and half-cape with its loose, sling-like sleeves. She unhooked the fastener at her neck and allowed the footman to slip it off and put it away for her. Her father had insisted on the new costly wardrobe before they had left for England. He'd had the gowns ordered from the House of Worth in Paris. It had embarrassed her to have such expensive things, but her father said they would be judged quite harshly based on their clothing. He'd reminded her that they would have to work twice as hard to fit in with the social crowd of London during the season.

To make the best impression, she had chosen a pale-rose evening gown with a low square neckline and sleeves that clung to the edges of her shoulders. Her gown was trimmed with live roses that had been carefully sewn in over the embroidered silk rosebuds on her skirts, draping from the high bustle at the back down to the front of her gown. A red silk bow exited the middle of her bustle, catching the viewer's eye to the pale-pink gown. It was exquisite, but Rayne wasn't used to such things, and she certainly didn't feel like she belonged in it.

At home in New York, she'd worn more serviceable, sensible clothes because she spent a great deal of time assisting her father at his office. She was fortunate to have a father who believed women were capable of working alongside men, but he was the exception. Most men in New York had laughed at her attempts to discuss business and politics, and she was afraid London would be no different.

As she and her father entered the ballroom, dozens of women were already eyeing her, whispering behind raised fans, their eyes glittering with curiosity or malice. She knew why—she was an American heiress, and every unattached man in the room would soon find a way to manage an introduction to her. It was a common practice now for the titled men of England to seek marriages with rich American heiresses. And that was the very last thing Rayne wanted, for a man to see her simply as a bank account. She didn't care if the man was a duke—if he was a fortune hunter, she wanted nothing to do with him.

She kept her arm tucked in her father's, and her other hand clutched her skirts as they moved through the thick crowds. There had to be close to seventy people inside the room. Musicians played in a distant corner, and waiters moved around the edges of the crowd, offering champagne to those not partaking in the dance. Rayne watched the dancers, trying to recognize the steps, wondering how best to match them. The only dance she felt comfortable with was the waltz.

"Mr. Egerton!" Lady Poole came over, beaming at them both. She had met Rayne's father a few months ago while in New York and had sent them invitations the moment she discovered they would be visiting England.

Her father bowed, and Rayne dipped into a curtsy. "Lady Poole." The fashionable Englishwoman was in her midforties and still quite stunning. The soft smile she cast toward Douglas didn't go unnoticed by Rayne. She'd wondered over the last year if her father and Lady Poole's frequent letters to one another might be leading to something more. If he found happiness again after losing his wife, Rayne was ready to support his decision to remarry. All the more so if he chose Lady Poole.

"How are you faring, Rayne, dear?" Lady Poole asked. Rayne smiled in genuine relief at having at least one ally here.

"A bit nervous, I admit."

"That's quite normal." Lady Poole tapped her closed fan in her palm. "Let's see if I can't make some introductions." She took Rayne from her father's arm and then towed her quickly around the room, introducing her to all the ladies in attendance. The names and titles became a confusing blur by the end.

"Stay here while I fetch some gentlemen to fill your dance card, my dear." She left Rayne at a spot near the wall with a group of other young ladies. They all shared sympathetic looks with her.

Rayne tried not to lose herself in shame as she watched a number of handsome young bucks prowl by her and the others left out of the dancing.

Heavens...I've become a wallflower so soon.

"Oh dear." The girl next to her shuffled her feet anxiously. "She's coming. Buck up, ladies," the girl hissed in warning to her fellow flowers.

"Who?" Rayne asked the girl, her stomach knotting with dread.

"Adelaide Berwick. Whatever you do, don't show any hint of weakness," the girl replied and raised her chin defiantly as a pretty young woman around Rayne's age came up to the group of single ladies. A trio of girls followed on Adelaide's heels, all twittering behind their fans.

"Well, 'tis a pity Lady Poole did not invite more young men. Quite silly to have so many left desiring partners. There's simply *nothing* worse than being a wallflower," she declared. Her soft blue silk gown, Rayne noted, looked as expensive as hers, but it lacked the flair of the roses. Adelaide seemed to notice this and sneered at Rayne.

"I do believe you're wilting." She pointed her fan at Rayne's dress. Rayne almost looked down but didn't. Even if the freshly cut roses were wilting, she didn't want to give the girl the satisfaction. She knew how she would respond in America, but here? She was well out of her depth.

Adelaide changed the subject. "I'm afraid we're not acquainted. You aren't familiar to me. Let me guess... A country cousin of Lady Poole's? She is always so charitable." Adelaide's friends giggled.

Rayne bit the side of her cheek. *Do not respond. You will embarrass Father.*

"Oh dear. Have you lost your tongue?" Adelaide continued. "The country mouse is too timid."

Rayne curled her fingers around her own fan, inwardly imagining bringing it down upon Adelaide's head.

"I have a tongue, Miss Berwick. You're simply not worth the breath or the words to speak to."

The wallflowers behind Rayne all gasped. Adelaide's brown eyes narrowed to angry slits. She tossed her auburn curls venomously.

"You are American, of course. You must be the

daughter of that rich old man everyone is fussing over tonight. Well, lesson one, *American*. I'm the daughter of Lord Berwick, so you will address me as Lady Adelaide, not *miss*." Her smugness was short-lived because Rayne was good and furious now at the girl's dig at her father. No one insulted him, especially not some twit like this.

Rayne took a step closer, plastering a smile upon her face. "My apologies, Lady Adelaide. I didn't see an earl's daughter here, only a spoiled little brat."

Adelaide bared her teeth as she readied a response, but Rayne wasn't done. She raised her voice a little so the girls behind her all heard.

"Be careful what you say next, Lady Adelaide, or I might ask my father to purchase everything you own. As you said, I'm the daughter of a very rich American. My father could buy half this country on a lark if it suited him."

Adelaide's face went ghostly white, and then her pretty face pinched and her cheeks turned a bright red.

"All the money in the world doesn't fix poor breeding," she snapped.

"I suppose you would know, seeing as how most old families in England are inbred," Rayne shot back without a second thought.

Adelaide looked ready to spew fire, but the trio of girls behind her pulled her away, steering her toward the table of refreshments. Rayne released a sigh of relief.

"You Americans really are as bold as brass, as they

say," the girl next to her said. She had stunning green eyes and dark-brown hair.

"I realize that may have been very foolish." Rayne blushed. Her temper was cooling, and as it did, rationality and doubt returned, along with embarrassment. She had just threatened the daughter of an earl. That wouldn't go over well.

"Could you truly do it?" the girl asked.

"Do what?" Rayne replied.

"Buy her family's estate and property like that?"

"Perhaps. What does her father earn in any given year?" She blushed again at the inappropriate question. The English thought it was so crass to talk openly of money.

"About forty thousand a year."

Rayne didn't even hesitate. "Oh yes, definitely. Twice over, I should think."

The wallflowers gathered around her then, all gasping and chattering questions all at once.

"Ladies, let her breathe," the green-eyed girl exclaimed. "My name is Zadie, by the way. It's a pleasure to meet you."

"The same," Rayne replied, relaxing a little at Zadie's warm smile. "I'm Rayne Egerton."

"Rayne, you told off Lady Adelaide, and that makes you my new favorite friend."

"I take it she terrorizes you all often?"

"Often," Zadie agreed with a frown. "She's the worst

sort of aristocrat. Not all ladies in her station are like that. I hope you won't judge the rest of us by her standards."

"Certainly not," Rayne promised. "I let people prove their worth before I pass judgment. And I think Adelaide proved she isn't worth anything."

The flowers flocking around her all laughed. Zadie introduced her to most of the girls, and she felt a stirring of hope that she might make a few friends tonight.

"So, how long are you in England?" Zadie asked as she and Rayne collected champagne from a passing footman.

"A few months. My father is here to buy stock in some steel companies."

"Oh? And your Christmas plans? Will you be staying in London?"

"No, we leave tomorrow by train for Inverness. Lord Fraser has invited us to a party there over the holidays."

"Lord Fraser's estate?" Zadie grinned. "I'm bound there as well. Only we leave in a few days, not tomorrow."

Rayne's heart soared. "You'll be there? Thank heavens, I'll have one friend at least."

Zadie chuckled. "Not to worry. I'll help you survive the end of the season and the holidays."

"Thank you."

"Oh!" Zadie suddenly looked toward a crowd on the opposite end of the ballroom. "I must go, I'm afraid. But I'll see you in Inverness." Zadie gave her a hug and rushed off. It was only as she watched her friend go that she noticed that Adelaide and the other girls nearby were laughing at Zadie.

She heard Adelaide say, "There's only so many ways to change the same old gown before a decent gentleman notices you can't afford a new one."

Rayne drew in a deep breath. If she wasn't careful, Adelaide might end up with her face drenched in champagne. Lord, Adelaide was testing the strength of her self-control.

Lady Poole plucked her from the wallflowers and sent her onto the dance floor. She had lined up a dozen young men to meet her. In between the twirls and whirls, they talked of her father and her holiday plans. Rayne tried her best to be clever, charming, and entertaining, and she found she wasn't a complete failure.

One man, Devon St. Laurent, teased her mercilessly until she was laughing. He reminded her of the brood of cousins she had at home who all worked for her Uncle Gerard's oil business. Those Egerton boys were delightfully wicked when it came to women, but fiercely protective of her like a little sister.

After an hour had passed, she sought refuge from the dancing in an alcove behind the refreshment table. It was a relief to have a moment alone to gather her thoughts. She'd never been overly fond of crowds. She preferred solitude and quiet study whenever possible.

Her father said she was like her mother in that way. Rayne's heart ached at the thought. They had lost her two years before, and her death had left her and her father clinging to one another in shared grief.

She was pulled from her thoughts at the rising sound of Adelaide's hateful gossip.

"I don't know why Lady Poole invited those *dreadful* Americans. They're so..." She lowered her voice to say something to her friends that made them laugh. "I mean, look at her dress. It's more suited to a pigsty. Perhaps that's where she grew up? Slopping her way around with the pigs? And her hair—such a lackluster shade of brown. Her face is quite ugly, don't you think? And those eyes—the color of mud."

That was no private conversation of hushed whispers. The woman had wanted her to hear. Had wanted to hurt her. Rayne bit her lip, holding in tears. Adelaide didn't deserve to see her cry. But she felt so helpless and alone. She needed air; she needed quiet.

She rushed toward the nearest door that led out of Lady Poole's ballroom and grabbed the arm of a passing footman in the darkened corridor.

"Please, is there a library here?"

The young man nodded, and he led her to a room a few doors down.

"Is there anything I can get for you, miss?"

"No, thank you. I just need a moment alone." She

slipped into the quiet sanctuary and instantly felt more at peace.

A library was the last place anyone would ever come to in the middle of a ball. It was a trick her mother had used when she first debuted in society and needed a moment alone. It was also how her father and mother had met. They had talked for a full evening and missed the entire ball. It had been love at first sight.

Just thinking of that story brought a smile to her lips and calmed her racing heart. She wiped at her eyes, hiding any evidence of her tears that threatened to cling to her lashes. She shouldn't have let Adelaide get to her, but the girl knew just how to hurt someone like her, where her confidence was at its weakest. At least they would only be here a few months. She could stomach that, couldn't she?

For Father's sake, I must.

The library door opened suddenly, and Rayne spun around, heart pounding. She feared Adelaide had followed her here, meaning to finish what she'd started.

CHAPTER 3

A tall, dark-haired man stood framed in the doorway, a dark silhouette against the noise and light from the corridor leading to the ballroom behind him.

He cleared his throat. "My apologies. I thought the room was unoccupied." His voice was pleasant, deep and smooth. It made her think of drinking a glass of brandy and how it made her warm all over. She summoned a polite smile.

"Oh... No, please, I don't mind."

The man hesitated an instant longer before coming inside. As he came into the room, the light from the gas lamps in the corridor outside illuminated him and made her catch her breath. With his intense emerald eyes and handsome face, he looked to be a long-lost prince from some childhood fairy tale her mother used to read. Her eyes moved over his broad shoulders and down to his tapered waist, taking in his tailored but slightly outmoded evening suit just as the strains of a waltz began to play in the distance.

Was this how my mother felt when she first glimpsed my father? A tiny thrill shot through her, like a lightning strike that rippled beneath her skin.

He stared at her for a long moment beneath the hanging oil lamps, and she wondered if it had been a mistake to let him come inside. There was an intensity about him that made her heart race. His green eyes made her think of Zadie, but he was older, perhaps in his thirties, and his features, well... He was striking, if that was the right word to use for a man.

"I could go, if you feel uncomfortable. I just came in here to find a moment of peace," he murmured, his tone all politeness despite the intensity of his green-eyed gaze.

The thought of him leaving, however, left her feeling strangely alone, even though solitude was the reason she had come here. "Please, stay. I suppose it's not at all proper, but..." She didn't finish.

The man chuckled. "I suppose not, but I won't tell a soul if you don't." He took a seat by the fireplace, where flames crackled over logs, and stared into the glowing light.

Rayne waited a moment before joining him. She carefully arranged her skirts and then sat in a second chair not far from his. Being alone with a strange man like this was exciting, a little frightening too. He made no move toward her, nor engaged her in conversation. He simply gazed at the fire as if the flames held the answers he was seeking. The firelight framed his handsome features, casting a melancholy glow about him that warned her he was deep in his own thoughts. She didn't wish to disturb him, so she took the time to study the clear-cut features of his face. Straight nose, noble chin, and a jaw chiseled from marble. He was possibly one of the most handsome men she had ever met.

"Do you find me interesting?" the man suddenly said.

She jolted a little and blushed at being caught in her secret study of him. "I..." She hesitated but then threw caution to the winds. "Yes, you're very interesting to look at. I'm quite sorry." She laughed a little, the sound slightly nervous. She knew it must be rude to admit such a thing, but this man had a way of drawing truths from her, even though they'd only just met.

The man's half-smile only enhanced his charm. "I suppose that's not a bad thing."

"No, indeed," she assured him.

"You're American?" he asked.

She nodded. Her accent was not what one would call fully American, but enough to be noticed. Her mother had sent her to a boarding school when she was younger, which gave her a more transatlantic accent. Her mother had hoped it would make her appeal to more gentlemen in the way of obtaining a suitable match.

"No doubt you needed to escape as well," he said. "Balls can either be wonderful or quite dreadful."

"Dreadful was my case."

"The same for me," the man said. "I wanted tonight to be wonderful, but I failed at that quite spectacularly..." His voice trailed off, his focus locked on the fireplace once again. He didn't finish his thought.

"I understand," she replied quietly. "I find myself flustered when I cannot say or do something, and balls seem to be a most limiting place for a woman."

This caught his attention again. He rested an elbow on the arm of the chair and studied her, his chin in his palm.

"And what is it you wished to say or do tonight that you did not?"

"You'll laugh at me," she warned.

"I may. Does that matter?"

Rayne nibbled her bottom lip, wondering how much she ought to say.

"I wanted to pull the curls off a woman's head and wallop her with a fan."

The man burst out laughing. Rather than be embarrassed, she started laughing as well. "Let me guess—Adelaide Berwick has created yet one more enemy?"

"How did you know?" Rayne demanded.

"That creature is the bane of many a ballroom-goer.

She can be merciless and gives no quarter to her victims."

"That does seem to be true," Rayne muttered. She still wanted to pull Adelaide's curls off her head.

"Aside from the challenges Lady Adelaide presented, were you enjoying yourself?" For some reason, she flushed with heat. He still watched her with interest. This man didn't know who she was, didn't know about her father's wealth—they were strangers in the candlelight. A whisper of a thrill stole through her, giving her goosebumps on her arms. He noticed her rub at them.

"Cold?" He removed his coat and moved toward her before she could stop him. He draped the black frock coat around her shoulders. She felt oddly shy as the woodsy scent that clung to the dense woolen cheviot cloth made her feel as though he were holding her, not the coat.

"Better?" He took his seat again, and she glanced down at the blend of fabrics, the dark coat against the vulnerable, pale-rose satin of her ball gown. Something about that, the heavy coat atop her, made her shiver again. The man noticed, but he didn't move from his chair again.

"Forget the ball," he said softly. The rich baritone of his voice pulled her focus to him, as though he'd cast some spell over her.

"Forget?"

"Yes. What would you be doing now if you were not here?"

She fisted her skirts nervously. "Now you truly will laugh at me."

"Honestly, tell me. We have the luck of anonymity between us. No one shall know or laugh at what we speak in this sacred realm of books." He raised a hand. "I vow it upon the sanctuary of the library."

Rayne laughed at his solemn expression, and his responding grin stole her breath. She had never seen anything so beautiful before. She saw the delight in his eyes as he looked at her. Aside from her father, she was unaccustomed to being paid attention to as though she mattered. As an heiress, men saw her as a prize to be won, not a woman to be loved.

"If I could be anywhere..." She thought out the answer carefully. "I think I would've liked to have seen the World's Fair at the Crystal Palace that was here earlier this year."

"Oh?" The man's face brightened. "An explorer of the world, are you?"

She grinned back. "Of sciences and the arts, certainly."

"My grandmother and grandfather attended the fair, or the great Exhibition in 1851. It was in Hyde Park then, before it was moved to Sydenham Hill. It was a city of glass and crystal, according to my grandmother."

Rayne leaned forward in her chair, captivated by him. "What did they love best about the fair?"

"My grandfather was taken with the trophy telescope used for viewing the stars."

"The trophy telescope? Why did they call it that?"

"He said it was because the telescope is considered the trophy of the exhibition, but my grandmother had a far more interesting item in mind." The man's eyes twinkled with mischief.

"More interesting than the telescope?" She couldn't imagine what that might be.

"A diamond captured her eye," he answered in a whisper.

"A diamond? How silly." Rayne laughed. She had no interest in gems or jewels. She was practical and valued knowledge above all else.

The man leaned forward a little, as though sharing the world's most important secret. "The diamond was called the Koh-i-noor, which means *mountain of light*. It is one of the world's largest cut diamonds and now rests in the vault of the Tower of London with the crown jewels. They say it is bad luck to any man who wears it."

"How did the queen acquire it?"

"In the Treaty of Lahore when Britain annexed Punjab in 1849. Ever since, the diamond has courted disaster, and its brilliance has been tainted with blood. Only a female of the royal household is allowed to wear it now." The man continued to speak softly. "My grandmother said it had been bound into an armlet for the queen to wear, with two smaller diamonds flanking it. It rests in a case within black velvet with gas lamps lit around it to make it sparkle. Yet the diamond was flawed and asymmetrical, you see. Prince Albert had it cut for Her Majesty a year after the Great Exhibition, but my grandmother said that day when she saw it, she looked at it head-on, and the uncut gem drew her in like a black cavernous hole, and she said..." The man paused.

"Said what?" Rayne was hanging upon his every word. "Tell me, *please*." She scooted her chair closer to his, until their knees touched.

The man still stared at her, his gaze fathomless as he continued. "She claimed that the diamond showed her half a millennium of bloodshed. Every man who'd held the diamond bore its curse and died. Then my grandmother saw it resting in a crown."

"But is it in the crown now?"

The man shook his head. "No, not yet. It is still in a bracelet that belongs to the queen. I've seen it myself. But I believe my grandmother saw the future."

Rayne gasped. "You've seen it?" Unthinkingly, she reached out to touch his hand on the armrest close to hers.

"Yes. The queen rarely wears the Koh-i-noor. She claims it makes her uneasy, but she still wears it to some state functions. I glimpsed it upon her wrist a few years ago." His gaze grew distant as he seemed to recall the memory. "The way the light glinted off it... I felt like a sailor lured to the rocks by a siren's call. Then I blinked, and the desire to possess it was gone. I felt as though I'd woken from a dark and terrible nightmare."

Rayne's lips parted in shock at the man's fantastic tale, wanting to believe he was teasing her, but she heard the truth in his voice.

"I wish I could've seen it. Not because I like pretty baubles. I do not, but..."

He chuckled. "You have no need of jewels. The beauty of your eyes and the brilliance of your mind are far more attractive than a diamond about your neck."

His frank words startled her. "You think I'm pretty?" Her face flushed, and a happiness blossomed within her in a way that had never happened before when a man praised her looks. Those men had only sought her money, but this man? He had no designs upon her fortune; he was simply looking at her. Longing stirred within her, and she knew for the first time in her life how a lady might easily be compromised by the right man in the right moment...a moment such as this.

"No, not at all," he said flatly. The blossoming hope inside her began to wither. She dropped her gaze, hoping to hide her dismay from him, but he lifted her chin with a finger. "I think you are *stunning*." That rich voice sent wild shivers through her. "*Pretty* is a word for young girls with bows in their hair. *You* are exquisite."

He reached up to trace her gently winged brows and

the slightly upward curve of her nose, then slipped his fingers over her cheekbones and down to her chin before resting on her lips. He brushed the pad of his thumb over her mouth, and a dark hunger she'd never experienced before stirred to life. She reacted without thinking, pressing her lips to his thumb and then flicking her tongue against it.

He froze and inhaled sharply. Their eyes locked. Rayne's stomach started to tumble inside her as she feared she'd let her newfound desire take her too far.

"May I steal a kiss, sweet stranger of mine?" the man asked, his low, hypnotic voice irresistible.

"I've never been kissed before," she admitted. And at that moment she wanted him to be the first. She wanted it more than she'd wanted anything in her entire life.

Her heart stuttered as his eyes darkened with desire. A devilish smile covered his face. There was a possessive look to it, one that said once he began to kiss her, she would beg him never to stop because she would be forever under his spell.

He lifted her easily from the chair and into his lap. Rayne grasped his shoulders, feeling the heat of his body pour into hers. She couldn't resist leaning closer to him.

The man cupped the back of her head, and she leaned into him. They both paused an inch apart, and she savored that building anticipation until his lips touched hers. Her stomach swirled as his warm mouth gently explored hers. It was a kiss of seduction in tender measure. The delicious sensation of their mouths moving together made her blood sing and her head light. Her corset tightened almost painfully as she struggled for breath. She drank in the sweetness of his taste, and a deep-seated need coiled low in her abdomen as he licked at the seam of her lips. She parted her mouth and gasped in shock as his tongue found hers.

The dreamlike intimacy set her heart to trembling anew. Her mind drifted deeper into his kiss. She imagined them seated just like this, her on his lap, a Christmas tree behind them and a kissing bough above them. The man in her dream looked up at her, and in his eyes she saw a future, a life she had never dreamed of before. A potent longing, so intense, made her stiffen in his arms, but she didn't pull away. A sudden fear of losing all this was almost overpowering.

The man held her tight, his kiss intensifying, and Rayne surrendered to the delicious, dark mastery he now held over her body. The fiery possession of his lips sent excitement like she'd never experienced before rippling through her. Her blood pounded, and her knees trembled. She was grateful to be on his lap, clinging to him with everything she had. His hands moved down her body, the heat of his palms seeping through the layers of cloth. A dozen emotions she could barely register whirled around her head as their lips finally, reluctantly separated.

The man was breathing as hard as she was. They

both smiled a little shyly as they looked at each other. His eyes roamed over her face, and there was a softness to his expression that made her heart flip in her chest.

"Thank you," he whispered as he grazed the back of his hand against her cheek.

"For what?" Rayne asked.

He was silent a bit longer before he replied. "For showing me what it could have been like."

Confused, she waited for an explanation, but none was forthcoming. The large grandfather clock in the corner struck the late hour.

"We should go before we're missed," he said.

Rayne slipped off his lap, her head a little muddled still from the stranger's drugging kiss. She couldn't find any words as she reluctantly removed his coat from her body and held it out to him. Their hands met as he accepted the woolen frock coat.

"I wish...," the man began, then gave a rueful shake of his head.

"Please... What do you wish?" She had to resist the urge to reach out and touch him again.

"I wish we could have met under different circumstances." The man cupped her chin and leaned down, feathering his lips over hers with one last ghost of a kiss. Then he brushed a finger along her bodice, and she gasped as he plucked a fresh rose from her décolletage and held it up to his nose, breathing in the scent.

"A token. To remember you," he said with a melancholy smile. Then, before she could stop him, he was gone.

Rayne stared at the open doorway, her heart racing with joy and yet strangely painful. Could she fall in love with a stranger and have her heart broken at the same time? There had been some magic at work, something that had drawn them together, and it left her feeling desolate now that he had gone.

She clutched her skirts and tried to calm herself. She waited a few minutes before returning to the ball. Everything around her seemed the same, yet she had changed. Some great change had indeed begun inside her, something that could not be undone, nor did she wish it to be erased.

If only...

OLIVER HELD THE ROSE BLOOM IN HIS PALM AS HE met his family on the stairs outside Lady Poole's home. The scent returned him to that memory of the mysterious woman in the library. He would have given anything to drop to one knee and ask her, whoever she was, to be his wife instead of Adelaide. He'd tasted desire on the woman's lips, had glimpsed her keen mind, and had seen a future with her as they'd talked. A future that could not be. Regret clawed a hollow space within his heart as he knew he would never see her again, nor ever know who she was.

He barely listened to his family's chattering as they waited for a hackney to take them to Grosvenor Square. They piled in after one came to a stop, and Everett jostled him with an elbow as he sat down beside Oliver.

"Well, how did it go?"

"Pardon?" Oliver was still replaying that lingering, too perfect kiss. He didn't even know her name, and that was all the better because tonight was all that they could ever have, an exquisite, life-altering kiss.

"What about Adelaide? Did you propose?"

Oliver cradled the rose in his hands as he looked up at the faces of his family. Guilt stabbed at his gut as he realized he'd failed them.

"I didn't. We spoke briefly, and I had every intention of asking her, but..."

"But...?" Everett prompted.

"I needed a minute to clear my head." *And then I met the most enchanting mystery woman in the library.* "And by the time I got back, she'd left."

That woman had changed everything for him. He had found a kindred spirit in her. The connection between them had been intense. He had spoken of cursed diamonds and old memories and lost himself in her eyes.

"Oliver." His mother spoke his name softly, but the concern in her tone caught his attention, pulling it away from the thoughts of the American girl in the pale-pink gown covered with real, blossoming roses.

"Are you holding a rose?" Zadie suddenly asked.

He glanced at his sister and nodded, still clutching the velvet-soft petals of the precious bloom. He had been unable to resist claiming the rose that had featured so prominently above such beautiful breasts. Her breath had quickened as he'd removed the rose from her gown. His desire—yes, desire, not simple lust—had been excruciating, but he had found the courage to walk away as the clock struck midnight, if only because he'd claimed this token of her. Zadie would've teased him for being caught up in a fairy tale or some other nonsense, but the magic in that room had been real. He wouldn't deny it.

"Where did you get it?" Zadie asked, her eyes still focused on the rose.

"I...," he stammered.

"Oliver... Did you take it from Miss Egerton?" There was a strange note of hope in Zadie's voice.

"What? Who?"

"Miss Rayne Egerton, the American. She was at the ball with her father tonight. She wore the most beautiful pale-rose gown with real roses sewn into it." Zadie pointed at the bloom in his palm. "Like that one."

"But what about Adelaide?" their mother interrupted. "Shouldn't we focus on how Oliver will find a chance to offer for her?"

Zadie ignored their mother as she stared at Oliver with a calculating look that bothered him. "You did meet her? Rayne, I mean?"

"We never introduced ourselves. We talked and..." He did not want to admit he'd kissed her as though he might not live to see the dawn in front of his sister and mother.

"Oliver," Zadie said, "Rayne is an *heiress*—far richer than Adelaide."

The occupants of the coach were silent as Zadie's words sank in.

"You mean..." Everett began to chuckle in delight. "We have someone else to choose from besides old Adelaide? Thank Christ!"

"Everett," Margaret admonished, then turned to Oliver. "Is it true? You met the American heiress tonight? Is she lovely?"

"The loveliest," he assured her, though he was still in shock. His beautiful stranger was an heiress and could be the solution to saving his family and his home. Surely life couldn't be that kind to bless him that way. He buried the sudden guilt at the thought that she might come to hate him if she ever learned how desperate he was to marry her. With Adelaide, she would have known about his situation and understood. Matches for wealth were common, but Rayne? She didn't come from a country that had titles or placed much value on them. He could only hope she'd believe his interest in her was genuine and that he wanted to marry her for more than just her money.

Margaret sighed. "How would we even find her again? These Americans always come and go on a whim, and we are due to leave for Lord Fraser's in a few days."

Zadie beamed in excitement and nudged Oliver. "She will be in attendance at Lord Fraser's house party too. She's taking a train tomorrow afternoon, and I think you should be on it."

"What?" Oliver asked. "My ticket is for three days hence with you."

Zadie shook her head. "No, you need to be alone, and you need to woo her on the train before she arrives at Lord Fraser's. We don't want Adelaide ruining your fortune hunting."

Oliver grimaced at the term. *Fortune hunting.* He didn't want to think of Rayne like that, yet trapping her in a tiny cabin aboard a train to steal a dozen more kisses... That was the sort of hunt he wouldn't mind at all, as long as he could ignore the creeping feeling of guilt about luring Rayne into marriage.

"Do you like her, Oliver?" his mother asked. "Only pursue her if you do. At least with Adelaide we know the kind of person we're dealing with."

His little brother snorted and winked at Oliver. "*Anyone* is better than Adelaide."

"Everett!" Margaret hushed him.

Oliver smiled, feeling hopeful for the first time as he

looked at his mother and siblings. "I do. I like her very much."

Now all he had to do was seduce an heiress on a train in two days to save his family and his home. How hard could it be?

CHAPTER 4

Rayne peered around at the imposing edifice of King's Cross railway station. Despite the fact that she wore a heavy gown with a black velvet dolman draped over her upper body, she was quite cold, and the breezy station only increased the chill. She stood with her lady's maid, Ellen Moore, a woman in her late thirties whom her father had hired to assist her while they were in England and Scotland. Ellen was quiet but kind and easy to be around, and Rayne felt they were forming a friendship, something she knew was very American, but she didn't care. Ellen passed her a thick black muff to tuck her hands in, and she smiled at her maid gratefully.

"What do you think of it, Ellen?" Rayne pulled her black dolman up around her neck, fighting the chill inside the station. "Quite an architectural marvel, isn't it?"

The maid's eyes roamed over the majestic temple that was King's Cross. It was a beautiful combination of functionality and architectural elegance. Brickwork and ironwork came together to create the vast station. Trains hissed, steam curled up from the tracks, and clouds of white smoke billowed out from the engines. Some people rushed frantically to board cars, while others said tearful goodbyes as they left for the holidays.

Rayne had seen trains before, but the red-and-black steel beasts here were more stately and less fierce than their American counterparts. Several mustached gentlemen in blue uniforms monitored the boarding passengers, checking ticket books and taking luggage when necessary.

"I've never been on a train before," Ellen confessed, her eyes wide. "I've been here plenty of times, but never to travel."

"It's quite fun," Rayne assured her. "The whistle is a little loud if you're close in the first few cars, but I like the motion of it, the vibrations beneath one's feet."

Ellen smiled with mischief. "My mother said that trains used to cause madness in her day."

Rayne and Ellen giggled at the thought. Thirty years ago, trains were fairly new to England, and there had been many silly beliefs that riding upon a train could cause madness and hysteria, especially among women.

"Ladies." Her father rejoined them. "Our train leaves in a quarter of an hour. I suggest we remove ourselves to the first-class refreshment room." Her father escorted them through the crowd to a red doorway with gold letters stating "First Class."

The refreshment room was a large open room with mahogany counters running the length of two walls. Behind the counter, uniformed men waited to serve drinks and sandwiches to passengers. Rayne and Ellen each ordered a glass of lemonade and some cucumber finger sandwiches, while her father purchased a pint of ale and a beef sandwich. Douglas was a fit, handsome man for his age, and it always amused her to see her father tuck away food without it ever adding to his waistline.

"What's our route, Father?" Rayne asked between bites.

He removed a small leather-bound book that had the words *Bradshaw's Monthly Railway Guide* inscribed on the cover and turned to a page he'd marked with a slip of paper.

"We leave London, then journey to Peterborough, which should take three and a half hours. Then we go to Doncaster in two hours. After that, Doncaster to York in an hour. From York to Inverness, it will be about thirteen hours. So we'll have two nights aboard the train."

"What do you think, Ellen?" Rayne asked.

Her lady's maid finished her food with a delighted

smile. "I was quite worried when I heard train food was all little gristly cubes and sawdusty sandwiches, but these were marvelous."

Douglas chuckled. "My dear Miss Moore, you're enjoying the benefits of first-class food. I'm told the third-class passengers fare far worse."

"Oh..." Ellen's cheeks were filled with color. "I'm very thankful indeed."

"I do hope our cooks in the dining cabin aren't too terrible. One never knows." Her father finished his ale and checked the time on his gold pocket watch. "Well, we'd best be off."

Rayne, her father, and Ellen left the refreshment room and crossed the bustling station to their train. Rayne paused, searching for a few coins in her reticule as she reached the W. H. Smith stand. The stand contained newspapers and a few books. Rayne purchased a copy of *Jane Eyre* as well as the *Morning Post* before catching up with her father and Ellen. Their luggage had been loaded earlier that morning and would follow them to their final destination. But Ellen and her father carried a few small suitcases to ensure they could change in their cabins for the next couple of days.

They boarded the first-class train car, and Rayne marveled at the expensive wood paneling, which was glossy with black and red paint. The glass windows that framed the cabins for day travel sparkled as she walked along the narrow passage after her father and Ellen.

"Here we are, ladies. Miss Moore, you are here in 6A. Rayne, dear, you are 6C, and I am 6B. I'm told the lavatories are at the end of the hall, and the dining cabin is two train cars behind us." Her father handed them each the keys to their cabins.

"I'll get settled and be right in to help you, Miss Rayne."

"Thank you, Ellen." Rayne entered her own cabin. It had a small bed, perfect for one person, or two people if they slept very close. A tiny closet was opposite the bed, where one could store luggage carried on board.

Rayne removed her dolman and unpinned her hat from her hair and set it aside, then looked down at her gown. It was dark-gray silk bustled gown with black lace that covered her sleeves and hem. Gray was usually such a dull color, but the silk in this gown made it seem almost iridescent. She brushed her fingertips over the silk and closed her eyes as memories of last night stole her focus again.

She had barely been able to sleep after returning from the ball. She had been giddy and at the same time burdened with sorrow, because the man she'd become fascinated by in so short a time was gone, and she would never see him again. She didn't even know his name. Her heart ached at the thought.

Have I missed it? The perfect man and the perfect moment?

Her eyes blurred with treacherous tears. She was not the sort of woman to cry, and this was twice now in two days. Rayne sniffled and reached for the newspaper she had purchased and folded it up for later reading. Then she heard the whistle of the conductor outside, signaling the last few minutes to board the train. She opened her sleeping compartment door to watch the bustle on the platforms and gasped.

A man was rushing across the platform. It was her beautiful stranger from the library! He looked dashing in a dark-blue woolen overcoat lined with dark-gold fur. The heavy braiding of his coat was secured with a series of divet buttons that spoke of his high-born class and good taste in fashion. The man dug into the right side pocket of his coat and pulled out his ticket booklet and showed it to the conductor who allowed him inside the first-class sleeping car. The man removed his top hat and brushed off a dusting of snow, then he glanced around and checked his ticket again before proceeding to the cabin next to hers.

Ducking back into her room just before he could catch sight of her, she closed her door, her breath coming fast and her corset stretched far too tight. He was staying next to her, sleeping one door away. The idea made her flush wildly. What should she do? Introduce herself? No, that was too forward, even for her. Arrange to bump into him in the small confines of the corridor? Maybe.

What are you doing, Rayne? You don't know him. He could

be married or engaged, yet you're indulging in romantic thoughts about him?

If he's engaged or married, that's the end of it, isn't it? she countered inside her head. *But what if he isn't?*

She knew she was being very foolish, but something about him made her want to take that risk. That kiss in the library last evening had awoken something inside her, and she didn't want to fall back into the sleep of what her life had been before.

She jumped when someone knocked on her door. She rushed to check her hair and face in the small mirror next to her bed before she answered. Her heart sank as she saw it was Ellen. Of course. Did she honestly expect him to come knocking on her door?

The maid entered her cabin, her eyes looking over Rayne suspiciously as she set down a suitcase of clothes.

"Miss? Are you well? You seem flushed," Ellen observed.

"Oh yes, I'm quite fine."

The train whistle shrieked, and then the train began to move. Ellen gasped and clutched at the wall, muttering about black deviled engines, and Rayne laughed, pulling her down beside her on the bed.

"It takes you a bit of time to adjust. You'll become used to the motion."

Ellen laughed nervously. "I expect it will take a bit of practice to walk while it moves. Your father has gone to the day-travel compartment if you wish to join him and read for a bit." Ellen leaned one hand on the closet door as she stood.

"I might like that, yes." Rayne reached for her books and newspaper. "I shall meet him there in a moment."

Her maid left Rayne to see to her valise and its contents in her closet. When she was done, Rayne gathered her book and newspaper in her arms and exited the cabin. She turned and collided with something—no, someone—and fell back onto the ground.

"Lord, I'm so sorry!" The achingly perfect voice made her look up to see her stranger standing above her.

He had removed his overcoat and was now wearing dark-blue trousers and a gray waistcoat that matched her dress. For some reason the idea of their clothes matching made her giggle. When she covered her mouth in embarrassment, she realized she had spilled her newspaper and dropped her book. He knelt and collected the items as she reached for them at the same time.

Their eyes met, and she saw gentle concern mixed with desire and fascination all at once as he recognized her.

"You... It's *you*," he murmured as he placed the newspaper in her arms and then wrapped his hands around her waist and lifted her to her feet as though she and her voluminous silk gown weighed nothing at all.

"I..." She stared up at him, both speechless and enchanted. He smelled wonderful, like a man who had come in from a snowy landscape outside and brought the scents of winter and man with him. No heavy colognes, no pomades. Just him and the fresh air. It made her a little dizzy with feminine delight, and she wasn't accustomed to that.

"Please, forgive me. I've gone about this like a damned fool." He still held her waist and didn't yet seem to be aware of it. They were standing far too close, and she liked it far too much.

"Shall we start again?" the man asked, and Rayne nodded, her mind and body still focused on his hands around her waist. He seemed unaware of the natural possessive gesture, and she liked it.

Please don't let go, she thought.

"My name is Oliver Conway, Lord Conway."

"Lord? Oh dear, what kind are you?" she asked. He tilted his head in confusion.

"What kind?"

"Lord, what kind of lord? I'm sorry, I'm dreadful at keeping all of the titles straight."

He grinned at her as comprehension dawned on his face. "Viscount Conway."

"Viscount. So above a baron but below a duke?" She nodded to herself. She could remember a viscount. She would have to look up his family in *Debrett's.*

The man chuckled. "*Far* below a duke. Above a baron and below an earl, if that helps." He grinned at her, and it hit her behind her knees, making her feel dizzy with delight.

"I'm Rayne Egerton. No title."

"You were quite the topic of discussion the other night." Oliver gave her a toe-curling smile that made her want to melt into a puddle at his feet.

"You don't mind that I'm American?"

"Why on earth would I mind?"

"Some people do. We're considered brash, bold, uncouth, and vulgar," she said, rambling on in embarrassment.

"Nonsense. You speak your minds, and you have, for the most part, open hearts. We Brits can be far too closed off and reserved." He still hadn't let go of her, and the feel of his warm hands spanning her waist made her tremble with excitement. His fingers stroked her sides a little, and it would have tickled her if she hadn't been wearing a corset. It felt as though he were playing with her, in the way a man would his sweetheart—the comfortable touches, the little caresses that Rayne had seen others exchange and had always wished to experience herself.

I want to touch him back the same way.

But she couldn't. Instead, she clutched her newspaper and book like a shield, even though she was tempted to drop them again to remove that barrier between them. Her eyes focused on his mouth, a mouth that seemed just as perfect in the afternoon sunlight as it had last night lit by oil lamps and firelight. A mouth that had delivered the most divine kiss.

Oliver Conway. *Lord* Conway. And she was trapped on a train with him. But she was bound for Inverness. What if he got off at Peterborough or Doncaster? How much time did she actually have to be with him?

CHAPTER 5

"Will you think me a terrible cad if I admit that I'm glad to have met you again, Rayne?" The man caressed her name in a way that made her body hum. She hadn't given him leave to call her Rayne, but she didn't want him to call her Miss Egerton either. Her given name had never sounded so sensual, so decadent, on anyone else's lips.

"I'm glad too," she admitted as she tilted her head back to look up at him.

"Last night was a memory I had planned to cherish and mourn since I did not believe I would see you again," he murmured. "But it seems fate has other plans for us."

"It does seem that way," Rayne replied, breathless. "Where are you headed now, Lord Conway?"

"Oliver, please," he said. "And I am bound for a Christmas house party in Inverness."

"Are you?" Rayne wanted to jump in excitement. "I am as well. My father and I have been invited by Lord Fraser."

"What a wonderful coincidence!" Oliver finally released her waist, and she instantly missed the connection. "I am Fraser's guest as well." He looked at her newspaper and book. "Are you bound for the day car, by any chance? I was about to go there."

"Yes, I thought I might read for a bit."

"May I join you?" Oliver asked.

Rayne's heart skittered and she nodded, feeling like a girl who'd fallen hard for the first time. And for her it was. She'd never felt under compulsion by a man before, to want to be near him. This was all a new and rather frightening experience.

"Just a moment." He vanished into his cabin and returned a heartbeat later, holding a book of his own. "Lead the way, Miss Egerton."

"Rayne, please, I insist," she replied.

As she started for the day car, she continued to look over her shoulder at him, feeling him close behind. The bustle of her gown flowed between their bodies, whispering against the dark-blue carpets and the wood panels of the narrow passageway. He followed behind her in a slow pursuit that sent her heart racing. He could so easily catch hold of her waist again, hold her against his chest and kiss her neck, her cheek...

The daydream temporarily distracted her as the train clattered and took a turn on the tracks as it departed King's Cross station. She stumbled and had a brief moment to see his face reflected in the windowpanes, a handsome god lit by winter sunlight as he dove to catch her.

"Got you," Oliver said as he held her up against the wall until the sway of the train car smoothed out and they were able to walk again.

The feel of his tall, muscled body pressed against hers, pinning her against the corridor wall, had left her breathless in a way that she was beginning to understand was dangerous. One of his thighs pressed between the front draping silks of her gown, and even that slight pressure created a low heat deep in her belly.

She tilted her head back to look up at him and smiled, but it faltered as something darker took hold of his features, something wholly masculine that warned her he wanted her, wanted to claim her in the most primal of ways. Every feminine instinct within her quivered at the thought. They were alone here. No one could stop him if he... The thought should have frightened her, but it didn't. Part of her wanted Oliver to ruin her in the best way, so much that it created a physical ache between her thighs.

"Are you all right?" he asked.

"Yes..." Her tone was girlishly breathless, but she couldn't help it. He stepped back, and they proceeded on toward the day compartment her father had rented, which was designed for passengers to sit in two rows facing each other. It was perfect to sit and read or converse with fellow passengers, whereas the Pullman sleeping cars were designed just for sleeping.

"Here we are." Oliver reached past, his arm brushing against her bodice as he slid the compartment door open. Then he leaned forward and gestured for Rayne to enter ahead of him.

Her father was seated beside the window, a newspaper in his hands. He folded the paper down to look at her. "Rayne, dear, there you are." He smiled at her, and then his gaze shifted curiously to Oliver behind her.

"Father, this is Viscount Conway. I met him at Lady Poole's ball last night."

"Conway?" Her father stood and held out a hand. "A pleasure, my lord. Please, join us. I'm Douglas Egerton." Her father nodded at the empty seats across from him.

Oliver shook his hand. "Thank you, Mr. Egerton."

Oliver guided Rayne to one of the two empty seats opposite her father. She tried to hide a blush as Oliver's hand lingered on her own before he sat down next to her. Her father watched them curiously before he spoke.

"So, Lord Conway, you are a friend of Lady Poole's?"

"Indeed," Oliver answered. "She and my mother are

good friends. My family no longer lives in London, but we made an exception to visit Lady Poole for her ball."

Douglas laughed. "That woman is quite hard to resist. I'm surprised no man has married her yet."

Rayne recalled that Lady Poole's husband had passed away five years ago. "Perhaps she enjoys independence," she suggested. "British ladies have less freedom than we do in America. I wouldn't blame her for choosing freedom to control her fortune and her destiny." She knew she had been too outspoken then by the silence that followed in the train car. Her father didn't mind her speaking out, but he was now studying Oliver, expecting him to react negatively.

"One more thing that makes America quite progressive," Oliver observed with an honest smile. "My mother and sister have often said as much. Of course, the women in my family have always been thinkers and learners. Women of the world, you might say."

Rayne couldn't resist inquiring more about his family. "Women of the world?"

He nodded and leaned back in the black leather seat of their compartment. "My great-grandmother was a duchess and married young at eighteen to my great-grandfather. She was a brilliant businesswoman and kept the dukedom of Essex quite profitable, and she also started an organization that still lives on sixty years later. They call it the Society of Rebellious Ladies."

"Sounds delightful. How does one join?" she asked. If

she ever had to remain in London for a longer length of time, she might consider applying for membership.

"I believe you must write an essay on what you believe a woman's place is in society. Station and class do not matter. Duchesses down to scullery maids are welcome, at least according to my sister. I've asked her what they do in the society, but she won't tell me. Something about being sworn to secrecy of a sisterhood."

"Your sister is a member?"

"She is. Zadie is very much like our great-grandmother, or so I'm told."

"Zadie? Zadie is your sister? I met her at Lady Poole's last evening."

His lips twitched. "You've met her?"

"I did." Rayne beamed at him. "She is wonderful. We had a brief moment to share names, but I never learned her surname. Is she traveling with you? I would love to see her again before we reach Lord Fraser's estate."

"She, my mother, and brother Everett are due to leave in three days. I have business with Lord Fraser that sends me north earlier."

"Oh? What sort of business?"

Her father cleared his throat and gave his newspaper a telltale rattle.

"My apologies, Lord Conway, I sometimes forget myself."

"Oliver," he reminded her gently, and she saw no irritation in the green depths of his eyes at her bold questions.

"Oliver," she repeated.

"To answer your question, my family may be leaving our home soon. We may move north to Scotland. Lord Fraser has some opportunities in trade for me that I wish to explore."

"Trade, you say?" Her father set his paper down to look at Oliver again, this time more seriously.

"Yes. Fraser deals with steel companies, and I'm rather interested in that."

"As am I," Douglas affirmed. "Good strong business, steel is. I recommend you invest now and buy stocks. It's a safer bet than railroad stock, yet the prices are building each day. You can double the value of shares in a matter of months."

"Thank you, Mr. Egerton, I will do my best to follow such sound advice," Oliver replied sincerely.

"Where do you currently live?" Rayne asked.

Oliver's mouth quirked up in an amused smile. "North Yorkshire. Do you know it?"

"No, I'm afraid not. I've seen it on maps, of course. It's in northern England. My father said our train will pass through York."

"Indeed we shall. My family lives near West Burton in a place called Astley Court."

"What is North Yorkshire like?"

A fond expression settled on Oliver's face. If he had been a woman, she might've called the look dreamy.

"It is a wild place, the landscapes dramatic, between the haunting moors and the dales. It's a land that had the Romans, Norsemen, and Normans leave their mark on it. In the winter, it can feel like a bleak endless place, and I like the way it feels to stand and look out across the moors. But in the summer, everything blooms or becomes covered in greenery. My brother and I used to run down the banks of the Walden Beck River before we tumbled past forested banks to the edge of Cauldron Falls. Water flows down and to the broken rocks, warming a crystalline pool sheltered by towering stones that make it look like a cauldron."

Rayne almost closed her eyes as she pictured the idyllic setting. "It sounds like you love it there."

"I do," Oliver admitted. "Astley Court, our manor house, has been in my family for two hundred years."

She leaned against the armrest between their two seats. "Then why are you leaving?"

Oliver's green eyes darkened to that of an English forest. "Sometimes one has to let go of the past in order to move forward. The time has come for my family to do the same."

"Oh..." For some reason her heart clenched at the thought of Oliver leaving a place he seemed so clearly to adore. "I'm sorry you have to leave." She reached over to touch his hand, and after a long moment he turned his hand over so their palms met. Then he curled his fingers around hers. Her heart pounded with a strange excitement as Oliver's eyes focused on her lips and she did the same in return. She began to lean into him and only stopped when her father coughed, reminding them both that he was still in the room with them. His paper still concealed his face, perhaps a small sign of his approval—within reason—so she did not pull her hand free of Oliver's, nor did he pull his away.

"What did you bring to read, aside from the paper?" Oliver nodded at the book that lay forgotten on her lap.

"*Jane Eyre.*"

"Ah. And what draws you to such a story? The Gothic atmosphere?" He was clearly teasing her, but she couldn't resist proving to him it wasn't only the Gothicness that interested her.

"Actually, I enjoyed the intimate first-person character viewpoint. We see that Jane's moral and spiritual development is colored by psychological intensity. The prose reveals her character through private consciousness as she faces issues regarding class, sexuality, religion, and being a woman in a world dominated by men."

Oliver's eyes twinkled. "Lord, and here I thought it was simply a good read. Those Brontë sisters, one should not be surprised."

"And you? What do you read?" She glanced down at the book in his lap.

He lifted the red-covered book up for her to see.

"*The Black Arrow?*" The shape of a black arrow was printed across the front of the book, as though it had been unleashed by some imaginary bow to land on the cover.

"It's a rather new book. Zadie read it a month ago and thought I might like it."

"What's it about?"

Oliver rubbed his thumb over her hand as he spoke. The intimate little touch thrilled her.

"It occurs during the War of the Roses, with the Plantagenet line of royalty battling the Tudors, who are usurping the throne. It's the story of a young man named Richard who rescues his lady love, becomes a knight, and avenges his father's murder. He joins a band of outlaws called the Black Arrow."

"That sounds romantic," Rayne sighed. "Like Robin Hood."

"There's nothing better than a tale of outlaws living deep in the English woods." Oliver chuckled. "Would you like to swap? At least until we reach Lord Fraser's?"

Rayne adored the idea, because it guaranteed her having to see him again, and she handed him *Jane Eyre* while she took his copy of *The Black Arrow.*

For the next couple of hours, she and Oliver read in silence, shooting glances at one another every few pages. Oliver would stroke light, teasing touches upon her hand, drawing invisible lines as though he were creating a private map between them. She peeked a few times to see what part he was reading, but when she did so, her skirts spilled over his left leg and their knees touched. When her boot brushed against his, she nearly jerked away, but when he moved his boot closer to hers, rubbing his foot against hers, she thought she might swoon like some Gothic heroine. Never in all of her life had she swooned, and yet here in a train car she was having trouble breathing as excitement gathered within her at each passing touch, each playful caress of his hands or foot. By the time she'd regained her focus, she realized she'd barely read any of the last page she'd been on.

After a while her father yawned, set his paper down, and stretched. Rayne carefully slipped her hand free of Oliver's so as to avoid her father's notice.

"I think I shall retire to my sleeping cabin for a bit," he told Rayne. "It was a pleasure to meet you, Lord Conway. Please join us for dinner tonight in the dining car."

"I'd like that, thank you," Oliver answered.

Now alone in the compartment, a sudden tension filled the room. She shifted, unsettled as she tried to focus on the book. It was rather good, but she was far too distracted by being alone with Oliver.

"For the first time, we begin to understand the wild game we play in life; we begin to understand that the thing once done cannot be undone nor changed by saying I am sorry." Oliver spoke the words she had been reading on the page.

"It is a beautiful passage about regret." She closed the book and tried not to think of the warning that it imparted to her.

"Do you have any regrets, Rayne?" Oliver asked as he set *Jane Eyre* down and cupped her chin, gently making her look at him.

"Regrets?" She hesitated. "A few."

"Name one." He stared at her lips again, and she felt that wild need from the library rise up within her. The need to connect to him in every way, like the moon pulling the tides.

"Letting you leave last night without..."

"Without what?" he asked, seducing her with his gentle deep baritone.

"Without more of this..." She leaned over and kissed him, and then she pulled back, shy and mortified at her forward behavior. But if she hadn't, she might have felt the world freeze beneath her feet forever. Oliver sat back, his eyes unreadable. It had been a mistake to assume that the madness that filled her whenever he was around was shared by him.

"I'm sorry," she whispered. "I shouldn't have done that."

He stood and turned to the compartment door, and she closed her eyes, waiting to hear the door click as he slid it open. Instead, she heard a soft whooshing sound.

She opened her eyes and saw he had pulled the blinds down on the compartment, making it completely private. Then he turned back to her. They stared at each other for a long moment.

"A person should do their best to live without regrets," he said, giving her a roguish smile that led to her heart again.

He crooked one finger at her, and she stood, leaning toward him. She was inches away. He wrapped an arm around her waist and tugged her into him. He captured her mouth in a feverish kiss that sent her senses spinning.

He kissed her like a man starved of life and her kiss would bring him back from the brink of death. The corners of her mouth turned up in a delighted grin as she curled her arms around his neck. The raw power of her attraction was astounding, but she didn't question it. He was all she wanted, all she could think about in that moment. He spun their bodies so that he pinned her against the closed compartment door.

"May I touch you?" he asked before he nibbled the soft lobe of her ear.

Rayne let out a tiny whimper of sharp animal need that tore through her. She had to have him touch her.

"Yes. *Lord, yes.*"

He barely stopped kissing her as he slid one hand down between their bodies. Then he curled up the voluminous skirts of her gown and slid his hand beneath them. She gasped as he caressed her inner thighs, and she moaned in shock and delight as he found her center and gently ran a fingertip through her wet folds.

"There… Do you like that?" he asked.

She slanted her mouth over his and raked her nails against the back of his neck. "More…," she demanded. He continued to stroke her, then slid that finger inside her, and she nearly jumped in his arms.

"Easy, love," he chuckled. "Let me show you how good it can feel. Do you trust me?"

"Yes… I do."

She threw her head back as he moved his finger in and out, slow at first, then faster. He used his thumb to brush the small bud of arousal on her mound. Everything seemed to explode around her. She could feel the entire world in that instant. The rumbling of the train upon the tracks, the wind whistling against the compartment windows. She inhaled the scent of Oliver and felt the blood in her veins surging inside her.

A frantic rhythm beat inside her chest. Had she any breath left in her to scream, she would have. But he kissed her again, his tongue sliding inside her mouth, and their mouths moved, mating almost savagely as she drifted down from the trembling perfection of that plea-sure he'd created within her. He withdrew his hand, and her gray silk skirts fell back down over her legs. She watched in dazed amazement as he sucked her juices off his fingers before he returned to her mouth for another kiss.

This was a wicked man, with a wicked touch, and Rayne knew she was losing herself to the stranger. His teeth scraped against her neck above the collar of her gown before he returned to her lips and brushed his mouth over hers. Then, finally, he drew back so he could look down at her.

Their breaths mingled in the intimate space of the train compartment, and Rayne knew if he let go of her, she would have trouble walking steadily. He had made her utterly weak-kneed.

"No regrets?" he asked.

She looked into his green eyes and replied without hesitation, "Not one."

"Good." He brushed the back of his hand against her cheek.

"You seem different from last night," Rayne observed.

"I feel different," he said. "Because of you."

"Really? I—"

Someone knocked on the compartment door. "Miss Egerton?" Ellen's voice disrupted them.

"Who's that?" Oliver asked.

"My lady's maid," Rayne nearly groaned.

"You should go to her. We shouldn't be staying too long in here with the shades down," Oliver said.

"I'll go first. Will I see you tonight for dinner?"

"I wouldn't miss it," Oliver promised.

Rayne collected herself and moved a hand over her hair before she exited the compartment and stepped into the hall.

"Time to dress for dinner," Ellen said. "Your father thought I ought to fetch you."

"Thank you, Ellen." Rayne wished the woman could've waited a few more minutes, but Oliver wasn't going anywhere. At least, not yet. They were on the train together and both bound for Inverness.

We have time yet to discover what lies between us.

CHAPTER 6

Oliver remained in the cabin for a few minutes longer, his heart racing. He licked his lips and smiled. He could still taste Rayne's sweetness there, and it gave him a heady rush. Everett had teased him last evening that the attraction would grow as the size of her fortune did, but Everett was wrong. Rayne was everything Oliver had ever dreamed of having in a wife, and he would have given up everything to be with her. It was simply good fortune that she was also an heiress. A flicker of guilt niggled him at the back of his mind for deceiving Rayne, but he had to ignore it. Rayne had desired him last evening and had been just as interested in him as he had been in her. And they had been complete strangers.

It was more than her beauty that drew him to her. Rayne was real and tangible to him in a way that other young ladies didn't seem to be. They presented a facade of what they *should* be instead of simply being who they were. Rayne had no such pretensions. It was as if he could reach out and touch her soft satin skin and feel her dreams through that simple connection alone.

Oliver smiled as he retrieved his copy of *The Black Arrow* from where she had forgotten it among the newspaper pages scattered on the seat. He stroked the book's spine and in his mind relived the sweet moment when he had her pinned against the door of the compartment. He had almost come undone himself as her face had revealed that intimate look of a woman in the throes of passion. There was nothing more beautiful than the way her lashes had fluttered or the way a heavy blush had stained her cheeks. He had wondered then what beauty there would be in seeing the rest of her flushed like that when she lay beneath him in a bed.

He took a long moment to let his ardor cool before he took his book and returned to his own cabin in the sleeping car. Dinner was in an hour, and he needed time to prepare. He had barely made it to the train on time. It had taken longer than he thought to have his ticket changed, and then he'd had to meet with the officers in charge of luggage. He had only a few days of clothes, and they would have to do until he reached Inverness.

As he reached the cabin, he heard feminine voices coming from next door and grinned. He'd paid another man on the platform almost twice the cost of the ticket to ensure that his cabin was next to Rayne's.

Oliver slipped into his cabin and then removed his valise from the closet and set it on the bed so he could retrieve his evening clothes. His valet, Benjamin, would catch up with him at Lord Fraser's in two days, but thankfully he had no need of him today. He donned his black trousers, which were cut narrower than his usual trousers and finished with black braid on the seam. Then he donned a lounge jacket that fell to his hips. It would be more suitable for dinner on a train than a coat and tails. No doubt Mr. Egerton would be sporting a tuxedo, which was all the rage in America at the moment. The British, however, were reluctant to embrace the look. Oliver knew his dinner jacket would be an appropriate compromise between the two dueling fashion trends.

He brushed his coat with the suit brush and carefully checked his appearance in the small mirror. He had only a handful of days to get Rayne to fall in love with him. A more cynical or mercenary mind might be focused on seducing her or trying to compromise her into marriage, but that was not his intention. He wanted Rayne to love him so that when he proposed she would be happy with him and not resent him for marrying her for her fortune. If he played the hand of cards he had been dealt in the right manner, Rayne would not care about his lack of fortune because she would love him, and he would endeavor to make her happy. Still...he couldn't quite shake the small dark cloud forming in the back of his mind that whispered he was going to hurt her when she discovered the truth. That was why he had to make her fall in love with him.

Though it was too soon for him to believe he loved her, she had captivated him with her mind and her body, and he truly believed his heart would pose little resistance in the days to come.

He opened the door to his cabin and stepped into the hall. Through the windows, he saw that the sun had set behind the distant hills, but the train would roll on through the night. They had left Peterborough one hour ago, and now the train was headed toward Doncaster and would pass through York overnight.

"Lord Conway?" The voice stopped him dead in his tracks. He spun to see a woman in a mauve evening gown. He stared at the woman, worry prodding his stomach at this unforeseen complication.

"Ellen? What are you doing here?"

Ellen Moore stared back at him in confusion. "I am accompanying my new employer to Scotland. And you, my lord?"

"Your new employer?" The dread forming in his stomach grew. "You wouldn't happen to be working for the Egertons, would you?"

She nodded.

"Christ," he muttered. "Come in here." He gestured to his cabin.

Ellen hastily followed him inside, and he closed the door. Then he faced Ellen, one of the women he'd had to let go from employment in his own home only two months before.

"How is Miss Conway?" Ellen inquired hopefully.

"She is well, but she misses you," Oliver said.

Ellen had been Zadie's lady's maid for three years, but due to their situation, Oliver had been forced to let go of half of his staff. He and Everett now shared a valet, and Zadie shared a lady's maid with their mother. Oliver had done his best to provide sufficient funds to let every servant have a chance to get by until they found new work.

"Thank you again for the references. It helped me obtain my position," Ellen said with a sad smile. "The Egertons are lovely people, especially Miss Egerton."

"I'm glad to hear it." Oliver hesitated. "Ellen, I must beg a matter of secrecy with you. Regarding my family's...situation."

Ellen's brows rose, then narrowed. "My lord, I would never speak untoward about you, but why are you so concerned?"

"Well, you see, I am attempting to court Miss Egerton. We met last night, and I'm quite taken with her." He would not say he was fortune hunting. He refused to call it that.

However, the lady's maid's shrewd gaze confirmed she had already made the connection. "You wish to…"

"Marry Miss Egerton."

"For her fortune—"

"Not entirely," he cut in. "Because I genuinely like her. I met her last night before I knew she was an heiress, and now, well, perhaps fate has a kindness planned for my family after all."

"Lord Conway, you know how much affection I have for your family, but surely there is another way?"

"There isn't. I went to see the banker in charge of our loans, and he could not give us any more extensions. I had been about to propose to Lady Adelaide when I met your Miss Egerton."

Ellen's face pinched. "Oh my lord, not her. She's the worst sort of creature. It would devastate Miss Zadie."

"It would indeed, but she is my only other choice. Please, Ellen, I beg you. I find myself faced with a horrible choice: an honest transaction with a woman I cannot love, or a chance at happiness that requires me to be dishonest for a time. It is not a quandary I take lightly. I don't wish to start a marriage out like this, it galls me to even think of hurting Rayne by hiding my financial state."

Ellen crossed her arms, eyeing him with a severity that was wholly inappropriate given their stations and yet richly deserved under the circumstances. "You truly like Miss Egerton?"

"I do," he promised. "She bewitched me last night long before I even knew her name."

"Then I will keep your secret, my lord, but you must win her on your own. You will have no help from me, not because I don't wish you well, but because she deserves a man who will value her as a person, not as an heiress. That is my only advice. Truly win her heart, my lord. She deserves to have a marriage based on trust and love, she shouldn't have to worry over whether you married her for herself or her money."

He'd managed to avoid feeling guilty about his motives for seducing Rayne until now, but Ellen had reminded him that what he was doing was what all fortune hunters did. But unlike those callous individuals, he wanted to love Rayne, wanted to be married to her not just for the money. Surely that mattered.

"I've always liked you and your family, my lord, but I know that desperation can turn even the sweetest fruit sour. If I come to believe your intentions are anything other than what you say, I will tell Miss Egerton the truth."

"That is fair, and I would expect nothing less from the woman who kept my dear sister away from more than one cad in her time." He opened his cabin door and let her slip into the hall, then made his own way a moment later.

As he stepped into the dining car, his heart stopped at the sight of Rayne. Her beauty was intoxicating, and he felt he could become drunk on the sight of her alone. She looked exquisite in a blue-and-pink plaid silk evening dress. Pale-blue three-quarter-length sleeves matched the pale-blue revers that separated the bustle from the front skirts, which were draped with pale-cream lace. She was a picture of perfection, as delicious looking as a dessert sitting in a confectioner's shop window. She turned, the pleated train trailing behind her as she laughed at something her father said.

He hadn't heard her laugh before, and he liked it more than he could say. She swayed as she walked farther down the dining car on her father's arm, and a bitter-sweet ache settled in Oliver's chest.

Ellen stepped in behind them, and the three of them proceeded to a set of tables. Oliver hurried to catch up with them.

"Oh, Lord Conway, it seems the dining car has only two tables left, each seating two. I don't suppose you would prefer to dine with Rayne tonight? I'm sure she's quite tired of listening to me talk and would love a charming younger dinner companion."

Rayne chuckled. "You know that isn't true, Father." Oliver didn't miss the fond look she sent her father's way. It was clear they were very close, and Oliver liked that, even though he knew it would make it more difficult for him to win the older man's trust.

Mr. Egerton's eyes twinkled. "Perhaps not, but I do

think you would enjoy someone new to talk to. I would be happy to dine with Miss Moore."

"Thank you, Mr. Egerton. I would be delighted." Oliver couldn't believe his luck. Rayne's father must have sensed that Rayne and he had a liking for each other and possibly approved, at least so far as to allow them time to converse at dinner.

Oliver saw the pair of open tables, which were across the aisle from each other. He offered Rayne his arm and relished the blush on her face as she slipped her hand in the crook of his elbow as he led her to their table. He pulled her chair back for her as she took her seat and then sat across from her.

"You look magnificent," he said softly.

She looked down, clearly embarrassed. "Thank you. I don't normally wear such gowns, but Father ordered them from Paris, and, well, it has been fun to wear them."

"What do you normally wear?" he asked.

"I do love a nice gown, but they tend to be a tad more practical," she reflected with a small smile, as though amused at the admission. "I work at my father's office a few days each week, and it is easier that way."

"You work with your father?" That startled him, though he didn't disapprove.

"I do. Most men find that unattractive, or at least inappropriate." She said this a little coolly, as if he was being tested. Well, luckily for her, he believed she would like his honest view on the matter.

"I find that very appealing. Idleness is nonsense in my opinion. Men and women alike are creatures who like to be busy, to be useful, to be innovative. What use are we to our fellow man if we do nothing to contribute? I know that sounds odd coming from a member of the landed gentry, but I have never believed that I should sit by and let others work while I do nothing but reap the benefits."

A waiter approached their table and poured them each a glass of wine. Rayne reached for hers. "So you don't mind a woman who works?"

"I do not," he promised. "As a son and brother to two very intelligent, driven, passionate ladies, I see only strength in women."

Rayne relaxed a little, and he knew he had won an important battle tonight.

"Tell me, what sort of work do you do?"

She laughed. "My father calls me an office manager. But it is more a mix of accounting, invoice collections, and correspondence with investors and clients."

"Incredible." Oliver meant it. Those qualities would make for a masterful mistress of Astley Court. Running an estate took skill, patience, and determination.

"I'm glad you think so," she admitted, that shyness now back in her eyes.

"As my sister often reminds me, it should not matter one whit what a man thinks."

She giggled. "All the same, I'm glad."

"Rayne…" He spoke her name softly. "Given last night and this afternoon, I am finding myself growing attached to you. May I…" He paused, wondering if now was the right time to ask or if he was rushing it. But then he mustered his courage and continued. "May I court you?"

"Court me?" she echoed in a surprised whisper.

"Yes. If you are not interested, I understand, but—"

"Yes." She cut him off, which made them both laugh at her eagerness.

"Yes?"

She nodded, a blush staining her cheeks, and then she took a large sip of her wine.

"Good, then let us learn more about one another," he said.

"How do you propose to do that?"

"We shall play a question game. You ask me a question, then I ask you."

She sipped her wine, studying him intently, and he wondered what sort of question she was brewing up.

"How do you take your tea?" She looked at him so seriously, he wanted to laugh again.

"A most penetrating question. A touch of cream, no sugar," he replied. "My turn. Favorite color?"

"Green."

"A sensible choice. Any particular shade?"

"The color of your eyes," she blurted, then covered her mouth.

He couldn't resist smiling. "Until yesterday I favored red, but now I'm bewitched by the color of *your* eyes. They are an enchanting shade, a diamond blue-gray." He meant it. Nothing he said or would ever say to her would be false. He needed to win Rayne's heart along with her hand, and he would not lie to her to do so.

"I dreamed about cursed diamonds last night," Rayne said in a scandalized whisper. Her eyes, so deep and clear, were full of longing and desire.

"Is that *all* you dreamed about?" he said conspiratorially as the waiter set plates of quail and potatoes in front of them.

"Perhaps. Perhaps not," Rayne replied with an impish smile. He nearly choked on his wine when she gave him a wink.

"I think I adore you," he whispered, and she blushed. She was a fascinating contradiction of a woman. Clearly passionate, but shy about expressing it, except when she wasn't. Given how society treated such things, he couldn't blame her for being inconsistent in her expressions. More likely than not, she was passionate and outspoken by nature, but society was continually reinforcing that a woman must be quiet and meek. He much preferred the former in a woman and not the latter.

"I'm not usually this forward, at least in regard to romance," she whispered back. They were both aware of how close the other diners in the first-class dining car were, and the fact that their conversation could be overheard. It was frustrating and exciting at the same time.

"Neither am I," he added. At least, he hadn't been in the last few years. He had put his days of roguish behavior behind him, but this woman seemed to draw that old devil out. If he wasn't careful, he would be seeking an invitation to her cabin tonight, and it was far too soon for that.

"I confess, I don't seem to be sensible around you," she said.

"I feel a bit wild myself. Perhaps that's a sign of something?"

"Perhaps it is simply lust at first sight?" Rayne asked, still lowering her voice as they ate their way through the first course.

"Lust, yes, but a desire that runs deeper as well, I hope." He was quiet a long moment. "Tell me about your home, your family."

Rayne's eyes darkened to a stormy color that made him think of spring rain.

"My mother passed away two years ago. My father was madly in love with her. I became more involved in his company to help him with his grief."

He knew what it meant to care for a parent who had

lost their spouse. But unlike Rayne, he'd had the good fortune of sharing that burden with his siblings.

"And who helped you? Losing one's parent is a difficult blow to one's heart."

"No one, really. I'm strong enough to bear it." But her eyes said otherwise. They became downcast, and her eyes began to shimmer. Rayne had taken her father's grief and carried it along with her own. That alone told him how strong she was, and he wanted to be the man who helped her carry those burdens from now on.

Oliver reached across the table to catch hold of her hand, forgetting that they were not alone.

"There is nothing wrong with relying on someone when you are hurting."

She didn't pull her hand away; she simply shrugged. "There isn't anyone to rely on."

He squeezed her hand gently, hoping she could hear his silent vow. *There will be, if you let me.*

When the waiter delivered two plates of blancmange for dessert, their hands separated. The milky white pudding was shaped into an artful mold surrounded by thinly sliced strawberries. Oliver watched Rayne dip her dessert fork into the blancmange and take an experimental bite. Her face lit with a glowing pleasure that stole his breath.

"I say, Rayne, this is rather good," Mr. Egerton said from across the aisle. Oliver was dragged back into the awareness that he and Rayne were not alone. It was so easy to forget that when he was with her.

"Yes, it is good," Rayne replied to her father. He nodded and returned to his meal.

"Tell me about your home," Oliver asked, hoping she would have happy memories to share.

"Home is... Well, not exactly a place for me anymore. My father's business has always kept us in New York, but that city never felt like home. I had no idyllic place to explore as a child, no enchanting waterfalls, no dusty old attics, no place to call my own."

"It's never too late to find one's home." He imagined she would fall in love with a place like Astley Court and quickly make it her home.

"It would be nice to have a place like yours," she said, seeming to read his thoughts.

"Perhaps you can. I would love to extend an invitation to you and your father to stay with us after Christmas." He hoped that she would be wed to him before then, but he couldn't wager on that.

"I would like that. I will ask my father this evening."

"Ask me what?" Mr. Egerton and Miss Moore had finished their dinner and had risen from their table.

"Lord Conway has invited us to stay at his house, Astley Court in Yorkshire, when we are finished with our visit to Lord Fraser's."

"Thank you for the invitation, Lord Conway. We would be delighted to accept." Douglas offered him a smile, but Oliver could see the man was appraising him. Perhaps he had overheard more of their conversation than he was letting on?

"Ladies, forgive me, I'm going to steal Lord Conway for a glass of brandy."

It was as Oliver suspected. Douglas was aware of Oliver's interest in his daughter, and now he would begin the interrogation.

"Oh..." Rayne sighed in obvious disappointment.

"Breakfast tomorrow?" Oliver volunteered, and she brightened again.

"Yes, that would be lovely." She rose from the table, and she and Miss Moore headed in the direction of the Pullman sleeping car.

"This way, Lord Conway," Douglas Egerton said.

Oliver knew this might well be the hardest battle for Rayne's heart. He did not wish to lose her because of her father's disapproval. He cast one last look at Rayne's retreating figure, and it gave him the strength to face her father.

I must win them both.

CHAPTER 7

Oliver sat down across from Mr. Egerton at the back of the dining car as a waiter brought them two glasses of brandy. He tried to remain calm, but damned if he wasn't a bit nervous. The atmosphere between him and Rayne's father had grown a bit cold, just enough to give him a slight worry as to what was to come.

"Well, I'm not one to beat around the bush, waiting to see what rushes out. Let's get to the heart of the matter. You are interested in my daughter, Lord Conway." It wasn't a question.

"I am, Mr. Egerton. She has consented to my courtship."

"And what about me? Do you care to ask me if I consent?" Douglas wasn't angry, but there was a gleam in the man's eyes that would have made Oliver nervous if he had been a younger man. But far too much was at stake for Oliver to be afraid.

"I am of two minds on that matter," he said diplomatically. "Rayne is a woman possessed of her own mind and desires and believes she does not need any man's approval for the choices in her life. I respect that. But at the same time, I do seek your approval for my suit toward her. I respect a father's need to look out for the best interests of his child. My intention was to come to you if Rayne and I decided to marry. But we have only begun our courtship, so I thought it imprudent to assume such an outcome was guaranteed."

Douglas sipped his brandy, remaining silent long enough that Oliver assumed the man was still testing him.

"How did you meet my daughter last night? I did not see her dance with you."

A clever *and* observant father. Oliver liked him far too much for that, even though it made seducing Rayne more difficult.

"We both sought refuge from the ball in Lady Poole's library. We met and conversed for a short while but did not exchange names. I did not think I would see her again, but she made quite an impression on me."

"The library?" Douglas's eyes softened. "Libraries are wonderful places, aren't they? I met her mother in a library. Jeanette was never one for crowds, and Rayne is a little like her mother in that regard."

"Rayne said she passed away two years ago. My condolences on your loss."

Douglas's gaze grew distant. "Thank you. No one prepares a man for losing a woman he loves with all his heart. It felt as though my own heart was ripped out and cast into a raging fire. Rayne is all I have left of her."

Oliver met his gaze and saw a flicker of pain there. "My father passed over a year ago. I wondered at times if perhaps he would come back to haunt me. We have such strong stories of hauntings here in England, but my mother told me something that put my heart at ease. She said the world has its ghosts, but they are not the phantoms we imagine drifting among the graveyard stones. She said the spirits of those we love never truly leave us. Once a soul is born, it can never perish—it merely changes form. She told me that my father's eyes were those of my own, that his laugh can be heard in my brother's voice, and his honest and loving heart beats within my little sister's chest. When my mother looks upon us, she sees the separate pieces of her husband, as though he were one being again."

Rayne's father gave a bittersweet smile. "My Jeanette is certainly within Rayne. It makes it hard for a man to let go."

Oliver knew what he meant. It would be hard to let

go of Rayne because she would marry a man and live her own life far away from her father.

"If she married the right man, you need not ever lose her," Oliver said, hoping he would understand that he would be a welcome member of the sometimes-boisterous Conway clan.

"And are you that man, Lord Conway? If you aren't, then you would be wise to leave my daughter alone before she becomes too attached."

The gauntlet has been thrown, Oliver thought.

"I would like to be that man. As a peer of the realm—"

"Titles mean little to me. I value a man's actions." Douglas threw back his brandy in one gulp. "Court my daughter if you wish, but if you break her heart..." Douglas fixed him with a powerful stare. The unspoken threat was nevertheless made abundantly clear to him.

"I shall heed your warning, Mr. Egerton." Oliver finished his brandy. "I will retire now."

He bid Douglas good night and returned to his sleeping cabin. He listened next door but heard no sounds coming from Rayne's cabin. It was hard to hear much given the sounds of the train. As he prepared for bed, he changed into his dark-blue jacquard silk dressing gown. As he was fastening the sash around his waist, someone knocked at his door.

As the night steward had not yet come by to check

the oil in the lamp in his cabin, he assumed that was who was there. Oliver opened the door.

"Good of you to come, my lamp is low—" His words died as he saw Rayne standing in her nightgown with a gold-and-black dressing gown over it. It made her look like a beautiful red admiral butterfly with the puffed sleeves near her shoulders. Her hair was loosely bound at the nape of her neck by a black ribbon, and she'd pulled her hair over her shoulder so it tumbled down in a riot of brown waves.

"May I come in for a moment?" she asked.

His mouth was too dry to form words as he stepped back to allow her entrance. Then he closed the door. The woman was far too lovely for him to keep his wits about when she was around.

"Did anyone see you?" he asked.

"No, the steward has extinguished all the lamps except the ones in the passageway between the train cars. I waited until he was gone."

"Good, I wouldn't want to cause any scandals," he said.

Rayne flashed that impish smile at him. "The scandal might be worth it."

Oliver almost laughed. He was supposed to be the heartless fortune hunter, and yet the little American heiress was the one sneaking into his cabin dressed so enticingly. It would be so easy to peel the dressing gown off her body and remove the filmy white peignoir she wore under it. And her body, with its luscious curves, would no doubt erase the last bit of his frayed control.

"I realize how silly this is," Rayne said as she reached up to hold her dressing gown closed. "But...I didn't want the night to be over."

The sweetness of her sentiment stunned him. She was impossibly innocent, yet not naïve. She'd sought him out because her heart called to his. The need to not be apart from him must have been overwhelming. He felt it too, that strange and wonderful pull toward her like he'd never felt for any woman in his life.

"I feel the same, so perhaps we are silly together." He gestured to his bed. "Come and sit. We shall talk."

He sat down opposite her in the small armchair beside his bed.

"What were you like as a boy?" she asked.

"Me?"

She nodded, excitement filling her eyes. Oliver couldn't resist laughing as he considered his answer. "Trouble. Certainly trouble. I was forever escaping the house to avoid my schooling. Once Everett was old enough, we would sneak out together to go into the woods and set snares for rabbits, or we'd go fishing in the river."

Rayne laughed at this, clearly delighted in his penchant for mischief. It made him all the more curious about her.

"And what was a young Rayne like?"

She looked down at her black silk slippers. "Trouble. Certainly trouble."

Oliver chortled. "You? Trouble? I cannot picture it."

"You should," she insisted with a mischievous smirk. "I was quite clever escaping my house as well, only I would go down to the stables and ride my pony. When I was older, I tried to go to my boarding school without my corsets. I may have burned one or two in protest."

"You burned a corset? Why?"

"Because they're impossible to breathe in most of the time. You become even a little bit excited and *poof*!" She made a gesture with her hands to show she was falling. "You faint dead away. It's no wonder men believe we're so delicate. If we were allowed to breathe normally, we'd be quite different during the day, I assure you."

"Surely you don't wear them *all* the time. I know that during afternoon teas, ladies do not wear corsets—it's why we men aren't allowed to attend those teas." Oliver knew women wore them most of the day, but he was curious to see what she would say.

"We don't wear them all the time. I'm not wearing one *now*."

"Dear God, woman, are you trying to kill me?" He was seconds away from creating the very scandal he wished to avoid.

Rayne left his bed and came over to him and settled herself on his lap. She kissed him, her small delicate hands framing his face. He gave up fighting his desires then. He had never been a saint, and he wasn't about to become one now.

A SMALL PART OF RAYNE TRIED TO WARN HERSELF THAT this wild, reckless behavior was a bad idea, but the rest of her was blissfully lost in kissing Oliver. When he had opened the door and she'd seen him wearing those silk sleeping trousers and his lounge jacket, she'd been both stunned and aroused. Something about Oliver in a state of undress made him twice as irresistible. Perhaps it was that the veneer of being a gentleman was gone and in its place was a man of flesh and blood, one of dark carnal desires. That was the Oliver she wanted now.

He cupped her face as he slowed their fevered kisses to look at her. She tried to catch her breath.

"Are you all right?" he asked as he stroked her bottom lip. "I'm not scaring you?"

She shook her head and licked her lips. "I came to you," she reminded him. She curled her arms around him and played with the strands of hair at the base of his neck.

"I know, and as much as I am enjoying this, love, I don't want you to think that I have expectations."

"But you have desires, I hope?" she asked. A sudden fear that she was the only one truly feeling this way made her draw back a little.

"Oh, I do. Great, *hungry* desires." His eyes turned dark, and she saw what she was hoping to see, that he was barely in control of himself.

"Could we...stay together tonight, just to sleep? I don't think I'm ready yet for..." It was hard to explain why, even to herself, but she wanted to lie beside him tonight and feel his heartbeat against her cheek and listen to the rhythm of his breath. Her mother used to say that people showed who they really were when they were asleep. If a frown marred their brow, worries troubled them; if they smiled slightly, their dreams were as sunny as their disposition. She wished to know what Oliver was like at his most vulnerable.

He groaned approvingly at her scandalous request and twined his fingers in the hair that spilled down her shoulders. "Of course."

She leaned in to press her forehead against his. "But...I would like a bit more of this first..." She pressed her mouth to his and delighted in tasting his laughter before he conquered her lips with his own.

Oliver Conway was indeed a master of kisses. He knew when to flick his tongue against hers, when to deepen the kiss, and when to pause and let her regain her breath. He held her full attention just with the power of his lips. She couldn't imagine what he would be capable of if he used the rest of his body on her.

She shivered with longing and pressed closer against him. It was strange and comforting to feel the train clacking along on the tracks beneath them. The sound was hypnotic and kept her bound in this perfect moment where she and Oliver had nothing but their endless kisses together. When the train came to a stop, she looked around in confusion. A distant whistle shrilled in the night.

"Doncaster," Oliver murmured before he nibbled her earlobe, and her body was once again under his magnetic thrall. Soon enough the train started moving again, and she knew they would be on their way to York next. York, where Oliver lived. She recalled his face as he'd mentioned having to leave his home behind, and it saddened her. Her heart ached, and her sorrow for him bled into her kisses. He seemed to sense her emotions as he pulled her closer, the embrace more comforting now than sensual.

When their mouths parted, he drew in a deep breath, and she saw his sensual expression fade a little.

"Are you tired yet?" he asked.

"Not quite... We could play cards and talk? That is, if you have some?"

"I do." He let her slide off his lap and went to retrieve a deck from his suitcase. "A gentleman never leaves home without a deck of cards." He looked at her with a wolfish smile. "Or a good book."

"It's rather nice to meet a man who reads. Most gentlemen I've been introduced to lately don't seem to know that books exist anymore. It's all horse racing or stock markets when we talk."

Oliver smiled, the expression confident and tinged with amusement. "You've been meeting all the wrong men. A good Cambridge man always reads. It's those Oxford bastards who don't."

She couldn't help but laugh. She'd heard more than once of the long-standing rivalry between the two elite British universities.

He slipped the cards from their box and began to shuffle them in his hands with the flair of a man who knew his way around a deck.

"You know how to play Bread and Honey?" he asked.

"I think so. I played once or twice. You deal all the cards one at a time facedown. And there are cards called blackbirds that determine what each of us can play following the reveal of a blackbird card so that we can gain more cards in our respective stacks?"

"Yes, exactly. The winner is whoever ends up with the most cards."

They sat down on the floor beside the bed, and Oliver deftly dealt the cards between them. Over the next hour, Rayne laughed as she and Oliver played. They talked about themselves, in between his teasing about her spectacular ability to lose the game, and she clung to the details of his life, how he had served for a time aboard a naval ship when he was in his twenties.

"It was the only real fight my father and I ever had,"

Oliver said as he turned over another card. "I thought at the time that he was trying to control me since I was the eldest son and heir, but as I grew older and wiser, I realized he was afraid that I might be injured or killed."

"Fathers can be like that. They want to protect you, but they don't realize you need to live your own life, make your own mistakes." Rayne thought of how her own father never tried to control her, but he had made it clear that he would not let her marry just anyone.

Her inheritance as his only child put her in a clear position to become wealthy beyond most men in America. They'd had many discussions about fortune hunters and the danger of being alone with men. Rayne wasn't naïve. She knew a man could compromise a woman and attempt to force a marriage. But she wanted love, wanted to find a man who would love her for herself, even if she was as poor as a church mouse. But how did one find a man like that?

Perhaps in a library?

That was why she'd been so attracted to Oliver. He'd had no idea who she was, and yet he'd liked her. Even now, he seemed unconcerned with her wealth, whereas most gentlemen would have pressed her with questions regarding her father's business, which always led to talk of money. She felt she could trust him too, in a way she hadn't been able to trust any other men, aside from her father.

Rayne focused back on the card game and cursed as

Oliver won the game by turning over his final card and adding it to his larger stack.

"Damn!" Rayne tossed her remaining cards down. "You have an unfair advantage."

"Suppose I do. I've been playing Bread and Honey since I was a child."

"See, advantage!" she teased and leaned back against the edge of his bed. She yawned, and then heat rushed to her face in embarrassment. Her mother used to remind her that it was rude to yawn in the presence of others.

"Tired?" Oliver's face was gentle with a hint of amusement, and her embarrassment faded.

"I am now." She had been so nervous coming here tonight, but, as always, being with Oliver was impossibly easy.

In some ways, it felt as though they'd been together for years, playing cards until after dark and whispering about their lives as the oil in the lamp burned low. Her heart quivered with a desire for it to always be like this, to have Oliver as a husband and...to have a life together with him.

He gathered up the cards and returned them to his suitcase before he pulled back the sheets of his narrow bed in silent invitation.

Rayne stood and removed the black-and-gold dressing gown she wore and stepped out of her satin slippers before she climbed in. Oliver watched her a long moment, allowing it to build with delicious tension before he removed his lounge coat and revealed his bare chest. She was left in a daze at the way the light from the lamp made his skin look soft and golden. He had a patch of dark hair at the top center of his chest and a trail of dark hair that started a few inches below his navel. Her gaze followed it down to the waistband of his satin sleep trousers. She swallowed hard as it became all too real. She was alone in a man's sleeping cabin. Alone in his bed.

Oliver extinguished the oil lamp, and darkness swallowed them up. Her heart hammered wildly against her ribs as he joined her in bed, but it eased as Oliver pressed his body against hers and slowly relaxed. The heat of his bare upper body soothed her, and she pressed her cheek against his chest. The beating of his heart was so steady that she could set a pocket watch to it.

After a moment, he reached to touch her hair, stroking it gently. That was how she knew she was lost to him. He was a blend of gentleness and fierce passion, and he cared about his family and his home. He didn't have a problem with a woman who worked or liked to learn about business. He was perfect—*too* perfect.

A sudden flicker of doubt was there. Could this be an act? Was he like the others?

Those men in dashing suits who brought flowers and gifts to her door, all in an attempt to woo her, to take her fortune and leave her brokenhearted? If that was the case, then he was the most clever one yet, because she was falling for him. He'd only been a gentleman with her thus far and had done his best to keep her from being compromised. Any other fortune hunter would have had witnesses ready in the library or in the day compartment to see them kissing and expose them to try to force a marriage, but that hadn't happened with Oliver.

He must be different. He must be...

CHAPTER 8

Morning arrived with sweet, slow awareness. Rayne had forgotten sometime during the night that she had come to Oliver's cabin and stayed there in his arms. As it came back to her, she felt her body nestled against his, and she almost giggled in delight at her own wicked behavior. What would those stodgy ladies in the Knickerbocker Club back in New York think of her?

Oliver lay on his back, one arm folded behind his head as he slept. She rested her chin on his chest and studied him. A night beard shadowed his jaw, making him so very human, so very masculine, and so very real in that moment. She reached up and traced her fingers over his jaw, feeling the slight scrape of stubble beneath her skin. The touch was so intimate, like something only a lover or a wife might do. Rayne was filled with a desire then to be Oliver's lover, to be his wife. She still knew so little of him, but she knew more about him than many people who got married.

He shifted beneath her touch, turning his face toward her hand and pressing a kiss to her fingers. Then he opened his eyes, and his slumberous expression toward her was incredibly intimate.

"Did you sleep well?" he murmured.

"Yes. You?" she whispered, not that anyone could hear them, given the train's noise.

"Wonderfully so." He settled his free hand on her lower back beneath the blankets. His palm heated her body, coursing through the thin fabric of the peignoir she wore. It reminded her of how little clothing was between them now. She moved to lie more fully on top of him, spreading her legs a little so she could press her heated core against his hips. He continued to lie still beneath her, his arm lazily propped behind his head as he studied her.

She placed a kiss to his chest, loving the feel of his warm skin beneath her lips as she kissed a path up to his mouth.

"What I wouldn't give to have you beneath me," he whispered between her kisses. His hand on her lower back slid down to her bottom, cupping it in a way that made her flood with wet heat.

She nuzzled his nose and stole a playful kiss. "Why don't you?"

"Because I am *trying* to be a gentleman. Something you're making very difficult, Miss Egerton." He caressed her formal name with a heavy layer of sensuality. His eyes in this light were a dark green that made her think of an English forest in the middle of summer.

She suddenly laughed, which made him laugh too.

"What?" he asked, both of his hands now settling on her bottom beneath the sheets.

"I was thinking of how things would be back in New York if we were courting there."

"Oh?" He stroked his fingers in playful patterns on her backside, toying with the thin material of the nightgown between her flesh and his hands.

"Yes, everyone in New York is so stodgy, the society rules so rigid."

"Worse than here?"

She heard a hint of amusement in his question. "Yes."

Oliver chuckled. "I find that hard to believe. Isn't America built upon the ideas of independence and free spirits?"

"Oh, it is," she insisted. "But there's a rather strong puritanical streak, at least in the northeast, that tends to control modes of behavior. Most of society is run by ladies like the infamous Mrs. Astor, one of the richest and most influential women in America. They belong to what my father says is called the Knickerbocker Club. It's all old-money families that's left them feeling in charge of everything and everyone. They dictate who may attend the balls every year and when social calls must be paid. Ladies have no higher aspirations than to seek a wealthy husband and own a brownstone in Washington Square or Gramercy Park and fill it with an acceptable amount of children. If they could see me now..."

"Mrs. Astor would die of a heart attack," Oliver finished with a wolfish smile. "I've heard my mother talk about her. Even New York society reaches our English ears. I heard she tries to control who can attend what balls."

"She certainly does. But there's always new money coming into New York, and she can't control the waves of the nouveau riche." Rayne grew serious again as she looked down at her tempting English gentleman. "Oliver... Are we moving too fast? I swear I am not a lady of easy virtue, but you make me a little wild."

He cupped her face with one hand. "I know you're not, love. Whatever this is between us, it's overpowering to us both. I won't claim to be a saint, but with you, I've tried to be."

"You don't have to," she said. "I want you to be yourself."

He moved his hand to her throat, curling his fingers around the back of her neck to draw her head down to his. "Even if that means I'm *very* wicked?"

"Yes, be wicked so I won't feel like I'm a temptress,"

she murmured against his lips before they shared a long, impossibly intimate kiss.

"Very well, my love. I warned you." And it was indeed the only warning she had before he rolled her body beneath his. He shoved the blankets off them, and he kissed his way down to her breasts. She still wore the thin peignoir, and he sucked one hardened nipple through the cloth. The feel of the wet satin and his hungry lips was erotic beyond anything she'd experienced in her girlish fantasies. His hand cupped and kneaded her other breast gently, pinching and rolling the nipple between his thumb and forefinger. Her breasts felt heavy, and her body burned with heat all over as he continued to play with her. Then he moved down her body even farther until he was kneeling between her parted legs, and he pushed her nightgown up.

Rayne tensed, both excited and frightened at being so exposed to him.

"Easy, love," he soothed. "I just want to taste you." He stroked her inner thighs. "Close your eyes. Concentrate on the touch of my hands and my mouth."

He kissed down the inside of her left thigh until he reached her now soaked center. She almost yelped in surprise as he flicked his tongue against the sensitive folds. She lost herself in the strokes of his fingers and the licking of his tongue. It felt as though he wanted to consume her, *all* of her. He explored her, teased and conquered her until she was begging in frantic pants for something she needed more than her own breath. A bold swipe of his tongue was joined by the insertion of two fingers into her tight channel. He stretched her, making it burn enough that she gasped. Then he thrust those fingers inside her, his pace quickened, and she kept her eyes closed, feeling wild and free in a way she never had before. Then he licked the bud of her arousal, and she exploded with pleasure.

Unable to stop, she reached for him, her hands finding his head, and she fisted her fingers in the silky strands of his dark hair. He continued to lick her and penetrate her with his fingers, drawing out a second, softer climax that stole a breathy moan of exhausted delight from her.

"Wicked..." was all she could whisper.

Oliver's chuckle was accompanied by more kisses as he slid back up her body and claimed her lips. He gave her lower lip a hungry nibble before he kissed her open-mouthed, the kiss raw and primal. It felt wicked too, as though no one should kiss like this, but it was the best sort of kiss. He made her feel beautiful, desired. Their mouths met again and again in a wet, coaxing way that blurred their pleasure into an endless loop for hours. But the sensation of the train coming to a stop dragged both her and Oliver from the sweet aftermath of their passion.

"Have we stopped?" Rayne's head was still fuzzy with desire as she tried to sit up.

"Hold on." Oliver rose and pulled on his dressing gown. He stepped out into the hallway, then returned with a frown.

"What is it?"

"We've stopped at Edinburgh's Waverley Station on Princes Street."

She sat up, pulling her nightgown back down over her knees. "Is that where we should be?"

"Yes, but I saw the conductor on the platform, discussing something with the stationmaster. Why don't you get dressed? I'll do the same, and we'll see what's happened."

Unease prickled at Rayne's insides. "You think something happened?"

"I do, but I'm not sure what."

She rose from the bed and put her dressing gown back on and pulled her cabin key from her pocket. She tucked her feet into her slippers and headed for the door, but Oliver caught her by the waist, pulling her to him for one more scorching kiss.

"Thank you for letting me taste you." He brushed his nose against hers before he pressed his forehead to hers and held her a moment longer before he let her go. Feeling so very vulnerable, she held him back. She hoped he would not think her a clinging sort of woman, but she had never given herself like that to a man, and it felt special for her.

I hope he feels the same.

Then she hurried back to her cabin. She stepped inside to brush her teeth and wash her face. A minute later, Ellen knocked on her door.

"Miss Egerton?"

"Come in, Ellen," she called out.

Her lady's maid entered and began to lay out a dress for the day. "Did you have a nice evening last night?" Ellen inquired.

"I did." She tried not to think about what she and Oliver had done, lest she give herself away with a blush. "And you?"

"Oh yes." Ellen grinned. "I caught up on my reading."

Ellen helped her into a day gown of violet satin. The bodice, sleeves, and white satin underskirt were embroidered with palmetto motifs resembling peacock feathers, made entirely of silver thread. The sleeves were long and the neckline square and low, which would keep her neither too cold nor too hot. Ellen placed a small gold locket around her neck, one that had belonged to Rayne's mother.

Once dressed, she and Ellen stepped into the corridor. She could make out Oliver's form alongside her father's through the windows. Both men were talking to the stationmaster.

"He is handsome, isn't he?" Ellen said beside her.

"Who?"

"Lord Conway." Ellen chuckled.

"He is rather magnificent, isn't he?" She pressed her

palm to the glass of the window, drinking in the sight of him. He wore dark-brown trousers and his navy woolen coat lined with fur as he listened to the stationmaster. He had left his top hat back on the train and casually ran a hand through his hair. She flushed as she remembered how it had felt to cling to his hair while his mouth created such divine pleasure inside her.

"Is it true that he means to court you?"

"Yes, how did you know?" She looked at her maid, a little startled.

"Your father mentioned it to me."

"Oh." She relaxed. "Yes, I've agreed." She paused, her eyes still on Oliver. "Do you think it very silly of me? To be so eager for him that I can't seem to think of anything else?"

Ellen grinned at her. "Not at all. So long as the gentleman is treating you well and is worthy of you. Is he?"

"I believe Lord Conway is. When I'm with him, I feel extraordinary, as though anything is possible."

"You do sound smitten by him. But if I might be so bold, sometimes it's easy to let emotions carry us farther than we intend. Could that be the case now? Or do you believe you're falling in love?"

Rayne bit her bottom lip. "I don't believe in love at first sight, nor do I believe I could love a man so soon, but there's something there..." She thought of when he had spoken of his home and his family and how he had seemed so supportive of her need for independence. It was hard not to love a man like that.

"Well, as long as you don't lose your head, I'd say you owe it to yourself to discover the nature of your feelings for him. Just be careful, miss."

Oliver and her father shook hands with the station-master before returning to the train. Oliver climbed back inside first.

"It seems the tracks on the way to Inverness are covered in snow. The railway workers are digging them out now, but it will take another day. We will be staying in Edinburgh tonight."

"Oh dear. Will we be able to travel tomorrow morning?" Rayne inquired.

"Yes, if all goes well." Oliver glanced at her father. "I've spoken to Mr. Egerton, and we've both decided it's less comfortable to stay on the train tonight. I've recommended a hotel to him at the base of Edinburgh Castle. We are having our luggage transported there now, and the four of us will take a coach to the hotel."

"I'll pack your valise, Miss Egerton," Ellen said and slipped back into Rayne's cabin.

"Go on ahead with Lord Conway, Rayne. I'll meet you outside with Ellen shortly." Her father returned to his cabin, leaving her and Oliver alone.

She tucked her arm in his as they stepped out onto the platform. Pale winter sunlight came in through the ornate glass dome of Waverley Station and illuminated the booking hall in different splashes of color. Rayne marveled at the unique design. It was prettier than any of the stations they'd seen so far.

"Where are we to stay?" she asked Oliver as they exited the station to hail a hackney.

"A place called the Witchery by the Castle."

"The Witchery?" The name conjured up vivid images of women bent over smoking cauldrons.

"It was built a stone's throw from the spot where convicted witches were burned to death on Castle Hill. The hotel is located in what's now called Boswell Court.

"Did witches used to live nearby? Or were they merely held prisoner at the Witchery?"

"Heavens no." Oliver burst out laughing, and Rayne was torn between laughing with him and jabbing him in the ribs with an elbow.

"The Witchery was formerly a merchant's home in 1595. Then it became a committee chamber for members of the Church of Scotland, then later a rectory. They stopped burning witches around 1720, and the hotel was built as a reminder of the innocent lives lost. I suggested it to your father because it has wonderful cuisine and a broody Jacobean atmosphere, which is not to be missed when you are here in Scotland."

"Jacobean?" The term sounded familiar.

"The Jacobites were Scottish rebels who resisted English rule. You'll see lovely tapestries full of Scottish history hanging there."

Her father and Ellen soon joined them, and Oliver waved down a coach. Rayne claimed a seat where she could pull back the coach curtains and look at the old town of Edinburgh. The city was beautiful, with old sandstone buildings and small narrow passageways between them, which Oliver explained were called closes.

"How do you know so much about Scotland?"

"My great-grandfather and his friends visited here quite often. I have relatives in southern Scotland at Castle Kincaid, and I spent many a Christmas journeying north from Yorkshire."

Rayne leaned against his arm. "That sounds charming."

He grinned, the boyish expression so different from the seductive Oliver she had lain with in his bed that morning, but she adored both versions of him.

"It was. My cousins would build snow forts, and we'd battle for hours until we collapsed in the snow, utterly exhausted."

Rayne's heart stung with envy. "I admit, I'm jealous of you. I have no siblings. I do have cousins, Lord help me." She smiled as she thought of the trouble Uncle Gerard's boys would get into.

"Not fun cousins, I take it?"

"They are, but they are older and all boys. I was left out of most things, including snowball fights."

"What a disappointment. We would have let you play no matter what." His eyes glittered with mischief.

"It is a pity we are too old for snowball fights now."

"Poppycock. You're never too old. How's this for a promise? A battle at Lord Fraser's?"

"Oh, could we?" She almost forgot that the two of them weren't alone in the carriage. She glanced across the seats to see her father and Ellen both watching them, her father with an unreadable expression and Ellen with one of slight worry.

Her father cleared his throat, and Rayne let go of Oliver's arm and scooted a few inches away from him. Her father grunted in approval.

"Well, Lord Conway, since you are so familiar with Edinburgh, what's there to do while we spend the day here?" Her father's gaze was steady on them both. Rayne tried not to think about how closely he was watching them.

"I suggest we take a tour of the castle on the hill. We'll be close to it when we reach the Witchery."

"A castle, eh?" Her father stroked his mustache. "I suppose we haven't toured *too* many of those yet."

"Father, you like all the English and Scottish history," Rayne reminded him. "You read a four-volume set of British history before we left."

Douglas's eyes twinkled. "So I did, so I did. Very well, Miss Moore, could we prevail upon you to join us for a castle tour?"

Ellen blushed and looked toward Rayne. "If you'd like."

"We would love it if you would join us," Rayne assured her.

From the moment they had hired Ellen, Rayne had insisted on making her more of a paid companion than a maid. Ellen had resisted at first, but Rayne had convinced her to embrace a more active role while she worked for them. This meant she had dined with them and attended operas and ballets. Only at certain social functions like balls could they not quite manage to get around the social barriers and allow Ellen to join them.

When the coach stopped on the cobblestone lane of Castle Hill, Oliver leapt out of the coach and was ready to catch Rayne by the waist to help her down. She held her breath as he pulled her close to whisper, "I swear you choose clothing to drive me mad." His gaze swept down the length of her body, focusing for a long moment on the low square neckline.

"You don't like it?" she asked, fishing for a compliment.

"You know I do." He winked as he set her down on the pavement out of the way of the muddy, snow-covered street. Then he assisted Miss Moore down, and Douglas followed behind.

They entered the hotel, where a smartly dressed set of young men greeted them before proceeding outside to collect their luggage from the coach. Oliver and

Douglas went to the front desk and collected their room keys.

"Should we all meet down here in half an hour?" Douglas suggested.

Everyone agreed, and they all climbed the stairs to their rooms. Rayne was at the end of the hall, and Oliver's room was beside hers. Their eyes met as they inserted their ornate brass keys into the locks on their doors and turned them at the same time. Oliver's lips curved in a slow, sweet, but also sensual smile before he disappeared into his room.

When she entered hers, she gasped. The room was nothing short of palatial. Red damask wallpaper and dark mahogany wood furniture made the room instantly seem warm and seductive.

Oil lamps by the bed and the fire in the hearth only made the accommodations even more cozy. The tall four-poster bed had gold brocade curtains pulled back against the posts, secured by gold corded ropes with long tassels. A red velvet coverlet draped down over the large bed. Rayne's body heated at the thought of her and Oliver sharing this bed together.

Was she bold enough to invite him here tonight? Yes, she was. Rayne smiled, feeling a little silly as she faced the fact that she was hopeless when it came to Oliver. He made her wild, irresponsible, and desperate for things that an unmarried lady should have no idea existed.

But what did it matter? They were courting now, and if she was honest, she wanted him to propose—the sooner the better. What she felt for him now wasn't simply lust. There were softer, deeper, purer emotions in her heart now. She was afraid to call it love just yet, but perhaps it was. Ellen was right that she should discover what her true feelings were for Oliver.

Her mother and father had fallen in love right away and married within a month. Neither of them had ever doubted each other or their quick marriage. It gave Rayne hope that she and Oliver might share the same good fortune.

She removed her hat and gloves and sat down on the edge of the bed. She took in the surroundings of the chamber. A portion of the wall suddenly began to shift and move, and she almost shrieked. Then the sight of Oliver's face peering around the edge of the door had her giggling.

She grabbed the nearest pillow and threw it at his head. "You frightened me!"

He pulled the door closed enough to shield himself from the projectile, and when he seemed certain she wouldn't throw another, he stepped into the room.

"Did you know the door was there?" she asked as he closed the door behind him. She could barely see the line in the wall, it had sealed so seamlessly.

"I *may* have been aware of it when your father and I requested rooms," he admitted with a devilish chuckle.

Then he stalked toward her, and she gave a shriek of laughter as he tried to pounce on her on the bed. She rolled onto her hands and knees and crawled away from him.

"How the devil can you move so fast in so much clothing?" he demanded as he circled around the bed and caught her by the waist, pulling her into his arms.

"Practice." She grinned at him as he swooped down and kissed her senseless. Then he simply held her in his arms, and his lips brushed the crown of her hair.

"Perhaps we can skip the castle tour," he murmured.

"As much as I would love to, my father would be sure to notice our absence."

Oliver chuckled. "That means I must marry you sooner rather than later so I can take you to bed anytime we wish without the fear of drawing parental wrath."

She looked up at him, hope surging in her. But what if he was only teasing?

"Oliver...," she began, not that she had the faintest idea what she wanted to say.

"Too soon, I suppose?" He smiled ruefully. "You deserve a lavish proposal on the top of some majestic mountain, or in the midst of a glittering ballroom—"

"Oliver," she said, interrupting him, "please don't tease me about such things, not when I..."

He cupped her chin. "When you what?"

She looked away, wanting desperately to hide her embarrassment.

"Tell me, love."

She burrowed closer to him, wondering if he would pull away if she told him the truth.

"When I wish for it." She paused. "That, and truth. A lady ought not to tell a man that, but I feel that way, and I want only honesty between us. We've only known each other for two days, and yet I feel a bit in love with you already. I hope it leads to more." *So much more,* she thought.

Oliver was silent a long moment, and when she finally turned her face to his, his eyes were soft and a green color that reminded her of freshly cut grass on the lawns of a beautiful estate. He made her think of summer garden parties where the ladies wore white frothy lace-trimmed gowns, and Rayne would play a bit of tennis with her cousins and bask in the glow of the sun.

"I wasn't teasing, Rayne," he said. "From the moment we met, I have wanted you, *all* of you. I have marriage in mind, and as long as you like me, I shall continue to woo you to that end, my love."

"To marriage? What if you decide I'm too tiresome or boring or—"

He silenced her with another kiss that left her feeling scorched in the best way.

"Somehow, I don't believe that's possible." He played with a lock of her hair that fell over her shoulder. She was all too aware that they were standing chest to chest, with her trapped against the tall bed.

"You tempt me, my love. Tempt me so much," he warned, then stepped back. "But unfortunately, your father will come searching for us if we don't meet him downstairs."

"I need a moment. I shall meet you in the corridor."

Oliver stole a final feathery kiss and left her alone.

Rayne pressed her hands to her flushed face and smiled...smiled like a fool in love.

CHAPTER 9

Oliver delighted in showing Rayne around Edinburgh Castle. A heavy fog rolled across the snow-covered grounds, and he had been lucky enough to steal her away into an alcove, unseen by her father and Miss Moore, for a quick, passionate kiss on more than one occasion. It had become a game for them, to see how many times he could corner his little American before they had to reappear and act as if nothing scandalous had happened.

He couldn't keep his hands off her. She was addictive. Her smile, her laughter, the way she focused so intently on learning the history of this place—it all fascinated him. He had spoken the truth at the Witchery, and while her fortune had allowed for the possibility of pursuing her, that fortune held no sway over how he felt. If he were the one with the fortune and she were penniless, he would have chosen her to be his wife without a second thought. He didn't want to think about what his life would have been like if he'd never met her at Lady Poole's ball. He was a slave to his circumstances, but good fortune had given him Rayne as a possible match, and he wanted her desperately.

His family would adore her. Zadie had already gotten along famously with her, and his mother would admire Rayne's intelligence and sweetness. Everett would appreciate her wit and playfulness. And Oliver? He loved all of her.

I'm a blessed man.

He followed her and Ellen now into a clothing store on the Royal Mile, where ready-made items were sold. The two ladies gathered around a rack of woolen tartan scarves in an array of colorful plaids.

"Oliver, come try on a scarf. You would look so dashing." Rayne plucked a scarf from the shelves as she glanced his way.

He reluctantly joined them. He could not buy anything. He'd spent too much already on his hotel room, but he had needed to impress Rayne and her father. If they suspected he was as destitute as he was, he could lose Rayne forever. And he couldn't bear that, because like her, he was falling in love. There was no other way to describe it. Whenever he was near her, it was like he was falling into orbit around a bright and beautiful star.

Yet I deceive her with every breath. The dark thought encroached on his happiness.

Rayne wrapped a red-and-green plaid scarf around his neck and eyed it critically.

"Ellen, don't you think this brings out his eyes?"

"It certainly does, Miss Egerton," Ellen replied, but she cast a worried glance at Oliver. He attempted to remove the scarf, but Rayne tutted and kept it around his neck.

"I shall get it for you," she said.

"Rayne, you mustn't—" he protested.

"For Christmas," she replied in a tone that brooked no argument.

"Rayne, *no*. I don't need gifts." He caught her wrist, hating the look of hurt he saw in her eyes. But what else could he do? When she found out about his financial circumstances, he did not want her looking back on this moment and seeing it as him using her. He was not after her fortune for himself. His family and his home needed it, but not him. He could continue to wear old clothes and not renew his club membership and even keep sharing his valet with his brother if it meant keeping Rayne in his life.

Rayne folded the scarf back up and set it down on the counter. She turned sharply away from him. This was going badly. He started to reach for her, but his hand dropped back to his side. What could he say to correct his foolishness? He looked at Ellen, and she was frowning at him, not in disapproval, but disappointment.

"I only meant... I don't want you to think..." But he found no way to finish his thought in a way that worked. Oliver left the shop and stood out in the cold next to Douglas, who was admiring the streets of Edinburgh.

"Everything all right?" Douglas asked.

"Yes, of course. I simply had to excuse myself before Rayne purchased half the shop for me. I think she wants to see me in a kilt." Oliver was not about to admit that he had upset Rayne.

Douglas laughed. "That does sound like Rayne, always a bit romantic."

"There's nothing wrong with that. It's simply too bloody cold for a man to wear a kilt with all this snow." Oliver watched Rayne and Ellen move through the shop from his vantage point on the street where he and Douglas could peer through the shop windows.

When the ladies emerged from the shop, the smile on Rayne's face seemed off somehow. They spent the rest of the day touring museums and galleries close to the Royal Mile, which led from the castle down the sloping hill. Rayne seemed to be in better spirits by the time they had dinner. Douglas was a man of taste, and he told Oliver he wished to try the cuisine in Scotland, which meant they feasted upon tasty meat pies and drank whiskey at a small and cozy restaurant. It was located across from Greyfriars Kirkyard—a cemetery—

which wasn't nearly as macabre as one might think. It was a relief to see Rayne's natural smile return as he explained the history of Edinburgh to everyone over dinner.

As evening fell, he could see Rayne and Ellen were growing weary from walking. He couldn't imagine them carrying their skirts all day to keep them out of the snowy puddles on the streets and pavement without becoming exhausted.

"Shall we turn in for the evening, since we'll need to be ready at the station tomorrow morning?" Douglas posed as the four of them entered the hotel lobby.

"Yes," Rayne sighed. "My feet ache something fierce, Father. All I want is to crawl into bed and sleep." Her nose wrinkled as she removed her gloves and her red velvet dolman. Oliver wanted to sweep her up in his arms and carry her to the nearest claw-foot bathtub, strip her naked, and join her for a hot bath. But he knew she was still upset, and he needed to explain, at least enough to tell her why she couldn't spend any money on him.

He returned to his own room and removed his gloves and coat before opening the connecting door between their rooms. He found her sitting alone at the rosewood vanity table, gazing at herself in the mirror with a lost expression on her face. Tears coated her cheeks, and her wet skin shimmered in the candlelight.

"Rayne, my love." She tensed at his words, and her

eyes looked to his in the reflection. She brushed the tears away and faced him, that same false cheeriness cutting him deep.

"I'm sorry, I was woolgathering." She focused on smoothing her gown, no longer looking at him. Oliver came over and knelt at her feet and clasped her hands in his, stilling that frantic nervous fluttering of her fingers over the satin.

"I want to apologize for today. But I cannot let you buy me things."

"Why not? Is it some silly English custom I don't know about?" She tried to sound as if she didn't care, but she couldn't hide the hurt in her tone.

"No." He drew a fortifying breath. "My family is not as wealthy as yours. We live more frugally, and I don't want you to ever think I want you to have to buy things for me. I already hate that I cannot do so for you, as much as I would like to."

"Oliver..." She pulled her hands free of his and cupped his face. "I'm sorry, I didn't know," she said, and much to his surprise, she leaned in to kiss him. It was not quite the reaction he'd expected.

"I was too embarrassed to tell you. You mean so much to me, and I was afraid you would think less of me because I can't buy you lavish gifts in kind."

She slid off the chair and fell to her knees in front of him. "I don't need lavish gifts. I only need you."

He placed his hands on her cheeks the same way she was with him. "I hope that never changes."

"It won't," she vowed.

Lord, he wanted to believe that. But it was one thing to admit he was not wealthy—quite another to admit he was destitute.

"Oliver, stay with me tonight." She stood and pulled him close. The woman was such a tempting bundle of sweetness and satin.

"If that is what you wish." He captured her lips with his, wanting to growl in heady desire at the way she melted in his arms.

"I do, and I want *more*."

He slid his hands down her back. "More?"

"So much more." She looked at him with those soft bedroom eyes. "I want everything."

"Then let me give it to you."

OLIVER KISSED HER DEEPLY, A SENSUAL PROMISE lingering between them. Rayne shivered. She wanted him, *needed* him tonight. And he'd promised to be with her. Her head swam a little, and she giggled. It felt like the first time she'd taken one of her father's bottles of sherry as a sixteen-year-old and sampled a bit too much of it.

Oliver began to unfasten the hooks at the back of

her gown as they continued to kiss. When her gown loosened, she shimmied out of it and slipped off the bed to stand in front of him. Then, with a nervous beat of her heart, she turned her back to him so he could unlace her corset. The second he began to pull the laces loose, she felt like she could breathe for the first time in ages. The whalebone corset dropped to the ground, and she turned to face him just as he began to lift the thin chemise she wore off her body.

She stood bare before him now, except for her stockings and boots. His gaze raked down her body, and she felt a flood of heat deep in her belly. He pulled her against him, her bare breasts brushing against his satin waistcoat.

"There's nothing more arousing than holding a beautiful naked woman in my arms." He kissed the shell of her ear in a way that made her quiver. Then he sank to one knee and began rolling down her stockings and unlacing her boots. By the time she was completely naked before him, he had soothed her trembling nerves with kisses and caresses. He was a master of this. He knew exactly what to do with women.

"Oliver, how many others have you been with?" This was more a matter of curiosity than jealousy. There was no way he could be this well versed in seduction without practice.

Oliver cupped her chin, and his free hand settled on her lower back. "There have been a few, but you are the one I feel I've been waiting my whole life for." His lips seared a path from her neck to her shoulders, and his words wrapped her heart in soft velvet. She stood on her tiptoes to kiss him back, and then she pulled at the buttons of his waistcoat. He let her undress him, let her explore his body, and all the while he caressed her, touched her, and left burning kisses on her skin.

Rayne had never touched a man like this before. She coasted her palms up his chest and bent her head to flick her tongue against his nipple. She smiled in delight at the way he groaned and held her close in encouragement.

"I'm going to make love to you tonight," he vowed as he unfastened his trousers and let them fall to the floor.

"You'd better." Rayne reached for him, sliding one hand from his corded abs to his hard length. She stroked him hard as he bent his head to hers for a kiss. Then he curled his fingers around her wrist and gently removed her hand from his shaft.

"But if you touch me like that, my love, I fear I won't last."

"Oh..." She blushed and then squeaked in surprise as he scooped her up and set her on the bed. She fell onto her back as he climbed up the length of her body and caged her beneath him.

She parted her legs, though it was a little nerve-racking to let his large body settle between them.

Despite his size compared to hers, he didn't crush her as he lay down on top of her.

"Touch me now, however you wish," Oliver said. He bent his head to her neck and kissed a spot that made her writhe under him.

"Oh, Oliver..." She arched her back and pressed close. His cock nudged her entrance, but she was still too nervous to let him inside.

He didn't rush her. He simply kissed her, and soon she was relaxing into his tender seduction. Before she could even think about it, she canted her hips up at the same time he guided himself to her and thrust inside. It felt natural, good, and then she whimpered at the pinching pain deep inside her.

Oliver's mouth continued to work its midnight magic on her, and the pain faded into memory. His soft breath fanned her face as he withdrew, leaving behind an ancient ache for more. Then he thrust back inside, and they shared a moment of deepest pleasure. She never wanted his body to leave hers. Their connection felt almost mystical. Her inner walls tightened around him as he surged in and out, slow at first and then faster until she could barely catch her breath and her heart was galloping away. Oliver continued to imprison her beneath him as he claimed her. She welcomed it, clung to him, and basked in the wild passion, knowing that he belonged to her in this moment too.

"Oliver, I...love you." She spoke the words and

couldn't take them back. His eyes widened, and he sank into her again. Stars burst before her eyes. Oliver cursed and breathed her name, his body rigid as he emptied himself inside her. She relaxed beneath him, sated in a way that defied all reason. When he next spoke, his words stunned her.

"Marry me, Rayne."

Her fingers dug slightly into his shoulders as she held on to him. "You mean it?"

"You love me, and I feel the same way. Why should we wait?" His eyes were still dark with passion, but she heard the sincerity in his voice.

"Then yes!" Joy fluttered inside her, and she kissed him. A kiss that spoke of the excitement and tender longing that had welled up within her.

"You've made me the happiest man." He kissed the tip of her nose. "Stay here a minute."

He moved off her body, and she missed his warmth right away. He stepped into her bathing chamber, and she heard the sound of bath taps turning on. Then he returned and scooped her up, carrying her into the bathing room, where he set her down beside the massive claw-foot tub. He tested the water, and when it was warm enough, he climbed in and motioned for her to join him. She winced a little as her lower body was still sore from their lovemaking, and he cradled her against his chest as the warm water spilled over them. Rayne closed her eyes and surrendered to the feeling of pure bliss.

"I didn't hurt you, did I?" Oliver asked. "I've never been with a virgin before."

"It hurt but a moment, and then you made it feel wonderful." She lifted one of his hands to her lips and kissed his long elegant fingers.

"I meant it, Rayne—I want you to marry me. But I don't want you to answer when you're overwhelmed with passion. Just think on it." He stroked a hand down her belly and caressed her mound beneath the water. Rayne whimpered as he slid one finger into her still sore channel.

"Yes. I want you, Oliver." Yes, she was overwhelmed by passion, but she knew her own mind and her heart.

"Tell me again in the morning. I won't be upset if you need time."

"Oliver, we've known each other but a handful of days, yet it feels like I've loved you my entire life. I won't need time."

"I feel the same." He kissed her cheek and wrapped his arms around her. She couldn't help but think everything was perfect. She was going to have a marriage like her parents, one full of love.

OLIVER CARRIED RAYNE BACK TO BED. SHE HAD

fallen asleep in the tub with him. Now she lay naked in his arms in her bed, and he brushed the backs of his fingers over her cheek, watching her sleep before he turned the oil lamps down to low.

But he couldn't find sleep. It eluded him as worries built in the back of his mind. He would have to talk with Douglas tomorrow and get his blessing. And he would have to find a way to make sure that Rayne approved of her dowry being used at once for his family and his home. The whole thought of it gave him a headache. He didn't want to think or worry about money with Rayne. He wanted to marry her, declare his affection, and carry her off to Astley Court, where he could give her a home and a family.

But what if it all went wrong? What if, when she learned the truth, she thought him a heartless fortune hunter? This and other thoughts haunted him well past when the fire died and dawn was on the horizon.

CHAPTER 10

Rayne fell in love with the Scottish Highlands as she descended from the train that afternoon and stepped into the city of Inverness. The train ride from Edinburgh to Inverness had taken five hours, but she'd enjoyed every minute of it. The countryside was defined by high peaks, heathery moors, and serene lakes—or lochs, as the locals called them—which spread across the landscape. Snow covered half the fields and topped the tall hills. The train had carried them through towns that had such delightful names as Boat of Garten and Feshiebridge. Oliver had told her that this far north in Scotland a mass of small villages were all tucked into a wilderness of pine and heather where bitter winters and hot summers divided the year.

Rayne now stood on High Street in Inverness, a cold wind teasing her heavy red velvet skirts as she took in the town. Oliver joined her as she studied the looming edifice of Inverness Castle. It was a bulky work of stone. A statue of a beautiful young woman stood at the front of the esplanade. The woman's face seemed anxious as she looked toward the southwest.

"What is she looking toward?" Rayne asked, drawing closer to it.

"The Isle of Skye. That is Flora MacDonald."

"Who's that?"

Oliver put an arm around her waist. "A very brave woman. She helped Bonnie Prince Charlie flee Culloden's battlefield and sail to the Isle of Skye."

Rayne stared at the stone woman, wondering how she must have felt as she helped the man who had almost ruled Scotland, but instead had fled for his life. "What happened to her?"

"She was arrested after Charles escaped. She was a sympathetic cause for many in England and was eventually released from the Tower of London. She married a captain in the British Army and lived on the Isle of Skye for a time."

Rayne looked once more at the baronial turrets of Inverness Castle and its pink sandstone walls. "Are we very far from Culloden?"

"Not far at all, actually," Oliver said. "It's an old moor, a quiet place. I visited there as a boy with my father. I swear I could feel the spirits of the clanspeople who had fallen that day. Their anguished cries seemed to drift up from the haunting grounds, making it hard to breathe. I was not proud to be English that day, I can tell you. To see the lonely place where the way of life in the Highlands was lost forever is enough to break any man's heart." He paused in quiet contemplation before continuing. "Though I do like coming here when I can. The Highlands have a quiet and natural peace. It reminds me of Yorkshire."

Rayne curled her arm in his as they turned away and headed for the waiting coach. Her father waved to them as they crossed the bustling street and joined them at the coach.

The ride to Lord Fraser's didn't take very long, and yet their imminent arrival brought out a fresh excitement for Rayne. Oliver had told her he planned to ask for her father's blessing once they were settled in.

Lord Fraser's manor house was nestled within an old forest. To Rayne, it seemed like a place one would find a slumbering wood god lurking within the heart of one of its massive trees. Perhaps it was a fanciful idea, but she rather liked the magical feel of these Scottish forests.

Lord Fraser's house was a lovely Georgian-era mansion that seemed to have been molded out of a medieval castle. When the coach stopped, a footman wearing the Earl of Fraser's livery came out to meet them. Rayne and Ellen were shown to their chambers, and Rayne changed out of her damp traveling clothes and into a pleasant day gown of blue faille brocade trimmed with aged cream lace. It was a more delicate gown, one best suited to being worn indoors. The blue and gold of the faille brocade made her feel warm, as though summer was upon her. As she left her bedchamber, she met a tall handsome man in his early forties in the corridor.

"Miss Egerton?" he asked, his Scottish accent rolling off his tongue.

"Yes?"

"I am Lord Fraser. I'm sorry I was not able to greet you and your father when you arrived. I was seeing to some business." He bowed over her hand and lightly kissed her knuckles. She admired his dark-brown hair, cut a little too long to be fashionable, and the hazel gleam of mischief in his eyes. He was a bachelor, according to all the gossip in London, but well sought after. She'd heard whispers that the woman Fraser had loved had married another, and he'd vowed never to love again. It was a pity that such a charming man wanted nothing more to do with love.

"It's a pleasure to meet you, Lord Fraser. I cannot tell you how honored we are to be here for the holidays."

Lord Fraser smiled and offered his arm. "Let me take you downstairs." He spoke about his home and the rich history of it, such as how his family had helped hide Bonnie Prince Charlie one night. He lifted his chin in pride as he spoke. By the time they reached the morning room, where some of the other guests were spending the afternoon, Rayne was in high spirits.

Until she saw Adelaide Berwick.

The moment Adelaide's eyes locked with hers, all of Rayne's joy and excitement evaporated. Adelaide's face was pinched with open displeasure as though she, too, was surprised at Rayne's appearance.

Rayne glanced around at the dozen or so guests, and her heart dropped even further. Zadie wasn't here yet, but then she remembered that Oliver had said they would be a few days late. What would she do without a friend to help her lessen the sting of whatever cruel things Adelaide had in store for her? She had handled Adelaide at Lady Poole's ball, but she hadn't liked being harsh to another woman like that. It wasn't in her nature to be mean-spirited, even to someone like Adelaide.

Now more than ever, Rayne wished her mother were alive to counsel her on how to handle this situation. She didn't see her father anywhere and had no idea where he'd gone. She knew no one else in the room except Lord Fraser, who was now conversing with his other guests. Even Oliver was absent. Feeling awkward and alone, Rayne selected a book off the nearest table and took a seat by the window. She didn't read; rather, she watched the reflections of the people in the room like faint specters in the glass.

Adelaide and her mother were talking, their heads bent together as they whispered. Rayne tried not to shift restlessly in her chair, but it was hard to ignore them. They were almost certainly talking about her. When she couldn't take it anymore, she stood and started toward the door, but Adelaide stepped in between her and the exit.

"I heard you arrived here with Lord Conway?" Adelaide's tone was far too sweet to be genuine.

"Yes. We did have the pleasure of his company. Are you acquainted with him?" Rayne was proud of herself for sounding civil. It wasn't easy. Adelaide seemed to bring out the worst in her.

"Acquainted?" Adelaide smiled. "Oh yes, quite so. His estate borders mine. We've been friends since we were children. His father and mine were old friends. We are excited to be uniting our families soon."

It took a moment for Rayne to understand what she meant.

"You are to marry Everett?"

Adelaide laughed, the sound as sharp as broken glass. "Everett? Heavens no. No, *Oliver* and I have been betrothed for years now. I'm old enough now that my father will let me marry. He wished for me to wait until I was twenty."

"You and..." Oliver's name turned to ash upon her tongue. Dread settled inside her chest like a dark cloud smothering all light and life.

"Yes, of course." She shrugged a shoulder as if what she had said was completely obvious. "After all, he needs to marry well, what with his family being in such dire straits."

Dire straits... The words echoed in Rayne's mind. Oliver had said they were living frugally, but that wasn't the same as dire straits.

Rayne tried to wrap her mind around what Adelaide was saying. Adelaide fixed her with a cunning look, as though sensing she'd found Rayne's weak spot.

"He isn't going to marry for love, only money. And I want him, so my father is more than happy to pay him the dowry he needs." Adelaide played with the lace cuff on her left wrist as she smiled too sweetly at Rayne. "They say his family will lose Astley Court in a month if he doesn't marry soon."

Rayne felt as though Adelaide had pushed her into a freshly dug grave and was now shoveling dirt upon her.

"Oh, I say, you look far too pale. Perhaps you ought to rest until dinner." Adelaide patted Rayne's cheek condescendingly. Rayne slapped her hand away and stumbled back, almost tripping over the train of her gown in her haste to escape this vile woman's poisonous touch.

Rayne fled the morning room, hoping to escape the stares of the other guests. But as she reached the entryway, she froze at the sight of Oliver in the hall greeting Zadie, a man who looked too much like Oliver not to be his brother, and a lovely older woman. His family had arrived early? A few minutes ago she would have been overjoyed, but now it felt as though she were hearing an old grandfather clock ticking away her doom as she would have to face the family of a man she could no longer marry.

"Rayne! Come meet my family." Oliver smiled at her, that warm, inviting smile that she wanted so badly to trust. Now part of her wanted to slap that smile off his face.

Two days—you've only known him two days. How could you be such a fool to fall for a fortune hunter?

Then she realized that love didn't come quickly, only lust. She had very foolishly confused the two and played right into his hands. Oliver wanted her money, not her. He must have discovered that she was a bigger prize than Adelaide.

"Rayne." Oliver came over to her and grasped her hands in his. "Are you all right? You look pale."

"I..." She didn't dare let him know that he had ripped her heart out of her chest.

"Come meet my family."

Everything inside her screamed for her to run away. But she was stuck. Zadie and the others came up to her.

"Rayne! It's so lovely to see you again!" Zadie hugged her, and Rayne returned her embrace, but she felt noth-ing. Had Zadie been the one to tell Oliver she was rich? Had she been scouring the London balls looking for someone exactly like her? A dozen questions were carried on black wings of despair, but she didn't ask them. She didn't want to know the answers.

"This is my mother, Margaret, and my brother, Everett." Oliver beamed at his family. Rayne wished with all her heart that she could have had this moment in truth, with no lies, no secrets.

"It's wonderful to meet you, Miss Egerton. Oliver was telling us all about you," Margaret said.

"Was he?" she asked faintly.

"Oh yes. He was singing your praises." Everett grinned at her, and Rayne tried to smile, but it was far too late.

"It's lovely to meet you, but I really must go upstairs and rest. I'm feeling rather faint right now."

"Please, let me help you." Oliver moved toward her, but she shrank back from him.

"No, please, see to your family." She rushed up the stairs, leaving him behind. By the time she reached her chambers, her vision had blurred with tears. What was she going to do? She couldn't marry him now—she couldn't. Not when he'd become the thing she'd always feared.

It was all so clear now. Oliver had sought her out on the train. Why else would he have traveled alone while his family came later? And Zadie knew she was rich—far richer than Adelaide. And he'd already sung her praises, according to Everett, yet they had only just arrived. All the dreaded pieces of a wretched puzzle clicked into place. This had all been planned. He'd hunted her with the cleverness of the most talented fortune hunter.

I should leave today. Board the train and return to London with Ellen.

Women traveled alone on trains all the time. She could wait in London for her father to finish his business with Lord Fraser and return. It would be rude to abandon the house party, but she couldn't stay here, not with that man staying here.

OLIVER STARED UP THE STAIRS IN THE DIRECTION OF where Rayne had gone, and he didn't like the sudden knot of dread forming inside him. She hadn't been her usual happy self. Not that he didn't expect her, like all people, to have an off moment. But what he'd seen in her face…it had been pain of a different sort. She'd looked at him with an agony he couldn't fathom having caused. What could have happened in the hour he'd left her alone while he'd gotten settled and scheduled a meeting with Lord Fraser?

"Is she all right?" his mother asked. "She looked very pale."

"Yes, I think so," he replied, but the words held the lingering bitter taste of a lie. Something terrible had happened, but he wasn't sure what. His mother watched him with anxious eyes.

"I know you are feeling pressured, but two days is quick, Oliver. You shouldn't rush this, not if you care about her as much as you say you do."

"I love her, Mother. I know it sounds naïve to say it so soon, but I do. I love her in a way I never thought I would love any woman. She is intelligent and passionate and sweet." But it was more than that. Rayne made life seem full of endless excitement. There was a steadiness to her, a feeling that he could spend his life with her and that even the soft, quiet moments would have their own intimate thrill.

"If you love her, then I know we shall as well." His mother embraced him before she looked to Zadie and Everett. "Let's get settled. We shall meet down here before dinner."

Oliver watched them leave and then checked his pocket watch. He was to meet with Lord Fraser shortly, but before then he had to find Rayne's father and ask for his blessing.

"Oliver?" A feminine voice stilled him just as he reached the base of the stairs.

He turned around. "Adelaide." He turned to leave, but she spoke again.

"Oliver... I know."

That knot of dread inside him only grew. "Know what?"

"About your family's unfortunate situation."

Adelaide's eyes seemed guileless, but he saw a faint hint of cruel victory hovering around them.

He came toward her, trying to rein in his temper. "And how would you know that?"

"Because my father is friends with Mr. Kelly of Drummonds. He knew that our parents always hoped we would make a match. Well..." She smiled prettily. "I am ready to accept your proposal."

The cold triumph within Adelaide's gaze turned his stomach. This was why he had avoided her, why he had fled to Lady Poole's library, desperate to avoid this moment, to avoid becoming her pawn.

"Adelaide, I'm sorry. I've already proposed to another, and she has accepted."

The smile slid from Adelaide's face. "It's that American, isn't it? I feared you might have a dalliance with her, but I thought perhaps you had better sense. Breeding is at least as important as money, after all." Adelaide spoke more to herself, but then her gaze focused on him again. "It's a good thing I warned her about you, then. She had no idea that you were fortune hunting. Fortunately, it seems I saved her from that fate."

A wave of panic caused Oliver's blood to pound inside his head. He almost stumbled with the dizziness of it.

"You did *what?*"

"I told her the truth. That you need money. That you need an heiress. You don't need love, but you *do* need full bank accounts." Adelaide smirked. "I believe the foolish little girl thought herself in love with you." Her tone now became accusatory. "How cruel of you to string her along like that. At least I understand how these things work. She's a stranger in these parts, and quite vulnerable to someone like you."

"She is, and I'm in love with her." He wanted to grab Adelaide and shake her.

A flicker of shock flashed on her face at the mention of his loving Rayne, but it was covered all too quickly. "You can't be. There is no room for love in our world, only obligation. You knew she had more money than my family, so I can hardly blame your choice, but honestly. Love? You can't love a stranger in only two days. Some people can't fall in love even after a lifetime."

"She isn't a stranger to me. Not anymore." He dragged a hand through his hair. "Adelaide, how could you do this to me?"

"How could *I*?" she hissed. "You were supposed to be mine, Oliver. From the moment I was born, my father and yours hoped we would marry. And you just tossed me aside for some American with no pedigree?"

Oliver stared at Adelaide in horror. "Do you wish to know why I wouldn't propose to you? It's because you're selfish and spiteful. Rayne is everything you aren't, and I would marry her even if she had not a shilling to her name."

"You don't fool me!" Adelaide snapped. "You need her money. *That's* what you love."

Oliver shook his head, his mind racing. It wasn't about the money, not anymore. That moment he realized what he said was true. The only thing that mattered to him was Rayne, and he couldn't afford to lose her.

"I don't have time for this. I have to fix the mess you've made." He spun away and raced up to the hall of rooms that had been prepared for the guests. He caught the attention of an upstairs maid whose arms were full of fresh linens.

"Excuse me, which room is Miss Egerton staying in?"

"The last room on the right." The maid gestured behind her.

"Thank you." He raced down to the end of the corridor and knocked on Rayne's door. He waited and heard the sound of a dress whispering on the carpets.

"Who is it?" Rayne's voice was muffled, but he could hear an unfamiliar roughness to her tone. Had she been crying? The thought tore him apart.

"It's me, Oliver," he said.

There was a long silence, and then, "*Please*, go away. I'm not feeling well, and I don't wish to see anyone."

"Rayne, please," he begged softly, resting his forehead against the closed door.

"No." The reply was firm and hit him like a slap to the face.

"Please. I spoke to Adelaide. If you just let me in, I'll explain."

The door swung open so fast he stumbled and clutched the doorjamb. Rayne stood there with tear-stained cheeks and puffy eyes.

"There is nothing to explain. You want to marry me for my money, and I don't want that. Our engagement is off, Lord Conway. You're free to marry your childhood sweetheart. I'm sure her family has enough for your needs."

"My childhood sweetheart?" He stumbled over the words in shock. "Adelaide? We were never... She wasn't..."

"I don't care either way what she is or isn't. I'm just glad I learned the truth before I tied myself to you forever." Rayne slammed the door shut, and he heard the lock slide into place.

Oliver leaned against the door for what felt like forever, his chest tight. He had lost the only woman he had wanted to make a life with.

"Oliver?" Everett's voice made him lift his head.

"Everett," he sighed. "I'm sorry. I'm not in the mood." He couldn't handle his brother's teasing just now, not when his chest felt like it had been cracked open and someone had stolen his heart from between his ribs. He could barely breathe. Everything had been going so well, and now all was lost—Rayne was lost.

"What happened?"

"I've lost her, Everett. Adelaide told her I wanted her for her money." He mumbled this confession against Rayne's closed door, feeling trapped more than he ever had in his life. Trapped because he'd lost the one thing that truly mattered.

Everett crossed his arms. "Don't you?"

"There was necessity to consider, of course, but I *never* only wanted the money. I wanted Rayne too." Oliver stepped away from the door and dropped his hand in defeat. Clinging to her door wouldn't make her change her mind. Nothing could do that.

"Oliver, if you love her, would you be willing to give up Astley Court, give up all we have?"

"I would, but I couldn't do that to you, Mother, and Zadie."

Everett stepped close and put his hands on Oliver's shoulders. "Forget the rest of us and just think. You and Miss Egerton. Would you give it all up for her?"

"Yes," Oliver replied without hesitation. "If she wanted me without a fortune, I'd live in a tiny cottage with one room just to be with her."

"Then do it." Oliver flashed a Cheshire cat grin. "Choose her, not the money. Her father could draw up a legal settlement that transfers most of his money elsewhere and gives her a tiny livable allowance. Then you can go to her and prove to her that it isn't the money you want and that you want to marry her without it."

"But what about you? What about Mother and

Zadie?" Oliver stared at Everett, shocked to see his rakish brother putting the needs of others before his own.

"Trust me, we will be fine. We would all prefer to live in poverty rather than have you brokenhearted and forced to marry the dreaded Adelaide Berwick. To be honest, I was not looking forward to spending the holidays with her."

Oliver's heart swelled with love for his younger brother.

"Thank you, Everett." There was so much else he wanted to say, but he couldn't seem to form the words.

"Now go. You've got a man to see about a bride." Everett laughed and gently pushed Oliver toward the stairs. Oliver rushed down to find a footman who could show him where Lord Fraser was. Once he had his future as Fraser's London steward secured, he would seek out Mr. Egerton. He prayed he could have it all fixed by tonight, and he would have Rayne in his arms again where she belonged.

CHAPTER 11

Rayne and Ellen had their luggage packed, and a footman was summoned to carry it down to Lord Fraser's coach.

"Are you certain you wish to leave?" Ellen asked as they stood in the entry hall, waiting for their dolmans to be brought to them.

The old Scottish manor house was full of Christmas cheer, with evergreen garlands covering the banister of the stairs and kissing boughs hung over more than one doorway. The wooden floors creaked, and the tapestries whispered with Christmas secrets. Rayne would have given anything to stay here, to embrace the magic of the holidays in a home like this, but she couldn't face Oliver again.

"Ellen, I can't stay," she whispered. "Everything I believed about Lord Conway was a lie."

She had confessed to her maid what had transpired between her and Oliver. Not everything, but enough that Ellen knew Oliver had secretly been a fortune hunter all along like all the other men who had wished to court her in the past and failed to win her hand. But this time, she had fallen hard. She'd been so careful before to never let a man play upon her affections in order to get at her money, but somehow Oliver had done it flawlessly.

Ellen was quiet as they put on their dolmans and walked down to the coach. Rayne had written her father a letter, as well as one for Lord Fraser, apologizing for her abrupt departure. She left them in her room for the house maid to deliver when she came to tidy up. Rayne knew that leaving would cause the ladies to gossip, but she wouldn't be there to care. She would return to London and wait for her father to join her. Then they would return home to New York. Life would go on as before, somehow.

They arrived at the train station ahead of schedule. For a while neither of them spoke, leaving Rayne to ruminate on her heartbreak and Ellen to look on uncomfortably. Finally, Ellen spoke and broke Rayne's painful thoughts.

"Miss Egerton, I feel I must tell you something. I hope I will not lose my position over it, but I believe it's important." Ellen touched Rayne's hand gently.

Something had clearly been vexing Ellen for the

entire carriage ride, but Rayne had assumed it was concern for her. "What is it?"

A frown creased Ellen's brow. "Before you employed me, I worked as a lady's maid for Lord Conway's sister."

"Zadie?" Rayne gasped.

"Yes." Ellen went pale with anxiety.

"You knew Lord Conway this entire time? Why didn't you tell me?" Rayne stared at her maid, wondering if Ellen had been working with Oliver somehow, helping to bring them together or to deceive her.

"Lord Conway asked me not to when he discovered I was on the train and I was working for you. I warned you to be cautious, not because he isn't a good man—he is—but I wanted you both to fall in love. I thought I owed it to him to keep his secret for a time until he could tell you himself."

"Another lie," Rayne muttered and closed her eyes. She felt so cut open, so hurt that her heart felt raw. Even Ellen, a woman she had grown to consider a friend, had played a part in this awful deception.

"No, you don't understand," Ellen insisted.

"What's there to understand? He's brought everyone around him in on his scheme to marry me for my inheritance."

"I simply wish you to understand, miss. Lord Conway's father died a year and a half ago. He hid his bad investments from his family, and it came as a harsh blow. The Conways were not one for extravagance before, but after, when Lord Conway—Oliver, I mean—began to unravel the mess his father had left behind, it almost broke him. His family had to make immediate cutbacks on their lifestyle. They have not had new clothes in over a year and have been unable to afford repairs to Astley Court. They even cut the staff down by half, including myself. They've done all they can to avoid ruin."

"Have they?" Rayne felt petty for asking that, but where she came from, a person had to work to earn his or her place. Marrying her seemed like an easy solution for Oliver, but not a fair one to her.

Ellen nodded. "Lord Conway came here not to celebrate Christmas, but to beg Lord Fraser as a family friend to offer him a position as an estate steward. Lord Fraser has a man in Inverness to handle his interests here, but he's been looking to hire a man in London."

"How do you know all of this?" Rayne asked.

"Before I was let go by Lord Conway, I heard he was planning to come here this Christmas with that goal in mind. He never meant to live off anyone's fortune. He planned to work, but the debt on Astley Court was too high, and he needed money quickly to save his family, as well as their home."

"Then he met me, and now he thinks he won't have to." Rayne knew she sounded spiteful, but clinging to her anger was the only way she could keep the sorrow from drowning her.

"I asked him what his intentions were toward you, and I told him he had to win your love. What does your heart tell you about him?"

Rayne could feel tears forming in her eyes again. "Ellen, you don't understand. I will never know if it was me or my fortune. That is no way to start a marriage."

Ellen's gaze dropped to the floor as the coach stopped and they climbed out.

"Let's go purchase our tickets." Rayne headed toward the ticket office. She got to the front of the line, where a man with wire-rimmed spectacles reviewed the train timetables.

"Next train leaves in an hour and a half, miss."

"How much?" she asked.

"Ten shillings per ticket."

She removed the coins from her reticule and paid the ticket man. He filled out two ticket booklets and handed them to her.

She and Ellen went to the first-class refreshment room to wait. She didn't miss the way her maid looked at her from time to time, her lips parting, then closing again as if she wished to speak but dared not.

"Miss...," Ellen finally said.

"Yes?" A headache started behind Rayne's eyes, a dreaded pulse beating in a pounding rhythm that would make her sick before long if she could not banish it. She wanted to pretend the last few days had never happened.

If I had never met him, never shared a kiss, or a bed... If I had never fallen in love...

Could she truly regret falling in love? The moments she had shared with him, the heated kisses, the late-night whispers, reading beside each other, the feel of their bodies merging into one another, the stories of their pasts... She didn't want to forget any of that. But every minute she thought about it made it hard to breathe.

"Miss, sometimes life is a complicated thing. Love, great love, can exist, even when money is involved. You are beautiful, intelligent, and kind. A man like Lord Conway could easily fall in love with you. I worked in his household for seven years, and I know him well. The way he was with you... He's never been like that with anyone."

"What about Adelaide Berwick?"

Ellen scowled. "Lady Adelaide?"

"Yes, they were childhood sweethearts. They were supposed to marry before he found out about me."

"What nonsense," Ellen said, then blushed. "Forgive me, miss. But Adelaide was a mere girl when Lord Conway was already a young man. She had calf eyes for him, but she was always a child to him. And she hurt Lady Zadie's feelings more than once, playing terrible pranks on her. If he was to marry her, it would be out of desperation for his family and his home. He loves Astley Court."

Rayne recalled how he had spoken of Astley with a fondness that warmed his eyes. He had spoken of a home and sharing his with her. She had been enchanted by the idea. A home special enough to truly belong to her had always been her heart's secret desire, right after finding a man who loved her for herself and not her fortune. All of Oliver's stories of Astley had seemed like fate. But now those sunny feelings were overshadowed by his deception.

"Why did he lie, Ellen? Why not tell me the truth from the start?"

Her maid met her gaze. "Would you have given him a proper chance? Any man paying court to you would realize soon enough that you wouldn't marry except for love, and you would avoid any man who looked even a little desperate. Not that anyone could blame you for such caution, but it would put him in a bit of a bind."

Rayne wanted to deny it, but she couldn't. Ellen spoke the truth. Rayne would have sent him on his way the moment she learned he needed a fortune for his home and family.

"He still lied to me," she said, though with less conviction.

"He did," Ellen agreed. "But given his motives, that doesn't make him a terrible person. When he spoke to me about you, he didn't want to deceive you. He's not a man seeking money for his own selfish desires, nor is he a man prone to vices. His needs are selfless."

"I so badly want to believe that what we shared was real..." Fresh tears trailed down her cheeks.

Ellen handed her a handkerchief. "It might have been, but you left before you could know for certain. Love sometimes requires a leap of faith."

A passage came back to her from Oliver's book, *The Black Arrow*.

"He began to understand what a wild game we play in life; he began to understand that a thing once done cannot be undone nor changed by saying 'I am sorry.'"

Could she forgive Oliver? Could she still go forward and see if what they had between them was truly love?

"Our train leaves in twenty minutes," Ellen said quietly. "We should board."

Rayne rose from her seat in the refreshment room, and they headed toward the waiting train. But each step seemed to become harder and harder, as an invisible pull tried to keep her here in Inverness, with Oliver.

Oliver exited Lord Fraser's study, his heart beating in excitement. Fraser had agreed to give him the London steward position. It would pay decently the first year, and if Fraser found his work satisfactory, he would receive a 25 percent wage increase the following year. It would be enough to keep his family in a small but decent townhouse in London. He had resigned himself to losing

Astley Court and everything within its walls, but if it meant he kept Rayne as his wife, he would give up whatever was necessary.

After seeing her so upset today, seeing how he had hurt her beyond imagining with his deception, he knew he would do anything to keep her, to make her happy and love her. She was a gift more valuable than any manor house, more valuable than anything aside from his family. And he wanted her to be part of that family. He was going to win her back.

He entered the billiard room, where several gentlemen were drinking and talking, including Mr. Egerton.

"Ah, Conway," Douglas greeted him. "Join us for a drink?"

"Actually, Mr. Egerton, I wonder if I might speak to you?"

"Of course." Douglas followed him out of the billiard room and into the room across the hall, which happened to be the library.

He got straight to the point, knowing that Rayne's father preferred that. "Mr. Egerton, I have asked Rayne to marry me."

"And you need my blessing?"

"Well, it's more complicated than that, I'm afraid. I need your help." He drew in a breath to steel his nerves.

"Complicated?"

"Yes. You see, I wasn't entirely honest with Rayne.

My family is destitute. My father made a number of ill-fated investments before his death, and they put us into debt. I spent over a year cutting down expenses and selling much of what we own, but it isn't enough. I came to Lady Poole's ball intending to propose to Lady Adelaide Berwick."

Douglas's gaze was stormy, but he continued to listen.

"Then I met Rayne, and everything was so perfect —*she* was perfect. I didn't even know who she was when I met her. I learned her name only after I left the ball. My sister, Zadie, had also met her and knew that she was…"

"An heiress?" Douglas supplied quietly.

Oliver swallowed. "Yes. I knew then that she was the one I wished to marry. I didn't tell Rayne about my family's financial situation. I should have, but I didn't."

"Does she know now?" Douglas asked.

Oliver nodded. "And she refuses to speak to me."

Rayne's father crossed his arms. "So you want me to change her mind and get her to take you back? I won't do that."

"No, that isn't—"

"You listen to me, Conway. I know all about American heiresses who buy titled husbands, but my daughter doesn't want a title. She wants love, like her mother. I will write a check for whatever amount you need to walk away. Her heart will be broken, but at least she will be free."

"A check?" Oliver echoed in confusion.

"Yes." Douglas's tone was brusque. "I can easily pay off whatever debts you owe. But once I do, that's the end. You leave her alone."

Oliver's stomach knotted with nausea. He'd come to Douglas for help, not money.

"Mr. Egerton, I don't want even a sixpence of Rayne's fortune. That's what I came to tell you. I want Rayne. Nothing else. I came here to ask you to draw up a settlement that gives Rayne an allowance but restricts me as her husband from using any of it. Leave your fortune to your brother and his sons. I want none of it—I only want her."

"You..." Douglas frowned as he tilted his head to one side. "You would give up millions of pounds to marry my daughter?"

"I intend to give up *everything*, including my home."

"So how will you support yourself and her if you don't have her fortune?"

"A few weeks before I met Rayne, I had plans to come here for the holidays to meet with Lord Fraser about employment with him. He needs a London steward for his property holdings. He has agreed to give me the position. If I do well the first year, he'll raise my wages by quite a significant amount. So long as Rayne is comfortable with a modest townhouse in London, I can support her, and she may use her allowance from you however she likes, with no interference from me."

"Do you know anything about managing property?" There was a subtle challenge in his question.

"I do. I may be a titled lord, but we do learn how to manage our estates starting at a young age. Some better than others. My father wasn't the most skilled, but I believe I am well suited for it."

"Hmm..." Douglas still had his arms crossed. "What if you agree to this and then change your mind?"

"That's where the settlement comes in. I thought we could draft it today and execute it before witnesses so there's no doubt as to my intentions."

"If you intend to trick me, Conway..."

"It's no trick," Oliver assured him. "I made a mistake by believing that life would bless me and my family twice with both love and money, but love is the only thing that *truly* matters. I was a fool not to see this before. Losing Rayne's trust today made me realize that I cannot live without her, and all the money in the world is a poor companion when a man loses out on love."

"How could you fall in love with my daughter in only a handful of days?" Douglas leaned back against the nearest reading table.

"She shared her heart with me from the moment we met. She held nothing of herself back from me. And everything about her feels like a miracle to me. A beautiful miracle. Her smile, her laugh, her wit, her compassion, and her bravery. She is a woman who lives to be loved. And it would be my greatest honor to be that man, if she'll still have me."

"You think that this settlement you propose will mend her broken heart? Or will she see it only as the start of another deception?"

Oliver curled his hands into fists at his sides, trying to control his desperation for Douglas to understand. He met the man's eyes with a steady gaze and unwavering words.

"I don't know, but I have to try. What we share isn't ordinary, and I need to prove to her that I will fight to win her trust back."

Douglas was silent a long moment, and for a second Oliver feared that he wouldn't help.

"Come, we'll have the paperwork drafted and witnessed. Then you can find Rayne and try to change her mind."

They got permission from Lord Fraser to use his study to draft the settlement. Once it was executed and a copy was made, Oliver carried the copy rolled up and bound with a ribbon. He went straight to Rayne's room. A maid was inside, tidying up the bed.

"Excuse me, do you know where Miss Egerton is?"

"She left, my lord." The maid bent over the bed, tucking in the sheets tight.

"Left?" Oliver choked out the word.

"Yes." The maid pulled a pair of letters from her

pocket and handed them to him. One was addressed to Lord Fraser and the other to her father.

A terrible numbness settled inside Oliver's chest as he carried the letters downstairs. He summoned Lord Fraser and Mr. Egerton to the hall to deliver the notes.

"What's all this?" Fraser said as he scanned its contents. "Egerton, your daughter is headed to London?"

Douglas opened his letter, which was much longer. "She's leaving from the Inverness train station and plans to wait for me in London. I apologize, Lord Fraser, for her rude departure."

"That's fine. Is the lass all right?" Fraser asked, his gaze shooting between Douglas and Oliver.

"I believe so," Douglas sighed. "Just a bit of a broken heart."

"Lord Fraser, may I borrow a horse?" Oliver cut in.

"Yes, of course." The Scottish lord's eyes narrowed. "You're going after her?"

Oliver nodded. "Her leaving was my fault."

"Ah. Then you'd best go now, Conway. There are several trains to London a day—you could miss her." Fraser sent him a meaningful look, and Oliver returned it. Fraser had loved a woman and lost her, so he knew what that felt like. It was a pain like no other, and he didn't wish it upon any man.

Oliver didn't hesitate. He ran for the door, the settlement tucked firmly in his coat. He couldn't let Rayne go, not without trying everything in his power to get her back.

"Godspeed, lad!" Fraser shouted as he rushed into the cold winter air.

I need one Christmas miracle. Please let me reach her in time.

CHAPTER 12

Rayne stood on the platform, watching the attendants load her and Ellen's luggage into the luggage compartment. They had twenty minutes still until the train left the Inverness station. Ellen stood beside her.

"Are you sure you want to leave?"

"I can't stay. Seeing him there for another week? I'm not sure my heart could take it." Rayne closed her eyes and then drew a deep breath. "Let's go ahead and board." They took their seats in the first-class compartment.

She stared unseeing out the windows. "I feel like I see him everywhere, Ellen. I see him, I hear him..." Would she ever escape the memories that were guaranteed to break her heart over and over?

"Rayne!" The memory of Oliver's voice intruded on her thoughts. She blinked away tears as she stared out the train windows.

Steam billowed up, casting shadows as figures moved onto the platform and sunlight shone down to the station's tall glass windows. It was a strange blend of worlds, the shadowy station and fierce, gleaming black-and-red engines momentarily illuminated by shafts of sunlight before they were swallowed up again by clouds of smoke and steam.

"Rayne!" The shout came again, and she sat up a little straighter as she realized someone *was* calling her name.

"Miss..." Ellen pointed at a figure half-shrouded in steam.

Oliver. He was here and running down the length of the train platform, calling her name. Unable to resist, she leaned against the glass as he approached her compartment window.

"Ray—" He stopped, staring at her. Then he rushed down to the first-class car's door and attempted to board the train, but two attendants held him back. They gripped him by his arms and dragged him away so he couldn't get inside.

"Rayne! Please, just let me speak to you!" he shouted through the window. Desperation marred his features, and it made her inner resolve to ignore him quake and shudder until it was on the verge of collapsing.

"I think you should listen to him, miss," Ellen said. "Otherwise, you'll always be wondering what he came all this way to say that wasn't already said. You still have fifteen minutes before the train departs."

Rayne nodded and, hands shaking, stood and left her compartment. Soon she and Oliver stood on the platform half a dozen feet apart, neither daring to breathe.

"Please... There's something I have to say. Then if you still want to leave, I won't stop you." He reached into his coat and pulled out a piece of ribbon-bound paper. "Read this."

She stepped toward him and collected it, carefully removing the ribbon. After she unrolled the paper, she read the words on the page, words she knew her father had written because she recognized his handwriting. It stated that Oliver would receive no money from their marriage and that she would have a livable sum each month provided by a trustee that Oliver could not use.

She looked up at Oliver, confused. Did he really mean to take her without her fortune?

"Oliver, why did you sign this?" she asked, her voice shaking. "Did my father make you?"

"No. I signed it because I love you. If that means giving up everything else, then it is an easy choice. You are the *only* thing that matters to me." There was no hesitation in him as he spoke.

"But what about your home and your family?"

"I cannot save Astley Court without paying off a

large portion of the debt by the middle of January. Lord Fraser has given me his London steward position, and I will earn enough to support both you and my family, but the money I earn wouldn't be enough to pay what's currently owed to keep Astley. However, we will be able to have a decent townhouse in London. We shall live frugally for a time, but well enough that there should be no shame in it."

Now he hesitated. "I wasn't honest with you from the beginning, at least not about my financial situation. Everything else about me, everything that we shared, was real. I would never lie to you again, not even a lie of omission, if you still wanted to be my wife..." He raked a hand through his hair and chuckled wryly. "I'm bungling this up, I know that, but the point I'm trying to make is that I adore you, Rayne, and I would give everything to call you my wife."

Rayne bit her lip as a dozen conflicting emotions battled for dominance. The train conductor blew the whistle and called out that there were ten minutes left to board.

She looked down at the settlement. "I..." If she wanted more concrete proof that he loved her for herself and not her fortune, there was nothing better than the document she held in her hands. It was already signed and executed. That meant her father must have believed Oliver, and that bolstered her own desire to trust him again.

She closed her eyes and listened to her heart. She had loved Oliver from the moment he had come into Lady Poole's library, a mysterious dark-haired prince from some fairy tale. When she opened her eyes, she handed the legal document back to him, and the look of hurt in his eyes almost broke her. He thought he had lost her. She stepped up to him and curled her gloved hands around his coat lapels, pulling him close.

"Yes."

His green eyes lit with a hope that burned so brightly it almost made her cry.

He wound one arm around her waist. "Yes?"

She nodded and buried her face against his chest. "Yes."

He pressed his lips against her forehead and the crown of her hair, murmuring sweet promises that melted her heart because she knew Oliver would keep them.

"Oh!" She pulled back suddenly. "My luggage!" She spun away from him to hurry to the luggage car, but she halted just as quickly. Ellen stood a dozen feet away, a stack of traveling cases already at her feet.

"Ellen, how did you...?"

Her maid grinned. "I told you Lord Conway was a good man. I believed he would make things right, so I went to fetch our luggage."

Rayne rushed to embrace her maid and whispered a heartfelt thanks to her.

"It'll be nice to work for the Conway family again," Ellen said as Oliver waved to a station attendant to help take their luggage. They would need to hire a coach, since Lord Fraser's coach had to be on its way back to the estate by now.

Once they were all seated, Rayne leaned against Oliver's side and tucked her arm in one of his. He rested his cheek on top of her head.

"Thank you," he whispered.

She lifted her head to look up at him. "For what?"

"For saving me from a life I would've regretted. That night we met, I was going to propose to Adelaide. I lost the courage and went to the library and found you. I thought we would never see each other again, but meeting you showed me what I really wanted in life. I wanted love, a real connection."

Rayne kissed him softly, her lips trembling. "Thank you for loving me, Oliver. After losing my mother, I have felt so alone, and you came into my life, lighting up the night sky like a shooting star."

She pressed her cheek against his shoulder. His woolen coat and the gold fur around his collar tickled her when she stole another few kisses.

Ellen, bless her, pretended to focus on reading a book and not to see what they were doing.

By the time they returned to Lord Fraser's home, Rayne felt as though she could fly up the stairs from happiness alone. Oliver assisted both her and Ellen from the coach and escorted them inside.

Lord Fraser and her father were just inside, waiting for them.

"Ah, so you've returned with your fair lass?" Lord Fraser said to Oliver, but he winked at Rayne.

Oliver's face reddened. "I have." Then he looked to her father and held the settlement paper out to him. Her father took it, but he was more interested in searching his daughter's face for any sign of unhappiness. He didn't find any.

"You're truly happy, daughter?" her father murmured.

"Yes, ridiculously so."

"That's all a father can ask for." He let her go and shook Oliver's hand. "Welcome to the family."

"Thank you, Mr. Egerton."

"Douglas, please." Her father smiled mischievously. "Now, seeing as we've been missing most of the festivities..." He nodded toward the corridor behind them, where the boisterous sounds of people singing carols came from one of the parlors.

Rayne followed Oliver as they entered the room, and dozens of eyes swept their way. Adelaide saw them, and anger flashed across her face before she masked it behind cool, practiced indifference. But when Oliver's family saw them, they all broke into smiles.

"Do they know about the settlement?" Rayne asked Oliver. "Will they be angry?"

"Everett was the one who thought of it. I was falling apart and couldn't think past the pain of losing you, but he knew what to do. I owe him for that. I'm sure he's told Mother and Zadie."

"I hope so. I don't want your family to despise me."

Oliver laughed. "They're your family too, and they won't despise you. They'll adore you, just as I do." He looked at her seriously. "I want you and your father to come stay at Astley Court after Fraser's house party is over. We won't have it for much longer, and I want to show it to you." He clasped her hands in his. "And please understand that I am not attempting to coerce you into trying to save it. I just want to share it with you."

"I understand." She clasped his hands in return, and then they joined the others.

Someone sat down at the pianoforte, and Everett began to sing "God Rest Ye Merry, Gentlemen" in a deep baritone, and Oliver soon joined him. Rayne's heart swelled as she watched the pair of them singing. But she suddenly tensed as Adelaide sat down beside her.

"So, he won you back?" To Rayne's surprise, her tone was more puzzled than venomous.

Rayne gave her a wary look. "Yes."

"How? Did you change your mind about the money?"

"No. *He* changed his mind. He decided I mattered more to him than his home. He went to my father and had a settlement drafted that gives him nothing. I will live on a small allowance."

Adelaide's Cupid's bow mouth parted in shock. "He truly did that?"

"He did." Rayne would have celebrated her victory, but something about Adelaide seemed broken now. Or rather, the broken part of herself that had been well hidden until now was finally beginning to show.

"I always thought I'd be the one to marry him," Adelaide said, her eyes fixed on Oliver, and some of her bitterness seemed to fade as a deep pain etched itself in her features.

"Lady Adelaide... There is still hope for a woman who turns her heart toward kindness. Love finds a way."

Adelaide glared at her. "Is that your way of telling me to be nice to you?"

"Not to me, to *everyone*. Men—the ones worth marrying, anyway—are attracted to ladies with open and kind hearts. You can still be fierce and proud in your way, but you need not be so cruel to others." Part of Rayne was baffled that Adelaide was talking to her after everything that had happened, but she pitied the woman for her unrequited feelings toward Oliver. Peeking a glance back at Oliver and Everett, she noticed Everett watching them both, but he hastily glanced away.

Was it possible Everett was...interested in Adelaide?

"What about Everett? Would you ever consider...," Rayne suggested.

Adelaide snorted. "That devil? Certainly not. He used to tease me when we were younger. Left tadpoles in my teacups, tacks on my chair, always shoving me and pulling my hair. He and Zadie always laughed at me when they managed to get me into trouble."

"Oh…" Rayne shot a glance at Everett, who was casting them a covert glance again. "Sometimes a boy doesn't know how to express his affection."

"Oh, Everett certainly does with women he likes. I am not one of those women. There's no love lost between us, I assure you. He practically crowed at me earlier that Oliver was never going to marry me. He seemed quite happy at the thought." Adelaide lifted her chin and changed the subject. "Did you really have a whole wardrobe ordered from the House of Worth? I was too afraid to ask my father for even one dress."

"Yes. They are expensive, though not as much as one would imagine."

"Well… I shall look forward to seeing your ball gown this evening after dinner. Lord Fraser is having a small orchestra come in to play for the dance this evening." Adelaide stood and drifted away to speak to some other ladies, pretending nothing at all was wrong and acting like her usual judgmental self.

Zadie took her place in the chair Adelaide had vacated. "Goodness, that appeared quite civil from across the room. Was it?"

"Indeed it was, and I am just as surprised as you are."

"Whatever will be the next Christmas miracle?" Zadie asked with a giggle.

"I'd settle for a snowstorm that gives us a white Christmas."

"Perhaps we'll get lucky?" Zadie leaned in and hugged Rayne. "I'm so happy we are to be sisters."

"Me too," Rayne admitted, but she bit her lip. "I'm sorry I couldn't marry Oliver without the settlement."

"It's fine, Rayne. We'll manage. I will admit I was disappointed when I first heard about the arrangement, but then I asked myself what I would do if I were in your position. I couldn't see myself accepting anything less. And Oliver's happiness will always matter more to us than money."

Later, as the orchestra played and people danced, snow began to fall outside. Oliver claimed her for almost every dance. Her father and Lord Fraser had claimed the others, and Everett, the delightful scoundrel, had swept in and stolen one of Oliver's, carrying her off before his brother could intervene. But now she was back in Oliver's arms as they spun in a waltz. Her red-and-cream gown flowed behind her, and she used one hand to hold part of her silk train out away from herself so she could twirl in his arms.

"You are utterly captivating," Oliver said as he held her a bit too close, though no one judged him for it. They were to be married tomorrow morning. Her father and Lord Fraser had spoken to the local minister, and all had been arranged. Rayne couldn't have been happier; it felt like her entire body was full of bubbling champagne.

As the music finally ended and sleepy people headed upstairs for the night, Oliver escorted Rayne to her room and stole a soft kiss, but as Rayne opened her door, she grasped his jacket and pulled him inside with her.

"An early honeymoon?" he asked as he slipped out of his coat.

"Does that bother you?" She knew it didn't, because his eyes were bright and heated with desire.

"Not at all, so long as you are content with a wicked husband teaching you all the delights and the most sinful pleasures he knows."

"Oh, that sounds lovely." She gasped as he spun her to pin her against the closed door and they faced each other. She clung to his shoulders as he pushed up her gown and unfastened his trousers.

"With our clothes on?" she asked in a scandalized whisper.

Oliver nodded and then stole her mouth with his as he lifted one of her legs to wrap around his waist. He shifted her body up, and then he was inside her.

Rayne opened for him, his thrusts sending waves of pleasure through her. The intensity of their lovemaking built higher each time Oliver thrust deep. This wasn't about sweetness and slow passions—it was a moment of wild madness, the need to reconnect after what they'd almost lost. He kissed her neck, his warm breath sending tingles down her spine and making her even wetter. She came apart a moment later, her inner walls trying to hold him deep and never let him go.

Oliver gasped her name, almost crushing Rayne against the door as he tightened and released himself within her. He buried his face in her neck, kissing the shell of her ear as he held her upright, then gently set her down on her feet, her skirt falling back down. Her legs wobbled like one of the towering molded jellies served at dinner. Rayne giggled and squealed as Oliver swept her up and carried her to the bed. He stripped out of his clothes and then took his time removing hers inch by inch.

"Such a shame to strip you of that gown, but I want you naked, my love." He tucked her in bed and climbed in beside her, pulling her flush against him.

Rayne let out a yawn, then smiled in embarrassment, her cheeks hot.

"I'm sorry. I feel today I have lived a lifetime of emotions, and it's exhausted me." She laid a palm on his chest, the feel of his heartbeat a steady reassurance.

"You have, and it was my fault. I'm sorry I kept the truth from you. I won't ever do that again. You have my word."

"Thank you, Oliver. I know it is asking much of you to give up your home for me. I will do everything to make you happy," she promised.

Oliver lifted her hand to his lips, pressing a kiss to her knuckles. "I'm giving up Astley Court in exchange for the love of my life. I'm the one who owes *you* everything." He laced his fingers through hers. "You're my Christmas miracle, Rayne. Never doubt that, or my love for you. I'm only sorry that I'm not able to offer you a more lavish lifestyle."

She raised her head to look at him. "I've never needed that. Truth be told, I've never wanted it. I've only ever wanted love and a true home with a family that my father and I could be a part of."

Her future husband grinned down at her. "Those are presents I'm certain Saint Nicholas shall deliver." Then he kissed her, and she forgot all her worries. Only love remained. Outside, the snow continued to fall, blanketing the Scottish Highlands in a world of white.

RAYNE MARRIED OLIVER THE FOLLOWING MORNING, inside an old Norman church that had a dozen tall stained-glass windows framed within the stone walls. The morning light shone through and splashed colors upon the wooden pews. A dozen guests attended, but Rayne was barely aware of them. She stood beside Oliver in an ivory silk gown threaded with hundreds of pearls upon the sleeves and bodice. The colors from the stained glass played over her gown, making her glow.

She felt like a princess, and she knew that wherever her mother was, she would have smiled right along with her.

"You look opalescent," Oliver said as he slipped a ring upon her finger. She trembled a little. Her body couldn't seem to contain her love, which was ready to burst out.

The minister cleared his throat, and Oliver wiped the smile off his face as they continued their vows. Rayne wanted to memorize this moment. The fresh smell of lilies at the base of the altar, the flickering candles in their tall silver holders, the feel of Oliver's hand on hers. How strange and wondrous it all was to marry the mysterious man from Lady Poole's library. Now she understood the shadows that had lingered in his eyes that night as he had to say goodbye. She couldn't help but think perhaps her mother had been there, a guiding spirit trying to bring two lonely hearts together, binding them by books and candlelight in the sanctuary of a library.

All shadows and doubts were gone now, however. There was only love and trust. They shared a kiss as they were declared husband and wife. And then everything was a blur of laughter and smiles, even a few tears as she and Oliver took a coach back to Lord Fraser's home, where they continued the celebration with a wedding breakfast.

Lord Fraser stood up and called for his guests' attention. "If you've all had enough cake, I'd like to initiate a challenge for you to join me outside."

"In the snow?" someone asked.

Lord Fraser nodded. "Precisely." Fraser shot Oliver a wink, which Oliver returned.

Rayne curled her hand around Oliver's arm, leaning in to whisper, "Is this what I think it is?"

"It is. And I challenge you, my love, to a snowball fight. Now go and change into something warm and meet me outside."

Rayne, Zadie, and half a dozen other ladies rushed upstairs to change. Rayne came back down wearing a bustled red velvet gown and sturdy black boots, ready for battle. The men had already started, pelting balls at one another, and when they spotted the ladies, they quickly joined forces and turned on them. Rayne ran at the men, throwing as many as she could manage, until she slipped on a patch of ice. Oliver caught her in his arms, shielding her from the next snowball like the gallant knight he was. He kissed her soundly, and when he pulled back, she smacked him with a powdery handful of snow.

"Minx!" He let her go to wipe his face, and she dashed away across the lawn.

Snow began to fall in tufts like bits of cotton, and Oliver came after her again, unarmed.

"Mercy, my dear lady, mercy." He held up his hands in surrender. The snow dappled his navy-blue woolen coat and dark hair. She flung herself at him, and he caught her by the waist, spinning them both around in a cloud of swirling snowflakes.

"Thank you for forgiving me," Oliver breathed, holding her close as they spun to a stop. "Thank you." The tight warmth of his embrace felt like a vow, one that could never be broken.

"We forgive those we love—it's what makes love the most powerful force in the world." She held him right back, letting him know they would always support one another.

"I won't ever deserve you, but I intend to spend the rest of my life trying to." Oliver gave her one of those kisses that melted upon her lips like sugar and lingered like the sweetest of wine. It was the way he stared at her afterward, as if she was indeed some kind of miracle.

She carried the memory of that look with her all the way to Christmas four days later.

After everyone had retired from the Christmas Day festivities, she and Oliver sat in bed, and he held out a velvet box to her.

"What is it?" she asked as she accepted it.

"It belonged to my great-grandmother, the Duchess of Essex. My mother was hoping I would find a bride soon, and this was something we both felt should belong to you. I hope you like it. It was one of the few things we couldn't bear to part with when we started selling much of our belonging this last year."

With shaky fingers, Rayne opened the box. A single strand of pearls lay there. They gleamed in the firelight with perfect shape and color.

"They're beautiful." She touched the silky pearls, listening to them click against one another. She grinned mischievously. "Are they cursed like the Koh-i-noor diamond?"

Oliver raised a brow in a mockingly serious expression. "*Terribly* cursed. Whoever wears them must suffer a thousand kisses before midnight."

Rayne fell back into the mountain of pillows as Oliver began to unleash that curse. But soon the kisses deepened, and she sighed in delight as he covered her body with his.

A long while later, Rayne slipped out of bed and put on her nightgown. She left Oliver in bed and went over to the traveling cases he had moved into her room. She dug through the contents of one case until she found the settlement agreement.

"Rayne?" Oliver muttered drowsily as he stirred in the bed. "Come back here, love."

She returned to the bed but did not climb in. She held the agreement in front of her and played with the ends of the black ribbon.

"I have a present for you too." She turned away and approached the fireplace. He sat up in bed, his eyes wide.

"Rayne, what are you doing?" He started to leave the

bed, but she was too fast and flung the settlement into the fire.

Oliver grabbed his dressing gown and pulled it on before he joined her at the fire to watch it burn.

"I know my father has a second copy, but I wanted you to see this. I changed my mind. I want to share my fortune with you. I want... I want to save our home."

"You've never even seen Astley Court," Oliver replied as he placed his hands on her waist and drew her back against him while they watched the paper burn.

"You love it. That's all that matters. You once told me that people should be able to lean on others for support. I thought you wanting my money was selfish, but I love you and it will be my home too. So that means I can be selfish and save Astley Court. The best way to do it is to undo the settlement."

Oliver held her close, his voice slightly rougher than before when he said, "I would never ask you to do this. I didn't want there to ever be a doubt I chose only you."

"I don't doubt you, Oliver." She turned in his arms. "You need to trust me now. Trust that I want this for us."

His green eyes were overbright as he nodded and kissed her. "I suppose miracles really do happen, don't they?"

Rayne brushed a lock of hair out of his eyes. "They certainly do. Especially when one makes one's own miracles." She grinned.

Oliver chuckled, and then he lowered his head to steal another kiss. "Happy Christmas, my love."

"*Merry* Christmas," she corrected with a laugh.

"You Americans." He swept her up into his arms and carried her back to bed.

EPILOGUE

Ten months later

A crisp fall wind blew red and gold leaves across the path that led up to Astley Court. Everett shoved his hands into his coat pockets as he moved up the cobblestone walkway. The towering rhododendrons nearly walled him off from the front gardens and kept his path concealed from anyone who might be waiting for him at the house. He was already running late for afternoon tea, and his mother would no doubt give him an earful.

A feminine voice gasped somewhere around the bend. "Ouch!"

Everett quickened his pace and followed the sound. He burst into the clearing around the bend, expecting to see his sister or perhaps his sister-in-law, but instead he found Adelaide Berwick. She was the last person he would ever have wanted to run into, especially alone in a garden. Perched on the marble bench, dressed in a bustled green satin gown, clutching her hand, Adelaide painted a pretty portrait of a damsel in distress, not that he was attracted to that sort of thing. He *definitely* wasn't.

"Adelaide?"

She jerked as he spoke her name, dropping a rose bloom to the ground in her haste. Given how close their families' properties were, it wasn't unusual to see Adelaide stray into the family gardens, just as he'd often hopped the low stone wall to go fishing in the little lake on Adelaide's land.

"Oh!" She rose from the bench to flee, but Everett caught her arm.

"What's the matter?"

"As if you cared," Adelaide snapped.

Everett saw a droplet of blood bead upon her fingertip. "So, you've learned you're not the only thing in the garden with thorns," he quipped, unable to help himself.

Adelaide's face twisted with a scowl as she pulled her hand free.

"Come now, I was only joking. Here, let me see." He caught her hand again and removed a handkerchief from his pocket. He pressed it to the pad of her right index finger and held it firm. They both stood silent a long moment. The heavy scents of late-blooming flowers mixed with the bite of an autumn wind stirring the golden trees around them wove a strange spell over Everett as he studied Adelaide's face. For a moment she lost that cold, hateful look, and there was a softness there that puzzled him.

"What are you doing here?" Everett asked.

"I wanted a few roses. The ones in our hothouse at home don't have that..." She struggled for the right words. "Well, it's a wild look, an untamed beauty that our roses don't have. I didn't think you would miss the ones I took."

"And why do you need to poach our roses?" Everett still held on to her hand, the handkerchief wrapped around her finger.

The openness of her expression vanished. "You'll only laugh at me."

Everett wanted to disagree, but in the past, he had found reasons to tease Adelaide. She was such a prickly little creature.

"I almost certainly will, but tell me anyway."

"I wanted to sew a few roses into my gown for tonight's ball." Her face reddened like a ripe strawberry at the admission. Her auburn curls gleamed in the dappled sunlight as she turned her face away from his. To his own surprise, he didn't laugh.

"Ah, I understand. You wanted to have a gown like Rayne's from last Christmas?" he guessed. His sister-in-law had worn an exquisite gown with actual blooming roses sewn into it for one night. It had caused quite a stir among the guests.

"I... No," Adelaide huffed.

He moved one hand to her waist, rubbing his fingertips along her corseted form. He'd never noticed how much her body curved before, and how it felt strangely exciting to be touching her like this. "You don't need fresh roses, Adelaide. You're lovely as you are."

"*Just* lovely?" Her brown eyes darkened with seeming despair.

"Lovely isn't enough?" Everett rolled his eyes. "You're bloody exquisite. There, are you content now, Maddie?" He used the old nickname he'd teased her with as a child. She hated that name, but that was the point. He wanted to see fire in her eyes, not sorrow.

She smacked his chest and tried to pull away. "You callous bully! Don't ever call me that!" He'd taken to calling her Maddie Addie because he used to tease her for being madly in love with Oliver. Then it had somehow along the way shortened to just Maddie, but she still hated it.

Adelaide stared up at him, fire flashing in her eyes, and something just...changed between them in an instant. Like a flash of lightning from a building storm.

Unsure of what possessed him, Everett pulled her against his body and captured her lips. Her hiss of indignation changed to a confused gasp and then softened to a sigh of longing. He absorbed it all, fascinated by her sweet taste. He had never kissed her before, not once, and now he deeply regretted that. This was a woman who ought to be kissed a thousand times a day. Her petal-soft lips were made for sweet seductions, and the slight curve of her spine left his hand resting perfectly on her lower back while he enjoyed the press of her breasts against his chest. Lord, he could have stayed right there and kissed her for days.

He wasn't sure why they finally broke apart, but suddenly she was rushing away. Then she stopped, looking over her shoulder at him, the train of her green gown rustling over the fallen leaves. She looked like a startled wood nymph, and he wanted her back in his arms.

That was madness. He was the mad one, not her. She was *Adelaide*, the spoiled little rich girl who lived next door. The girl who'd followed his older brother about with big doe eyes and never looked his way, not even once. He despised her... Didn't he? Then she was gone, vanishing down a garden path back to her estate. Everett stared at the leafy rhododendrons for a long second and then resumed his walk back to Astley Court.

"Everett!" Rayne and Oliver called out his name in unison as he came up the steps. Rayne held a bundle of cooing joy in her arms. A little boy born only a month before. Justin Conway, the future Viscount Conway.

"Sorry I'm late." Everett held out his hands. "Now, let me see the little fellow." He took the babe from

Rayne's arms and grinned down at him. Justin stared up at his uncle with a serious expression, his green eyes focused intently on Everett and his tiny brow furrowed.

"Hello there, old chap," he teased, then looked at the new parents. "How is everyone?"

"Wonderful," Oliver said. "Douglas and Lady Poole just arrived. Everything is set for their wedding this afternoon."

"Excellent." Everett hadn't been the least bit surprised to learn that Rayne's father and Lady Poole had formed an attachment. They were both bighearted and well suited to one another. After Rayne and Oliver had married, Rayne's father had decided to stay in London and not return immediately to New York, and naturally, he'd been pulled into Lady Poole's social activities, which had led to the widow and the widower falling in love.

"Are Zadie and Mother here?" Everett asked.

"Already inside," said Rayne. "Zadie is fending off the attentions of my cousins. They all seem quite taken with her."

"They do?" Everett narrowed his eyes. "Need we worry, Oliver?"

Oliver shook his head with a mirthful laugh. "Far from it. Zadie is holding court like a queen, and they've been fetching her tea and biscuits for the last hour. I believe they're ready to don the old suits of armor and ride out to battle for their fair lady's affection."

Everett snorted. Zadie did have a way of managing men when she wanted to.

"Margaret was surprised you weren't here first to eat all the sandwiches," Rayne teased. "I'm sorry there aren't many left. My cousins have almost eaten them all."

"Not to worry—Mrs. Mead always has a few tarts left in the kitchens for me."

Everett gave the baby one more loving squeeze and a smile before he slipped Justin into Oliver's waiting arms. Oliver stared down with bemused fascination at his son and then lifted the baby's impossibly tiny hand to his mouth and pressed a kiss to it. The sight tugged at Everett's chest. He had no desire to marry, at least not yet, but seeing Oliver so content, and embracing fatherhood in this way, made Everett long for the peace that had taken over his brother's life.

They entered the house, and Everett glanced once more toward the gardens in the direction of Berwick House. He could still taste Adelaide's lips, and a sudden longing tightened his chest.

I must be mad to want her.

Yet he couldn't forget that singular kiss. Something had changed in him, because he knew he would dream about her lips tonight. He would perhaps dream of a bit more than a kiss too, and that was a dangerous thing.

ADELAIDE REACHED HER HOME, STILL CLUTCHING THE white handkerchief. She unwound it from her fingers and studied the initials *E. C.* sewn into the fabric with deep blue thread and lined with gold. A single bright red dot marred its center. She pressed her throbbing finger to her lips but didn't taste any fresh blood.

She felt like such a fool. Picking roses to look more like Rayne... Why had she done that? She had been jealous, that's why. Rayne always managed to look perfect, in her gowns with fashionable new designs from the House of Worth in Paris. Most ladies like Adelaide wore more sensible and pretty English dresses, but not stunning or risqué like the Parisian Worth dresses.

It was no wonder Oliver had fallen for Rayne. Adelaide must have looked as common as the other ladies compared to the American beauty. That night she'd first met Rayne, she'd been green with envy. And so she had done what she'd always done—resorted to meanness. It was what her mother had taught her, to strike out first at those you fear. Hurt them before they hurt you. It had proven to be effective. But now? Now she was thinking over and over about what Rayne had said last Christmas, about choosing kindness, not cruelty.

Adelaide squared her shoulders and looked back across the lawns of Berwick House toward Astley Court. She couldn't banish the memory of Everett kissing her. Everett... A man she'd loathed since childhood. As an adult, he'd become tolerable to talk to when necessary, but... no.

"Little Maddie Addie, little Maddie Addie..." She could still hear him teasing her from their childhood.

How she hated that name. It seemed so silly and common. And Everett knew she hated that nickname.

He was a bullheaded, stubborn bully, but that kiss... That kiss had been like the most wonderful dream. Not that Adelaide knew much about kisses. This was only her second one after a kiss from a stable hand years ago when she'd been sixteen. There was no need to compare the two experiences. Everett's mouth had set fire to her blood and made her dizzy. Wasn't that how a good kiss was supposed to be?

But instead of it coming from a handsome, polite suitor holding a bouquet of rare flowers, it had come from Everett Conway. Life, it seemed, always found new ways to be cruel to her.

Adelaide brushed her fingers over her lips and closed her eyes, wishing she could forget the feel of his mouth, and yet also wishing that he had never stopped kissing her. She clutched the handkerchief to her chest. A smile stole over her lips, but it soon faltered.

She couldn't fall for Everett. She *wouldn't*. Because she'd vowed to hate him for the rest of her life. The man had made her childhood miserable, and one kiss wouldn't change that, no matter how wonderful it had been or how she was likely to dream about it and him tonight.

"Damn you, Everett," she muttered. "Damn you."

THANK YOU SO MUCH FOR READING *SEDUCING AN Heiress on a Train*! I hope you loved Rayne and Oliver's whirlwind Victorian romance! If you haven't read my book *Wicked Designs* yet, you might want to check it out because it's the love story for Oliver's great-grandparents Godric and Emily!

Be sure to turn the page to read my exclusive author's historical note where can read a little more about cursed Indian diamonds, train engines and the haunting true history of the witchery in Edinburgh.

AUTHOR'S HISTORICAL NOTE

Sometimes a story takes you by surprise, and you never know what magical things will be uncovered. Rayne and Oliver's Victorian-set romance was a true delight and an adventure for me in ways I never imagined. Between cursed diamonds, rumbling train cars, and the haunting and seductive atmosphere of a witchery at the base of a castle, there was plenty for me to explore with the story and, more importantly, with history. Below I wish to share with you a bit about some of the fun things I researched while writing this book.

When Oliver and Rayne share their secluded moment in Lady Poole's library, he mentions his grandmother seeing the Koh-i-noor diamond during the Great Exhibition in 1851. This is in fact all true, right down to the description of the diamond's viewing and the fact that it was later cut down to a perfect shape at the direction of Prince Albert. It is also true that Queen Victoria never felt fully comfortable wearing the cursed diamond, and its history is indeed shrouded in bloodshed and mystery going back centuries. And when Oliver mentions his grandmother saying that to gaze upon it was like looking into a black abyss, that is actually true as well. Accounts from viewers during the Great Exhibition mentioned that strange and eerie phenomenon while viewing the diamond. This was a scene that surprised me, as the characters themselves revealed the Koh-i-noor in all its haunted beauty as I wrote. Just as Oliver's Grandmother predicted, it did end up in a crown a few generations after Victoria died. It was even in the crown which rested on the coffin of Queen Elizabeth II's mother while she lay in state.

As for the train scenes, I hope you all enjoyed that! I found the Pullman sleeping cars and the discussion of first-class refreshment rooms to be rather interesting. The history of trains is an extension of the history of stagecoaches, which is why train cars were originally called *coaches*. Another fascinating tidbit of truth is that people did believe early on that riding on or even being near those terrible black engines belching smoke and fire would actually drive a person mad. There was also a belief that the vibrations of the train and the rhythm of it would send women into "hysterics," which was a silly

Victorian way of describing sexual arousal for women. It was still widely believed by many that women could not experience pleasure during sex (yes, I laughed outright at this too and then sadly shook my head). Naturally, the idea of women traveling on trains wasn't seen positively for this "hysterical" effect, but later on, train travel actually proved to be quite liberating for women and was one of the few places where women traveling alone without men or chaperones was allowed. Trains, in a way, were quite a powerful force for the movement toward independence for women.

Rayne as an American heiress marrying an English lord in the late 1880s was quite a common thing. "Buying a title," as they called it, was a frequent thing. New York was flooded with oil money and other fortunes, while the English economy was weakening by comparison. The English Nobility were trying to maintain landed properties without selling the land. Men like Oliver were responsible for supporting local farmers and their families, but with the economy changing, that way of life wasn't surviving. Many landed gentry and titled lords lost their homes and were forced to sell their estates due to mounting debts. Therefore, many Englishmen were happy to chase American heiresses to save their homes and their families. Men like Rayne's father, Douglas, were, however, very clever in protecting their daughters through settlements with the husbands. Sometimes the

Englishmen were successful in getting their money, sometimes not.

The bewitching setting of the Witchery by the Castle is indeed a real place! My one bit of fiction about the Witchery is that it didn't start operating as a hotel until 1976. However, the building, with its brooding Jacobean atmosphere, has been there for several hundred years. The history that Oliver tells Rayne as to the building's usage is indeed true—it simply didn't become a place someone could stay as a hotel guest until the twentieth century. You can stay there today! So the next time you're in Scotland, you can stop by the Witchery by the Castle to dine at their restaurant, or you can spend the night in a room just like Rayne and Oliver did.

I hope you all enjoyed *Seducing an Heiress on a Train* as much as I enjoyed writing it, and I hope you liked the small historical details I worked in to enrich the story.

Happy reading, my lovelies!

Lauren Smith

Wait! This isn't the end...I know you were panicking there for a minute right?
Well don't worry! The best way to know when a new book is released is to do one or all of the following:

Join my Newsletter: http://laurensmithbooks. com/free-books-and-newsletter/

Follow Me on BookBub: https://www.bookbub.com/ authors/lauren-smith

Join my Facebook VIP Reader Group called Lauren Smith's League: https://www.facebook.com/ groups/400377546765661/

Want three free books?
You'll get *Wicked Designs* (a historical romance), *Legally Charming* (a contemporary romance) and *The Bite of Winter* (a paranormal romance). Fill out the form at the bottom of this link and you'll get an email from me with details to collect your free read!

Claim your free books now at:
http://laurensmithbooks.com/free-books-and-newsletter/,
follow me on twitter at @LSmithAuthor, or like my Facebook page at https://www. facebook.com/LaurenDianaSmith.
Join my PRIVATE Facebook VIP Reader group at: https://www.facebook.com/ groups/400377546765661/

I share upcoming book news, snippets and cover reveals plus PRIZES!

Reviews help other readers find books. I appreciate all reviews, whether positive or negative. If one of my books spoke to you, please share!

ABOUT THE AUTHOR

Lauren Smith is an Oklahoma attorney by day, author by night who pens adventurous and edgy romance stories by the light of her smart phone flashlight app. She knew she was destined to be a romance writer when she attempted to re-write the entire *Titanic* movie just to save Jack from drowning. Connecting with readers by writing emotionally moving, realistic and sexy romances no matter what time period is her passion. She's won multiple awards in several romance subgenres including: New England Reader's Choice Awards, Greater Detroit BookSeller's

Best Awards, and a Semi-Finalist award for the Mary Wollstonecraft Shelley Award.

To Connect with Lauren, visit her at:
www.laurensmithbooks.com
lauren@laurensmithbooks.com

OTHER TITLES BY LAUREN SMITH

Historical

The League of Rogues Series

Wicked Designs

His Wicked Seduction

Her Wicked Proposal

Wicked Rivals

Her Wicked Longing

His Wicked Embrace

The Earl of Pembroke

His Wicked Secret

The Last Wicked Rogue

Never Kiss A Scot

The Earl of Kent

Never Tempt a Scot (coming 2020)

The Seduction Series

The Duelist's Seduction

The Rakehell's Seduction
The Rogue's Seduction
The Gentleman's Seduction
Standalone Stories
Tempted by A Rogue
Bewitching the Earl
Seducing an Heiress on a Train
Devil at the Gates
Sins and Scandals
An Earl By Any Other Name
A Gentleman Never Surrenders
A Scottish Lord for Christmas

Contemporary
The Surrender Series
The Gilded Cuff
The Gilded Cage
The Gilded Chain
The Darkest Hour
Love in London
Forbidden
Seduction
Climax
Forever Be Mine

Paranormal
Dark Seductions Series
The Shadows of Stormclyffe Hall

The Love Bites Series

The Bite of Winter

His Little Vixen (coming early 2020)

Brotherhood of the Blood Moon Series

Blood Moon on the Rise (coming soon)

Brothers of Ash and Fire

Grigori: A Royal Dragon Romance

Mikhail: A Royal Dragon Romance

Rurik: A Royal Dragon Romance

Sci-Fi Romance

Cyborg Genesis Series

Across the Stars

The Krinar Chronicles

The Krinar Eclipse

The Krinar Code by Emma Castle

Buy these books today by visiting www.laurensmithbooks.com

Or by visiting your favorite ebook/paperback book store!

Lauren
SMITH
TIMELESS ROMANCE

www.ingramcontent.com/pod-product-compliance
Lightning Source LLC
Chambersburg PA
CBHW031617180726
48284CB00005B/1590